For Belinda

2017 Rabbooks Publishing First Edition

Copyright © 2017 Alexander G.James

ISBN-13: 9780998247410

First Edition

Book Design and Illustration by Alex James.

www.rabbitstudios.blogspot.com

flamingjackasspizza.blogspot.com

FLAMING JACKASS
In Love

Alexander G. J.

ACKNOWLEDGMENTS

Special thanks to all the people who helped in one way or another, either by inspiration or perspiration, to place this book in your hands.

A special thanks to Melissa Ehman and Luke Neher for their tireless editing and support.

CONTENTS

Part One
Puffy Nipples

The craftsman dug the multi-needled instrument into Erin's shoulder blade, one of the body's most sensitive spots. *Anyone who says tattoos don't hurt is either a masochist or a moron*, Erin thought. *Tawnee was right, the nipple would have been less painful.* Erin had been skeptical about a tattoo artist without a parlor, especially one who would work for a thank-you and a six-pack of beer, but this man seemed to know his job. He'd brought new, plastic-wrapped needles and wore rubber gloves and had an impressive design library to choose from. Erin had chosen a Celtic four-leaf clover because of her Irish heritage, and because she liked the idea of carrying a bit of luck with her.

"Let me know if it stops hurting," he said as he filled the reservoir with green. "Because it means I've killed you."

"Ha, bloody ha."

He started filling in the lobes and Tawnee, sitting behind Erin on one of the kitchen chairs, tried to distract her from the pain by talking about her own many tattoos, working at Ripped to Threads, and boys. The last didn't work. Talking about boys made Erin tense up, especially after hearing Peter's name.

"What did you say?"

"I said Peter asked about you." Tawnee repeated.

"What? Why?"

"Dunno. I never told him that I knew you."

"I wonder who did? I bet it was Fabrianne."

"How's living with Mary Jo working out for you?"

"Great, she's a gas. Don't change the subject, what did he say about me?"

"Oh, just normal shit: What are you up to? Are you seeing anybody? Blah blah blah."

"Why does he want to know if I'm seeing anyone?"

"You guys can't be using me as a mediator. You should talk to each other."

"You bought it up."

"I was just trying to distract you from the pain."

"And a fine job it was," the artist interrupted. "Finished."

Erin got up. Tawnee held a hand mirror so Erin could see without craning her neck too much. "It's a lot bigger and brighter than I thought it'd be, but I like that you can probably tell what it is from a distance." *This is a long way from those crappy tattoos that look like they were carved in prison with ballpoint pens, or those faded purple blotches that used to be black panthers.* "Cool."

"Thanks, Sean." Tawnee kissed her ex-boyfriend on the cheek.

Erin liked that about Tawnee: she was friends with all of her exes, even the ones who'd cheated on her. *Why is my ex showing interest in me? Knowing Peter, he's just horny.* While Sean instructed Erin on how to care for her intentional scars, she walked around the kitchen to stretch her legs.

Roger walked in. "Nice tits."

Erin quickly grabbed her shirt and covered up. Roger laughed.

"You forget I live with three women. I've seen them all in various states of undress, and a sports bra ain't nothing."

Fabrianne entered behind Roger, waved to Tawnee, and hugged Erin.

"Ouch."

"Oh, I'm sorry. I forgot. Is it finished? Let me see it."

Erin exposed her back cautiously, eyeing Roger as if his seeing more of her flesh would spark a mad frenzy of lust.

"That's open-out, Sean! See, Erin, didn't we tell you the North Side has better tattoo artists?"

"Definitely got a knack," Erin agreed politely. After moving here a month ago Erin had begun to notice just how prideful the people were: the Northerners, looked down on Southerners as if they were Hillbillies. Rents ran almost double those in the South, and businesses here had to either be unique and offer quality products or be large chains instead to survive.

The thrift stores and bargain havens on the other side of the bridge could never sell enough to make it here. *I might as well be on an island where the inhabitants speak a different language: I still haven't figured out "that's got ass" and "that's open-out".*

Even with her shirt on Erin felt underdressed and ratty. People here strove for a fashion edge of some kind: the women looked like they got up two hours early just to pick out the right earrings, the businessmen dressed like Armani ads, and the gutter punks spend their begging money adding piercings and tats. *Even the homeless are hipper than me.* In addition to this tattoo she had recently gotten two new ear piercings, but still felt "country with a K." *I thought working at the Acid Pit would be my edge, but people here seem to know what I'm just figuring out: it's as impressive as bagging in a grocery store. The Pit's exciting to the patrons drinking and dancing, and for the performers onstage, but my new opinion of the dance floor is something that constantly needs cleaning, and the stage is a time suck that always needs assembling and disassembling. And when I do see cool popular musicians, I'm not allowed to stand around and talk to them or even stop working long enough to watch them. In short, the Acid Pit's become as much a job as F.J. Pizza.*

After Sean left, Roger turned to the girls. "Who wants to watch a show one of my classmates is in?"

Fabrianne opened a cabinet and pulled out a bag filled with other bags. "You know I hate TV. I'm getting groceries. Want anything?"

Roger was already leaving the room, which Erin thought rude. Fabrianne didn't seem to care and went out. Tawnee was following Roger so Erin fell in line. Roger turned on the set.

"I only got cable so I can watch community-made TV shows," he announced.

As he flipped through the channels Erin noticed at least two, showing breasts. She raised an eyebrow at Tawnee, who rolled her eyes and pumped a fist. Roger stopped at Channel Z and sat down beside them. The corner logo announced they were watching Tear Shit Up! Over a heavy metal soundtrack, two guys wearing paper bags over their heads were currently smashing a pile of TV sets with baseball bats.

"Eh," Erin said, "I think I'll leave you guys to your entertainment…"

"I'm not watching this shit!" Roger said defensively. "The girl in my Communications class does the next show."

"Is she hot or something?" Tawnee asked, smiling coyly. "She one of the ladies you always clubbing with?"

"Here it is," Roger said.

Shut Up, America! With Donna Etcheverria flashed onscreen. Erin expected more guys tearing more shit up. Instead, it opened with two people seated in front of a very cheap blue-screen of a waving American flag. The woman, assumedly Donna, was around twenty years old, with a longish face, prominent nose, and short curly hair. *Lesbian?* She introduced her guest, an older gentleman around fifty who lived a completely self-sufficient lifestyle: he grew his own food, used solar and wind power, and had a well for water.

"You know, that show's title is a little misleading," Erin commented, "I was expecting some ultra-right wingers or more guys in bags. You know—Shut up, America! Or else!"

"No, dumb-ass. It's just a title. She doesn't focus on one thing. Last week she had some lady that was a witch or some shit."

"I think if you're gonna have a title like that, then it should be more radical—and don't call me dumb-ass!" When Roger laughed Erin took his beret off and hit him with it.

"Cut it out. Don't you have someplace to be?"

They turned their attention back to the show. The guy was explaining the nuance of outhouses.

"A perfect cue to depart. Later, guys."

Tawnee got up and followed Erin to the door. "He's such a pig. You know he ain't watching that show for outhouses."

"That girl is kinda cute."

"I think her sister is Tamara Etcheverria."

"Oh, I knew that name sounded familiar. So I guess that means she's loaded, too?"

"Probably. She drives a beemer."

"How do you know all this?"

"I see her shop at Ripped To Threads sometimes." They stepped out onto the porch.

"Why would someone with money like the Etcheverrias be so into art and cable access shows?"

"Bored, I guess."

Erin tried to look at her new tattoo. "Well, thanks for the artist."

"Sure, it looks good on ya, girl." The two hugged and Erin left. The tattoo still hurt, but she had no regrets. *I want to fit in with the Northerner Neos, but in a town full of weirdos trying to be as outrageous as they can, everyone starts getting tattoos or doing what was hip a few months ago and how can you keep up? I'll bet even kindergarten teachers in the North have nipple piercings.*

Erin wanted to explore before walking back home. There were tons of new restaurants and shops. Because she had been blowing through twenty or more dollars a day, she had started trying to cook and exercise more restraint. As she forced herself past the shoe store, Boutique de Chaussures, she realized she was near Jolly Roger's Videos. Since moving in with Mary Jo, she had also begun saving money by watching more videos instead of going out so much. She ducked inside to see what was new. At the counter a handwritten sign read: "If You Can't Find it Here, it Ain't Shit!" The girl behind the sign, a shorthaired blonde in overalls wearing nerdy glasses, smiled at her. It took Erin a second to recognize it was April, who'd helped her sneak into the Jelly rave.

"Hey, I didn't know you worked here."

"You never asked where I worked."

"Oh, yeah."

"That's okay, it's a good conversation starter." They laughed. Erin gave her a little hug.

"How's things?"

"Ça va bien, et tois?"

"Wha?"

"French, and you?"

"I'm good. You speak French?"

"Have to. Living with J.J., she's part French. There's actually a lot of French people in Neo."

"That partly explains the attitude."

"Ah, it's just how people in big cities act."

"I guess. The people in Prague were nice, though."

"You've been to Prague?"

"Yeah, for a few weeks."

April had been there too, and they began discussing the city. She and Erin had also frequented the same movie theater, and when Erin mentioned her love of Czech animation, April dragged her to that section. Erin was amazed at the vast collection of films by Jan Svankmajer and other East European artistes. Several films sparked her interest but were already rented. Erin held up the empty cases.

"Hey, when will these be back?"

April checked the computer. "Actually, a guy ahead of you's already reserved them."

"What? Who?"

"Can't tell you that. What if you requested Butt Pirates 4? You want me blabbing that around?"

"I guess not. But can you tell me when they'll be back? Maybe I can flirt them out of him."

"What's so important about those videos?"

"I saw one of them when I was going through a really bad time and it made me feel better."

"Well..."

"Come on April, I'll do you a favor."

"Like what?"

"Free pizza?"

"Your supervisor's one of my best friends."

Erin thought for a second. "Acid Pit for free?"

"We always sneak in."

Damn! Once again the Acid Pit isn't good for anything but a job. And I have absolutely nothing else to bargain with. God, why don't I have any assets? April's not going to help me out, either; she's a shrewd businesswoman. Right before she was about to launch into begging, April's face took on a distressed look.

"Hey! No masturbating in here!"

Erin turned. Whoever had got April's attention was disappearing behind the curtain separating the porno section from the merely offensive section. April grabbed a pair of pliers from under the counter and tore off to investigate further. Curious, Erin started to follow until she realized the computer screen was still up. She leaned back to read the name of the person who shared her animation taste. For some reason the name didn't surprise her. If possible, Kevin had just become even more of the perfect man for her. She smiled and sighed. The trench-coated masturbator and April came from the back.

"Dude, I'm telling you, if you want to bop your baloney, you gotta see this." She handed him a copy of "Glad He Ate Her" the guy examined the box like a sommelier looking at a fine bottle of wine. "Just hold on—no pun intended—until you get home." She walked back around the counter, acting as if nothing had happened. "Now, what were we talking about?"

"I uh, forgot."

#

Returning to Mary Jo's, Erin took the long way. Every time she'd taken a walk in North Neo she'd seen something interesting, and this time it was a group of skaters who had set up a wooden half-pipe in a parking lot. She sat down and watched them take turns, going up and down the U-shaped device. Some were pretty good and could do small tricks; others were not much better than she had been. *I wish I hadn't thrown my skateboard into the river as part of my ritual to exorcise Peter. I wonder why he's asking about me?* One of the bad skaters wiped out, sending him rolling down the pipe. He held his knee and moaned in agony. Erin got up and left. She wasn't much of a rubber-necker when it came to accidents. She almost prided herself on getting away from bad things.

As she crossed the street and headed toward Kenwood, she thought about another bad situation she had escaped: her mother. So far Carolyn had not tried to call her. Erin pictured her, without a kid to worry about, living it up with Dan. *If Mom asked my brother, she would know exactly where her daughter is living right now. So why hasn't she called? How does she know that I'm safe? If I were staying a few blocks further into Kenwood, I'd be in a building with drug dealers and guys who wear big puffy jackets even in summer.*

Mary Jo's apartment was literally across the tracks from the bad part of Kenwood, though those tracks were now paved over with asphalt and called The Rail Trail. Erin turned onto it at Trade Street, joining the many joggers, walkers, and bikers who traversed it daily. As she got closer to home, the crowd began to thin. In the North Side, neighborhoods could change from block to block. A Neo yuppie could live next door to a ghetto but stroll two blocks opposite for an overpriced latté. Only the daring stayed on this stretch of the trail, and Erin was one of the daring. *Most of these guys hanging out here are thug types for show. If someone wants to rob you, he's not gonna announce his presence with a boom box and a brightly colored jacket. A quiet one hiding in the shadows, though...*

She made it home without incident. Mary Jo was sitting in the living room watching TV and eating a bowl of Trix cereal. "Hey, roomie," she called out cheerfully.

"Hey." *Why does it always smells like pot in here?* Is that your dinner?"

"No way. This is an appetizer. Cake's for dinner." Erin wondered if this was a joke. She had discovered only forty-five percent of the things Mary Jo said were true. "Your brother called."

"Dave? I already talked to him yesterday. Wonder what he wants."

"I don't think it was a Dave, I think it was Joe-something."

"Josh?"

"Yeah, that's it."

"Oh my God, Josh never calls me. Oh, no! Someone must be dead!" Erin searched through her backpack for her address book. "Damn it! Did he leave a number? I don't even know if he's in the same place."

"Just press star sixty-nine. He was the last to call."

"Good idea." Erin walked toward her bedroom. "You know, they charge money for using that."

"Really? What about 911?"

"Not yet." The phone redialed what she assumed would still be his Manhattan phone number.

"Hello?" a woman answered. It was Kelly, his fiancée, and Erin wasn't really in the mood to talk to her. The last time they'd had a conversation, she'd kept asking Erin about her getting arrested and being on the news. It hadn't come off as curiosity, more as trying to tell Erin, "You see what happens when you don't go to church, dress nice, or vote Republican?"

"Hi, this is Erin. May I speak to Josh?"

"Hi, Erin, how are you doing? So nice to hear from you." Her voice hinted more at sarcasm than concern.

"I'm fine, Kelly."

"That's great. Josh is in the garage. Josh!" Kelly yelled. "It's so nice to hear from you, Erin. Are you still a punk rocker?"

"No, Kelly, I'm more into Death Metal," Erin lied.

"Oh, you better watch out for that music. Boys who listen to that stuff shoot at cops, and the girls...well, I guess they tear up empty condos." Kelly laughed at her own dig. "Here's Josh, it's been nice talking to you."

Erin flipped Kelly a long distant bird. *We did the wrong condo.*

"Hey Skipper, how's it going?" Josh said, more cheerfully than Erin expected.

"Josh, what's going on?"

"Just called to see how you were doing. Mom said you moved out without telling her where you were going."

"How did you find me?"

"David." Erin felt betrayed. "So are you okay? Are you still working at that pizza place?"

"Yep, sure am. You still do whatever you do?" With that question, Josh began to tell Erin about how he had made advances at his brokerage firm, his engagement to Kelly, his vacation house in the Hampton's and the bounty of blessings bestowed upon him. After 10 minutes of this, Erin had to remind him of the long distance expense. "Oh, oh yeah. I forgot. You're like on a student budget or something, right?"

"I'm not a student."

"What? You're not in school? What do you do in your spare time?"

"Well, I am working two jobs. Did Dave tell you that?"

"No, but that's good. A little extra cash. But do you want to be doing that the rest of your life?"

"Of course not." To her, he sounded just like her father. She was not in the mood to talk with her father. "What's that?" Erin yelled at Mary Jo. "...I gotta go, Josh. Something's on fire."

"Ah, okay. Sure thing, Skipper. I'll talk to you later."

Erin hung up the phone and looked at Mary Jo, sitting on the couch with a shocked expression on her face. "What is it?"

"Am I on fire?"

#

At the pizza parlor business was picking up: waves of students returning to or starting school flowed in and out. *I remember when I moved here and had no idea where to go. I wish I had time to tell you kids all the cool places and—*

"Man, did I get trashed at the Pink Barn last night," a girl told her friend as she paid for her slice.

"Aw," her friend whined. "I tried to get in but we got there too late and the line was all stretched, so we went across the street to Smitty's Lounge but it was doubled out."

"Where are those places?" Erin asked Jeff Carlito after the girls had walked away.

"Beats me," he called back as he went out to bus the tables.

Erin fumed. Not only were more and more places and scenes she's been into becoming either passé or closed down, now, the eighteen year-olds were discussing clubs she'd never heard of. Even 10th Street was starting to be talked about as if it were just another tourist attraction; East River Valley was turning into the new hip hangout. Erin's eyes shot daggers at the two girls. *Look at them in their C.F.M. outfits trying to look like early Madonna, complete with exposed bra.* Two guys dressed as glam rockers, minus the big hair, joined them and started chatting about leopard skin pants. Lashell walked over, followed Erin's gaze, and crossed her arms.

"Can you believe people wearing that: 'Come Fuck Me' shit? I'd never wear a bra outside," Lashell said.

"I never thought that shit'd come back."

"Actually, it's on it way out," Jeff called out from the prep table.

"So what are people into now, Mr. Hip?" asked Lashell.

Jeff pointed to a group of girls wearing baseball jerseys with Japanese letters on them. "Obscure sports team jerseys."

"Those are cool!"

"Yeah, I guess. I prefer more cleavage, myself."

"Of course you do," Erin said. "Where can you find them?"

"Probably at Frankenstein's Closet."

"Where's that? On 10th?"

Jeff looked at Erin as if she had said something incredibly stupid. "It's not on 10th. It's in East River Valley."

Erin looked at Lashell.

"Don't look at me. I don't live here."

"The last time I was down there, it was nothing but projects and check cashing places."

Again, Jeff gave her a look. "Those projects burned down last year. Don't you watch the news?"

"I rarely watch TV. So what? They put some condos there now?"

"No, it's just a few stores and a vacant lot, but some hippie-dippies started a communal garden and painted murals on the walls. It's kinda nice."

Well, Jeff is the type who discovers scenes right after the gays and minorities but before the artists, and way before the hipsters and laggards. I trust him. "I think I need to see this."

"When are you going?"

"Well, I was gonna go to the Pit, but you know what, they don't even notice me if I show up or not, so fuck it, let's go after work."

"Say what?" Lashell protested. "You sure about that? They gonna fire yo' ass."

"Big deal. Other people come and go whenever they want. This one girl, Bebe, supposed to be there at noon. She shows up at 4 with a hangover. No one says shit to her."

"Better be careful."

"Believe me, I'm one of their best workers; they're not gonna fire me."

"Then why is Bebe full-time and you ain't?"

"I don't know. Maybe she gives great head." *Damn, why is that? I work hard and yet I'm still part time. Buddha warned me that he let people go because they had drug problems or demanded full time status. And with their small army of odd-jobbers, someone quits there's a bright-eyed, minimum wage replacement, waiting in the wings. So how did Bebe get full-time? I'll bet I'm right.*

Jeff jerked as if he'd just realized something. "You guys gonna go to East River Valley?"

"Ah, yeah." Erin raised an eyebrow.

"Could I get a lift?"

"I guess." *This is odd. Mr. Hipster's never expressed interest in hanging out with us. Maybe he revealed too many secrets of East River Valley and is tagging along in order to kill us.*

#

At six the girls plus Jeff, departed. During the drive, Lashell filled them in on the social studies classes she was taking.

"I'm definitely going into some kind of psychological field," she concluded.

"I need to figure out what to do," Erin sighed. "Talking to my jerk-off brother made me realize I can't work at a disco and a pizza parlor for the rest of my life. I need to get training, but unless I work full-time I can't afford to take classes, and if I take classes I can't work full-time."

"You should check out the community college work-study program," Jeff suggested. "They basically give you a tuition break if you work in what you're studying."

"But I wanna study jewelry making. They don't teach that."

"No, you have to go to the Academy for that."

#

Erin parked near what used to be the projects. A year ago, she wouldn't have stopped here without a six pack of mace, but now the neighborhood was quieter. The young gangers on the corner had been replaced by a Rastafarian selling carpets with Malcolm Xs and tigers on them; the projects themselves were now a debris-free field with a sign which read: 'What was once filled with violence and no hope is now planted with violets and artichokes.' Erin saw neither of those plants in evidence, but she still liked the idea. The three leaned against a fence, admiring the sunflowers, tomatoes, and pumpkin blossoms framed against a mural of racially diverse children engaged in pro-earth activities.

"That's rad," Erin said, turning to Lashell. Jeff was staring at her; not the kind where someone is assessing your reaction to a situation, but something else. She walked around him to Lashell.

"Where's the new stores at?" Lashell asked.

Jeff startled, as if just awakened from a dream, and began walking. "Uh-ah, they're on Fourth Street, this way."

Deeper in the neighborhood Erin noted the number of White people. *I guess now they're not afraid of having their cars broken into.* Lashell pointed at another cheerful mural by the same artist on an abandoned building.

"My grandfather use to have a barber shop there," Lashell said.

"What happened to it?" Erin asked.

"Black-owned businesses and jazz clubs thrived here until the 70s, then those Summer of Love fools up on 10th Street started gettin' their dope from here and it turned all druggy."

Erin caught Jeff staring at her again. She sped up until they arrived at the up-and-coming neighborhood's new heart: a bar, a cafe, a clothing store, a jewelry store, and a laundromat.

"Is this it?" Erin asked. "I expected four blocks of coolness, like 10th Street. And the stores are clos—ooh!" She pressed against the window of Frankenstein's Sister's Closet. Everything she saw—foreign baseball shirts, serial killer lunch boxes—she wanted. "Holy shit! Look at those devil-head Red-Hots dispensers. I want one."

"If you like that, you'll love this." Lashell pointed to a silver, three-sixes necklace in Neon's.

"Cool. We've got to come back here when they're open."

Lashell pointed to an entire section of nose rings. "This place was designed for you."

They moved on to Buck-Buck Oink, a cafe. The displayed menu focused on breakfast and brunch.

"Shit, they're closed too."

"The bar's open," Jeff said.

Erin narrowed her eyes. *Is it me, or did his voice just hint that he knew everything would be closed and this is where he really wanted to go.* "Lashell doesn't drink, and I'm actually more hungry than anything."

"They have a kick-ass pinball machine," he said in a singsong accent.

That's odd. How did he know that I liked pinball machines? Well, could just be a coincidence. She turned to Lashell, who had zero interest in pinball, and shot her a "don't leave me alone with Jeff' face. "Join us?"

"O-kay," Lashell said slowly enough to convey she had understood Erin's expression, but her tolerance had a very low threshold before expiring.

There was nothing particularly "kick-ass" about the Las Vegas themed pinball machine, with as much excitement as the bar itself. Wally's bar had decided to buck the Neopolitan norm by offering no unifying theme, bar snacks, and no blaring music. Unsurprisingly, they had no crowd, just a sad-eyed bartender.

Strangely enough, Erin felt rather content and relaxed. After playing the machine for an hour, she finally got her ball between the royal flush area and earned the bonus game. She let out a yahoo.

Lashell rolled her eyes. "What-the-fuck-ever, let's go someplace else."

"There is no place else," Jeff responded.

"That reminds me, Jeff," Lashell said, her face reading of expired tolerance. "You wanted a lift here. What for? You just been hangin' out."

Jeff panicked as if he had forgotten his name. "Oh, I was just coming to, you know hang, out."

"Right." Erin checked the wall clock. *Two hours from my shift at the Pit being over. Should I show up at all?* She glanced at Jeff, who was meandering near her as if he were waiting on something. *For what? Ain't shit gonna happen in this dump unless we start drinking or dancing.* "Ready to go, Shell?"

"Hell ye—hold up, who's that?" She pulled out her buzzing pager, checked the number and smiled. "Ah gee, it's P.J."

"P.J.? I thought you let him go 'cause he always had money and no job?"

"I did. But apparently he now has a job and a new car."

"So, you gonna take him back?"

"We'll see. Where's a phone around here?" Jeff pointed to the phone booth outside. Once alone with Jeff, Erin avoided looking at him, she could feel his eyes, scanning her like X-rays. She considered just walking away but she was curious what he was going to say next. *Is he going to talk about other hip hangouts? Ask me out?* He remained silent, apparently waiting on her to do something. Erin searched for a reason to escape. At a table, near the window sat a young lady reading a book. Since her arrival ten minutes earlier, Erin had been trying to place the girl's vaguely familiar face. This curiosity was a good excuse to leave. "Hey, Jeff, I know that girl. I'll be back."

Before reaching the woman Erin looked back. Jeff remained at the bar, glaring. Apparently he was guessing what Erin already knew: she was not coming back. Erin took a deep breath and interrupted the reading girl.

"Hey, you look familiar, don't I know you?"

The girl shook her head. "No. Do you go to Neo Tech?"

"No, no. Wait, you know a guy named Roger?"

"Roger? Black beret and sun glasses?"

"He's the one. He told me you're in his class and you're on that cable show." The girl smiled. "I hope this doesn't offend you, but I thought something called 'Shut up America' would be more like that show with those guys with bags on their heads."

"Tear Shit Up?"

"Yeah."

"No, it's about taking control of your life by being self-sufficient instead of going around complaining about things."

"That's cool." Erin peeked back to see if Jeff was still there. He was and had got himself a drink. "Are you majoring in Communications, too?"

"I'm actually going to go more into the business part of radio and TV."

"Right on. I'm Erin, by the way."

"Donna." They shook hands. Donna invited her to sit down. Lashell returned, was introduced, and joined them. Jeff remained on his perch, looking angry.

"So, what's up with P.J.?"

"That muthafucka said he wants to keep a casual relationship. Like I'm gonna be some kind of booty call." Donna's face lit up as Lashell talked, as if she were hearing French.

"So, you're not going to see him?"

"Hell naw! Hey! Why's Jeff over there?" Lashell started to raised her arm to call him over before Erin stopped her. "What? Why not?"

"He's been scope'n me out all day."

"Say what?"

"We gave him a lift, but he's still hanging out and he keeps looking at me, like he's waiting on something."

"I thought he had a crush on Brenda?"

"I thought so, too. But we both know she wouldn't give him the time of day."

"Are you saying you're easy?"

"No, but he's acting weird." All three girls looked over at Jeff. He turned away in embarrassment. Lashell and Erin laughed. "Speaking of boys, I discovered that Kevin likes Czech animation like I do. Could he be any more perfect?"

"Dang, girl. Always after that gay boy."

"You're going after a gay guy?" Donna asked. She had the fascinated look on her face, like she had with Lashell.

"He's not gay." Lashell blew through her lips. "So, Donna, you live around here or are you scoping out the new hip hotspot? At least according to Jeff, over there."

"I like to come here because it's not all crowded like 10th Street."

"I can see that. We're not harshing your peace, are we?"

"Oh, no-no-no. I was actually wondering if you girls wanted to get something to eat?"

Okay, what's she want? Horny lesbian threesome? "What do you think, Lashell?"

"Don't you have to be at work?"

"Well, maybe. I really don't think they'll notice."

"Where do you work?"

"Acid Pit."

"Wow! That must be so cool. All those musicians you get to meet."

Wow, she really does look impressed. Finally, someone who finds my job interesting. "You'd think, but I'm so busy running errands that I see the bands less than the audience does."

"That's bad."

"It is. That's why I'm debating even going in."

"Well, I'm going to X'emplé. You wanna come?"

Whoa, yuppie alert! Why would someone with a furry pink purse want to enter their lair? But, she doesn't seem very yuppie-like. Maybe I should experiment. "Okay. Lashell?"

"Fine. Maybe I can get breadsticks."

"Don't worry, it's taken care of," Donna said.

#

Erin stopped her car on the crosswalk, forcing annoyed pedestrians to walk around it. "What did she mean, 'taken care of?' Is she gonna pay?"

"She is rich, so maybe paying for dinner is like buying gum for her."

"But, she just met us, and she invites us to dinner?"

"So? We just met her and we're going to dinner with her."

"I'm just glad Jeff didn't want to tag along."

"You didn't invite him," Lashell laughed. "Girl, you didn't even wave goodbye."

"What else could I do? He might have invited himself along."

Lashell giggled. "You're one cold bee-ya. It's so funny—whenever men chase after you, you treat them like shit."

"I do not. If a man has confidence and looks like Kevin, he's in." Lashell gave her a skeptical look. "It's true, don't give me that look."

"Okay, the next time a cute boy shows interest in you, you go for it."

"You think Jeff is cute?"

"Hell naw! He's a toad. But he was showing interest."

"Whatever. I have no interest in the F.J. Pizza boys."

"Not even Tojo?"

"He's kinda cute, but one time, he was giving me a neck rub and Roger and Cliff started razzing him like, 'go lower, man' and shit like that, and he stopped."

"I remember that."

"Yeah, like how would you stand up to them if we were dating?"

"True. Okay, Pat is out. Doug is out. Roger is out..."

"Roger would be out even if he weren't dating."

Lashell grinned. "That leaves Cliff."

"No, thanks."

"What's wrong with Cliff?"

"You mean besides being an asshole, a racist, a sexist, and a homophobe? Noth'n."

"So what about boys at that glamorous job you're 'sposed to be at?"

"Coke heads, speed freaks, gutter punks, or they only chase after Brenda types."

"Sounds like you've put some thought into this."

"Nothing else to do while I'm working. It's so monotonous. All I do is: take this to there, clean this, change that. I know it's what I get paid for, but geez, why bother working there? Might as well be working at another pizza parlor."

"Well, soon they'll fire yo' lazy ass and you won't have to do nothing."

"Oh, well." Erin sighed while looking for a place to park. She spotted Donna getting out of a two-seater BMW convertible. "Holy shit, I guess she is loaded. Look at that thing. Maybe I should park this piece of shit around the corner."

"Oh no! Don't you start covering up who you are. She wants to have dinner with Erin and Lashell, and that's what she's gonna get."

"Okay. But no burping or farting."

"I ain't promising shit," Lashell said before burping.

#

X'emplé looked like artist Antonio Gaudí had designed it personally: curved doorways, ornate mosaic tile-work and an absence of sharp angles transported the diners to the heart of Barcelona. On the walls hung framed photos of Park Guell, La Sagrada Familia and his other masterpieces. It was crowded, but not by as many yuppies as Erin had expected. In fact, the people at the two closest tables had dyed hair and tattoos. The hostess, with her Betty Page hair cut and long black dress, lifting and pushing her cleavage together, could easily pass for a goth. Donna, like a dozen others in the restaurant, was on her cell phone. She hung up, lifted her arm, and waved to a waiter, who had apparently been on the other end of the line. He walked over.

Erin thought the man, whose light goatee and short dreadlocks framed a dark-caramel colored face, was very cute. If he hit on her, she was prepared to prove Lashell's theory wrong. He kissed Donna on the cheek.

"Hey, guys. This is Duncan Torres. Duncan, this is Lashell and Erin."

Duncan zeroed in on Lashell. "The shell? That's cool. Where did your name come from?"

"My mom couldn't decide between my two aunts: Lashanda and Sheryl." Duncan laughed until Lashell shot him a dirty look.

"I'm sorry, I just think that's such a cute story."

Erin sucked in a breath. *Nice try covering your tracks, but it was still rude. Minus twenty points. Now, if Lashell can just restrain—*

"Aight, Duncan DOUGHnuts," Lashell sneered.

"Oh no, I didn't mean to insult you." He seemed genuinely apologetic. "What can I do to make it up to you?"

"How about a table?" Donna suggested.

"Right, right." He went away to talk to the goth hostess. Erin wondered how he could get them a table in the overly packed eatery.

"Don't be so hard on Duncan; he puts his foot in his mouth a lot," Donna told Lashell.

"Make fun of my name, I'll put more than his foot in his mouth."

Erin laughed. "Gotta admit, he's pretty cute."

"I think so too," Donna agreed. "It's a wonder that he's not seeing anyone."

Erin looked over at Duncan, wheeling and dealing with the hostess, who looked up from the reservation book at their group. She smiled when she spotted Donna. Donna waved. The woman gave Duncan a yes nod and he walked back over.

"All set, follow me."

"What? How'd you do that?" Erin looked at the line of people who'd been waiting when she'd arrived.

A man detained Duncan with an arm grab.

"Hey! We've been waiting forty-five minutes for a table, how come they just walked in and got one?"

"They have reservations."

"I have reservations, too."

"Tell you what. I'll look in the book and see if I can move you up higher on the list, what's your name?"

"Oaks, party of three."

"Okay I'll be right back." He continued to lead the three girls to their table. "Hope you like waiting another forty-five minutes, Mr. Oaks." He seated them at a table intended for more than three diners. Erin imagined a pissed off party of six. Duncan had held Lashell's chair, but she seemed unimpressed. "Can I get you guys anything to drink?"

Erin, imagining the prices, was about to order water when Donna jumped in. "How about a bottle of cava?"

"What's that?" Erin asked.

"It's like sparkling wine."

Lashell jumped in. "Not like Champagne, right?"

"Yeah, is that all right?"

"Cept for the fact that I don't drink and we can't afford it."

"Oh, that's right. I forgot that you don't drink."

"Tell you what, how about a cherry soda?" Duncan suggested.

"Fine, unless it's ten dollars."

Donna put her hand on Lashell's shoulder. "Don't worry about it," she repeated.

Duncan winked at Lashell as he left. "I'll be back, making you like me again."

Erin scanned the ornate tile mosaics and the barstools made from twisted black metal. "This place is cool."

"I like how they did this place so close to Gaudí's style," Donna said. "Have you ever seen his work?"

"Naw," Erin said cautiously, "I've never been to Mexico."

"Mexico?…" Donna looked confused. "…Have you ever been to Spain?"

"No. I didn't get down further than some town in the south of France. Spain is below France, right?" Donna nodded. "Yeah it was some small town. I forgot the name of it… Coursac? The woman I stayed with went to pick up some cases of wine for her job…or was it vinegar? Anyway, I tagged along. It was nice, got a great baguette there." Donna wore her interested expression again. She turned and smiled at Lashell, who looked bored hearing about Erin's adventures in Europe. *Hey, over here, I'm talking.* "What about you, Donna, you been over the pond?"

"Some."

"Like where? France?"

"We use to go every year, but we sold our house there."

"House?"

"Yeah. How about you, Lashell? You done any traveling?"

"Girl, I rarely get out of this city."

Duncan returned with the cava, two glasses, and some bread. Another male waiter followed, carrying Lashell's soda, little white plates, and some fried plantains.

"How's your soda? Duncan asked Lashell as soon as she'd taken a sip.

"It's aight.

"Want something else?" He reached for the glass.

"No, it's fine. It's cool."

"Great. You guys ready to order?"

"We haven't even got any menus yet," Erin said

"That's okay, I know what to get," Donna interrupted. "Calamars Romana, xoricets fregits, gambas, and the spinach salad."

Lashell raised her eyebrows. "Dang, Roseanne Barr, you gonna eat all that?"

Donna laughed. "No, silly. That's for all of us. Oh, I forgot —anyone here a vegetarian?" Erin raised her hand. "Okay, beet salad, olives barrejades, plantain soup, and some portobello skewers." After Duncan left she turned to Lashell. "They're all tapas."

"You didn't just say 'tacos', did you?"

Donna laughed. "No. Tapas is Catalonian for 'little meals'. Small dishes we all share."

"You been to, where you call it? Catawhatzit?"

"Barcelona." She turned to Erin. "I go there before we hit Ibiza."

"Ibiza? I've heard of that. It's like a big rave on an island, right?"

"Yes."

"Course you'd hear of anything drug-related," Lashell remarked.

"Hey, screw you! Donna bought it up. She's the raver. Am I right you're into the 'E' thing?"

"Not as much since I started school. Although I am curious about this alphabet party next month at River Shore."

"A what?" Lashell looked to Erin, the human drug encyclopedia.

"No idea."

"It's like a rave," Donna answered. "After you pay to get in you can choose different drugs. They split up the letters from A to Z and you get a teeny tiny sample of each so that you can still function. A's for acid—or alcohol, if you don't want to freak out. B's for buds or beer. And so on..."

"Whoa! That sounds fucking awesome!" Erin praised. "How far have you got? What's past 'B'?"

She started doing the drug alphabet on her fingers. "...Buds, cocaine, Demerol, ecstasy.... After that I'm not sure. I've never made it past...cocaine. And I don't know anyone who's made it past heroin."

"Fuck! They have that shit there?"

"The one I went to didn't, just hash, but you never know."

Lashell sighed. "Can we talk about something else?"

"I take it you don't do drugs, either?"

"Lashell doesn't even drink coffee."

"Neat. Neither does Duncan. Is it re..." Donna's cell phone interrupted her Duncan sales pitch. "Hi...I'm at X'emplé. You should swing by...Erin and Lashell...They're my new friends...yes...yes...I don't think so...yes, come by...Ciao." She hung up and called someone else.

Erin took the opportunity to talk to Lashell. "So, Duncan's nice, huh?"

"He's okay."

"Okay? He has a job, doesn't drink or smoke, he's cute. You better go after him before someone else does."

"Like who, you?"

"He's shown no interest in me. It's all you, sweetheart."

"My friends Kim and Art are coming," Donna announced.

"Art a cutie?" Erin asked hopefully.

"He's...nice. Kim is cute."

Whoa. I hope my friends don't tell people I'm nice in that tone. "Kim a guy? Or are you into girl-girl action?"

Donna giggled "No. It's a Korean guy."

"That'll work."

"You seem to be very adaptable. I like that."

"We call it flakey," Lashell amended. Erin sneered back.

Erin got tired of waiting for someone else to drink first and tried the cava. *Likable, but if it sparkles, it all taste like Champagne.*

Duncan flourished the tapas onto the table. As Lashell and Donna sampled the little meat dishes, they gave orgasmic moans. Erin dug into the soup and the portobello skewers. *These are the best things I've eaten in over a year.* Her companions sang the praises of the spinach salad, and its bacon bits were a temptation to come home to meat, but Erin stuck to the beet salad. *Good, but my mom actually makes a better one. I bet she knows through Dave and Josh I'm all right. Isn't it a parent's job to check up on their children? Or is that only up to twenty-one?*

Kim and Art arrived. Kim Yi—short, with black wire frame glasses and a colorful vest—was cute, but in more of a stuffed toy way. Art Santos was heavy, with scruffy hair on his face and long in the back to offset a balding front. He wore a black T-shirt with the letters H.F.S. over what looked like silhouettes of potatoes with halos having sex. When he saw Erin, his face lit up as if he had found money. After introductions, Art sat next to Erin and tried her soup and salad without asking. *I know we're were all sharing, but he shouldn't have assumed.*

"What the hell is H.F.S.?" Erin asked as he helped himself to more of her soup.

"Holy Fucking Shit. It's a band."

Huh. So not potatoes. Well, that satisfies my curiosity about all things Art. She turned her attention to Kim, but he seemed content to talk just to Donna, as if no one else was around. Duncan re-appeared with another bottle of cava. Erin liked it. Her face didn't feel numb like it usually would after three glasses of Champagne. Duncan asked Lashell if she would forgive him if he bought her some salmon. She said she'd think about it, which was enough for him to run off and retrieve it.

"Wow, Shell, he's literally waiting on you hand and foot. You gonna cut him some slack?"

"Depends on how this salmon taste."

"Oh, you'll love it," Donna assured. "He picked a good meal to seduce you with."

"Be cheaper with a beer and pizza," Art said, finishing off the Calamars Romana.

Erin found his little joke funny but she didn't want to encourage anyone that muscled in on her soup.

"Does anyone want more food?" Donna asked.

Erin pointed to a plate of croquettes on another table. "Those cheese things look good."

"No problem. Hey, Erin, are you into comics? Art works in a comic book store."

Erin grew queasy. *Surely Donna's not trying to hook up me and Art. He's no Duncan.* "Not really. The only thing I ever read was Richie Rich and Archie."

Art gave a snort.

"What?"

"Nothing."

Erin narrowed her eyes. *If you're going to insult my childhood literature, be man enough to do it to my face.*

"You work at F.J. Pizza, right?" Donna asked.

"Yeah."

"Get any free pizza?" Art asked

"Not enough to seduce anyone with."

Everyone laughed at her unintended joke.

"She also works at the Acid Pit," Donna added

"Probably not anymore," Lashell said.

Erin didn't feel worried. *There's no punch clock at the Pit and no one to report to when I show up. Only a few will seek me out for a specific task, like Paul, and lately, he's been too busy in the office.* She watched the sea of guys in beige pants trying to mingle with those in hip, black attire. *I never thought that I'd like the food at any place frequented by yuppies or hipsters. But here I am, ordering more food and not sure how we're going pay for it.*

In addition to the croquettes, Donna ordered two more tapas for Kim and Art, and a dessert and two glasses of sherry for her and Erin. After Duncan brought their order, Erin leaned over to Lashell.

"Doesn't look like that salmon got him in."

"Too oily, but I won't hold it against him."

"Oh, my God, he should get you this flan. This is the best I've ever had." The aged sherry pushed her right into intoxicated. Absolutely content, she glanced over at Art, eating a bowl of mussels with his hands. *Nope, even if I smoked crack, I wouldn't hook up with him.* Her sudden attention set him off talking to her about how he broke up with a long distance girlfriend of some sort, and Batman. *Why is he talking to me? Should I tell him that I'd never date anyone who tries to offset his or her balding by growing it long in the back? Okay, let's end this.*

She turned to Donna. "So, you guys all go to Tech?"

"Just me and Kim. Duncan is Kim's next door neighbor, and Art is taking computer classes at the community college."

"I knew I've seen you somewhere," Lashell told Art. "So, Duncan's not in school or nothing?" Lashell had a disappointed tone in her voice.

"No, he dropped out of State."

" 'Cause of grades or finances?"

"Neither. He got into an argument with a professor who was out to get him or some stuff like that. I don't know the full story. But don't hold it against him, he's a cool person."

Lashell looked doubtful. When the subject of the conversation made an appearance, Erin reached into her backpack and found twenty-two dollars. By her calculations the bill, including tax and tip, should be at least $168. Donna looked the slip over and dropped her credit card beside it. Erin guessed they were going to consolidate everything through her.

"How much do we owe you, Donna?"

"Uhmm, how about eight dollars?"

"What? Are you covering or something?"

"No." She handed Erin the bill. Not including tip, it was an even forty. She perused it like a detective examining a murder scene. Duncan had left off three quarters of their items. *So that's what she meant by "Don't worry about it."* Erin chipped in for an extra big tip for Duncan. When he said good-bye to Lashell he kissed her hand. She didn't seem impressed, so Erin swooned for her.

"Oh, my God, he is so cute."

"Yeah, but he screams of effort."

"Jee-zuss, Shell. What do you want: Romeo or homeboy?"

"A Romeo that doesn't pine away at the bottom of no dumb-ass balcony."

"Hey," Donna said as they squeezed past Mr. Oaks to the door. "Do you have any plans tomorrow after work?"

"Well, Lashell is off and I guess I'm fired from the Acid Pit, so I guess I'm free. Why? What's up?"

"There's this band playing at my sister's cafe that I want to see. After that we could go to a restaurant in Bistro Alley."

"What kind of music?"

"Grime rock."

"Leave me out," Lashell protested

"Lashell hates local music," Erin said, patting Lashell's shoulder.

"Only that fucked up shit you listen to."

Donna still appeared surprised Lashell had said no to her. "Oh. That's too bad. Erin?"

"I'm there." Erin exchanged numbers with Donna. Art and Kim also agreed to attend.

As Erin drove Lashell across the bridge, they talked about the group they just met. "Art seemed confused that not only did I not ask him for his number, but I didn't initiate any physical contact while saying good-bye."

"I can't figure how an odd group like that could be friends. It's like Donna's their leader or something."

"Well, she did set up a pretty mad bill on that dinner."

"That's another thing: we wouldn't give someone cheap pizza we just met. She doesn't know us. We could be purse-snatchers or something."

"Like I said, money is probably no big deal for her. Maybe her whole thing was to find a date for Duncan?"

"Now you're scaring me. Like drag'n two hookers off the street."

"Great. She thinks we're trash."

"That's not what I meant. It's just there's something weird about her. You notice how she don't cuss yet she's all down with the drug thang?"

"So she's proper."

"Proper, hell. She's a dabbler."

"A what?"

"Dabbler. You know, those Neo yuppies that hang out in the rough parts of town, have lots of cool, fucked-up friends, but when the party's over they go back to the safety of their lofts."

"Hey, she ain't a yuppie."

"I bet she'd say the same thing."

"Hey, I like her. She gave us a kick-ass meal."

"That's cool, but I never judge a person on what they got or give, but who they are."

"Dang, Shell! You're harsh. She was just trying to make friends."

"Then why didn't she ask me for my number?"

"Uh, I don—because you didn't want to go to the concert?"

"Perhaps."

Erin dropped Lashell off and made her way back to the West Side bridge. She stopped off at the Acid Pit to see if she were fired. The theme night, Techno Cowboy, didn't seem to be much of a success—the parking lot was less than half full and there were more employees outside than patrons trying to get in. *Shit! With such a low crowd, of course they'll notice my absence.* She took a deep breath and walked up to the entrance. One of the doormen was Maxx, from the Riverview boarding house she'd stayed in, and by unspoken agreement they ignored each other. Inside, the first person she saw was Paul.

"Erin? What are you doing here?"

"Er, ah...."

"Didn't Toad tell you to go home?"

"Say what?"

"Yeah, it's so dead I sent some people home early. I guess you must have missed her."

"Yeah, I was cleaning up something."

"Gee, I'm sorry you've been working all this time." He grabbed some posters out of a cardboard box near the ticket booth and handed them to her. "Here, you can have some posters from our next shows." Erin unrolled one of them.

Underneath the words 'Bitch Night' a muscular guy in a black, leather thong was getting his ass bit by a woman in military dominatrix wear.

"Cool! Thanks Paul." Erin returned to her car, resisting the urge to dance or scream triumphantly. Not only had she gotten away with skipping work, but she was rewarded for it as well.

When she got home, Mary Jo was watching TV as usual. Moving in, Erin had expected to have a more crazy, outgoing roommate. *She's more crazy at work than at home. And how does she find time to do artwork and have interesting friends and yet watch so much TV?* After exchanged greetings Erin went into the bathroom. Mary Jo called out something unintelligible through a closed door and pee hitting water. She ignored it and continued her bedtime closing ritual. When she'd reached the teeth-brushing phase, Mary Jo knocked on the door. Erin spat out the foam. "Yeah?"

"You got some letters."

"That's nice. Could you leave them on that mannequin head, coffee table thing of yours?"

"Hey, these were dropped off by your mom."

At lightning speed, Erin opened the door and grabbed the stack of envelopes. "What the? Why didn't you tell me when I walked in?"

"I never check the mail until you come home. That way, if it's sad news, I have a shoulder to cry on."

Sighing physically and mentally, she slipped the handwritten note out from the rubber band. *"Erin, I'm dropping off some old mail of yours. Love, Mom."* Is there any hidden meaning? Bringing the mail physically instead of forwarding it. Love, Mom? She's obviously making an attempt to reestablish some kind of dialogue between us. Erin considered calling and thanking her but the thickness of one of the envelopes distracted her. Pulling it out, she saw 'Welcome to Capital American' and a Visa logo.

"No fucking way!" she said opening it. Inside was something she had no idea that a girl working at a pizza parlor and only $86 in the bank could qualify for. But there it was, with 'Erin P. Pierce' embossed on its golden surface: her first credit card. "Holy fucking shit!"

"Do you need a shoulder to cry on?"

"No, just a mall!"

#

On Erin and Lashell's day off from F.J. Pizza, the first thing she did was piss off Lashell by calling at eight o'clock in the morning to go shopping. Lashell set her straight, with a stern name-calling; she was not to be disturbed until noon. Erin was too excited to wait. She left the apartment, searching for something to buy. *The only thing I know would be open is the 24-Hour cafe, and they only take cash. Neopolitan is definitely a night person. You have a better chance of finding a cup of coffee at three AM than a few hours later.* Walking in the nicer part of Kenwood she found a place that bucked the trend: the red, white-trimmed monster of gentrification, The Coffee Barn.

Inside, she discovered they had abandoned the faux-barn decor, complete with hay bails for the every-popular yuppie generic. She got in line behind a guy who looked about twenty-three. *If he wasn't wearing those beige pants with a light blue shirt I might consider him cute.* He turned and smiled. She returned an 'as if' look which seemed to dash his hopes enough so he didn't attempt conversation. After he had slunk off with a soy milk carob latte made with decaf beans infused through bottled water and the whole topped with low-fat whipped cream, Erin pleased the girl behind the counter by ordering a plain cup of coffee. Informed that the minimum purchase was five dollars for credit cards, an over-priced cranberry muffin joined the meal and her first adult transaction was complete. She took a seat in the corner and watched the yuppie drive off with the coffee cup on his roof.

On her trip to Europe, the first thing she would do on arrival in a new country, was go to a cafe or bar, order coffee, and sit in the corner, getting her bearings as she watched the locals and listened to them talk about the current events or the weather. The Coffee Barn was not a good place for her technique: no one sat together and talked, and those who did merely asked for the sports section of the paper. By the time she'd finished her cup, Erin was bored. She still had three hours until she could call Lashell. She returned home to watch the morning talk shows.

She passed an unfamiliar man coming downstairs from her floor. Her woman alarm tingled, imagining Mary Jo alone with a possible stranger, but she tried not to make too much of it. What did alarm her was Mary Jo sitting on the living room floor with a stack of twenties beside her elbow on the coffee table. More alarming still was the huge, open garbage bag full of pot next to her roommate's legs. Erin looked at it, then at Mary Jo, then the pot, then Mary Jo. This went on for at least fifteen seconds.

"Oh, you're home," was all Mary Jo said.

"Yeah."

"Oh shit! That's right. You're off on Wednesdays."

"Uh, yeah. Er-ah, how? Or why?"

"What?"

"Mary Jo! THERE'S A HUGE PILE OF POT ON MY APARTMENT FLOOR!"

"I kept forgetting to tell you about this."

"That you're a drug dealer? What's with F.J. Pizza and drug dealers?"

"I'm not a drug dealer. It's just the one bag…Who else is selling at work?"

"That's irrelevant! Mary Jo! People can get two years for just an ounce of this shit…" Erin pulled some out and smelled it. "You fuck'n have at least 1000 YEARS WORTH! Where did this come from?"

"The Cannabis Club."

"The Cannabis Club! Mary Jo! This stuff is for old people and AIDS patients! What are you doing with it?"

"Remember the old club on 14th Street?"

"No, but I'll take your word for it."

"Well, my roommate, who worked there, gave me a couple of bags to hold in case Nazi-Man raided them. When they did, they didn't get this but they got her on some bullshit parking tickets so she spent some jail time. She told me to go ahead and sell the stuff to help cover rent and give her something to live off of when she got out 'cause she was now unemployed. By the time I'd sold through the first bag, she'd gotten out of jail and left to go on a spiritual journey to Tibet. So now I have this bag."

"JESUS! Do you know how many years you can get for selling? Do you know that they can jack me up, too?"

"That's why I didn't tell you, so if they asked you if you knew anything, you could say no and it'd be open out."

"Oh yeah, that'll work on the Feds. Mary Jo, you gotta get this shit out of here."

"I can't. I need it for my art."

"ART MY ASS! You just like the extra income. And speaking of which, why aren't you at work?"

"I called in sick."

"JEE-ZUSS! This can't work M.J. As much as I like this stuff, I'm not going to prison for it."

"What can I do? Throw it away? If someone else finds it, they'll just sell it and then they'll be making the money I could have made, and selling it to kids."

"And how much is that?"

"Currently, $45,000."

There was a long pause. "You have $45,000?"

"Well, my grandma in Tennessee has most of it. She saved her farm with it. I just keep enough to do my artwork and pay rent."

"Then what the HELL is F.J. Pizza for?"

"To keep the bank from asking where I get money from."

"My God, I don't believe this. My roommate is a drug dealer! What do you do with the Pizza money?"

"I give that to charity."

"Oh..." *She's not into selling the pot for profit. She sees it as something to let her to live a decent life. But the police won't see it that way.* "Mary Jo, you gotta get this stuff out of here! If the cops come in here they'll take us both away."

"What can I do? I gotta support my art. A bronze cast costs a lot of money."

"What bronze cast?" Erin asked, looking around. "Where?"

"It's at my studio. I'm making a six foot bronze cast of a cock."

You mean a rooster?"

"No, a dick. A six foot, erect penis."

"That's interesting. But I don't know if even the Neo M.O.M.A. would display that."

"It's not for them. It's for people that like to look at giant six-foot bronze cocks."

"And where...never mind. Mary Jo, the pot has to GO! I don't care if you sell it or not, but it can't stay here!"

"Well, technically, the pot was here first."

"Oh... I see. So you'd rather keep it here and lose a roommate?"

"I'd rather keep both."

"You can't! I like you and I like living here, but I'm not going to jail for you!"

"That's too bad. It sounds like you're the one who has a decision to make."

Erin thought for a moment. "If you get caught, I'm not gonna lie for you!"

"I wouldn't expect anything else."

Erin went to her bedroom, shut the door and sat on the bed. *I can't believe I'm in another bad living situation. I don't want to go through the whole moving disaster again, but there's no way I'm risking jail. I could threaten to turn her in. No, even Mary Jo knows that's not going to happen. My only option is moving on.* She lay back on the bed, reached over the side, and petted Buster's head. In spite of Lashell's warning, she called her again. This time she answered in a more cheerful tone.

"Hey, Shell? I'm sorry. It's still before noon, but I have to get out of the house."

"That's okay, I'm up. Some dumb-ass called me early this morning and I haven't been able to get back to sleep."

"Bloody ha-ha. I need to talk to you. Are you ready to come over?"

"Why should I come over? Haven't even had breakfast yet."

"C'mon, I'll buy you breakfast with my new card."

"Okay, but why you in such a hurry to get me over there?"

"Shell, I just discovered that Mary Jo's a drug dealer."

"...Meet me at the train station in 40 minutes."

#

At Buck-Buck Oink, Erin picked at her huevos rancheros omelet. Her stomach was too full of anxiety to fit more. Lashell had gotten her second wind and had no problem finishing off her crepes. She drank the rest of her orange juice and leaned back in her chair.

"You got that same stressed look on your face as when you was apartment hunting. So, what you gonna do?" Lashell asked.

"No idea. I dread going through the whole moving thing, again."

"Well, if you think about it, minus the bag of pot she's not a bad roommate."

"Whatever. I can't stay there. I don't feel safe. Like, any moment now some Lars-type is gonna come over to take out the competition and I'll be the one that's home."

"True. This is a stone cold trip—Mary Jo, slanging. Maybe you could blackmail her and she'll have to cut you in."

"Knowing her, she'd kill me and turn my body into a sculpture or some shit."

Lashell laughed. "That's so true. Maybe cover you with all that bronze she's buying."

"Right, grabbing on to a six-foot cock." They both laughed until Erin sank back into her funk. "This blows donkey ass. What am I gonna do?"

"I say ignore it like you know nothing until you find a place. If cops or dealers come to visit, maybe they'll be smart enough to know that you're just the roommate."

"Right. That's why we have drive-bys, 'cause drug dealers do research."

Lashell nodded. "Hmm. Hey, you going out to that concert-slash-dinner with the dabblers?"

"They're not dabblers—and yes, I still think you should go."

"No way. Using me as an escort service for Duncan Doughnuts—Shee-it!"

"It must be nice being rich. She can buy whatever she wants and not have to worry about it."

"I'm sure she has plenty to worry about. All people do."

"'Cept the money thing."

"Sure she does. Look at Bill Gates. Motherfucker make thirty-five thousand dollars an hour and yet he still keep on working. Me, I'd work for one day and retire."

"Well, he may also have to pay fifteen thou an hour to live like he does."

"Exactly. How the hell did he get in that hole? He live like us he could use his money for a party everyday for everybody in Neo. But nooo, gotta have a solid gold toilet seat with hot and cold running water."

Erin laughed. "Oh, speaking of toilets, I should walk Buster. You wanna go to the park?"

"Sure, walk off those crepes."

#

Central City Park didn't have a special dog area, so Buster had to be leashed. As they made a loop around the pond Erin told Lashell about the note her mom had left on the mail.

"I agree. She's probably calling for a truce. You should call her."

"Maybe. I wanted things to be good when I called her. To show I can do well without her help."

"Things are fine. You ain't gonna reach no point where they're perfect."

"I know, but wouldn't it be nice?"

Erin steered toward the gazebo to sit and chat, but someone was sleeping in it. Just as she prepared to turn away, she realized she knew the person.

"Hey, isn't that Doug?"

"Really? Hey! Doug!"

Doug raised his head and squinted his eyes. "Hey, whassup?"

"What the hell you doing here, man?"

"Sleeping."

Erin and Lashell looked at one another. "Aren't you supposed to be at work?"

"I am, to my house."

"What? I don't get it."

"I played a gig up in Mountain Springs 'til four last night. I needed to catch some z's so I had Sam call in a pizza delivery for a far-off location. Now I got to get at least an hour to crash, two if I say I got lost."

"But won't you have to pay for that pizza?"

"Sure, but now dinner's taken care of."

"O-kay. Well, I guess you wanna get back to sleep, so we'll just move along."

"No, it's cool. About time I should be heading back."

The girls and Buster joined Doug as he walked to his car. *What a bizarre day: one of my friends is a drug dealer and another is lazy and cheating F.J.P. with a plan I wished I had thought of.*

"Hey," Erin said, "how's your girlfriend?"

"Still pregnant and growing."

"You sound like you ain't looking forward to being a daddy," Lashell said.

"On what I make at F.J. Pizza, I'm not."

"I think having a baby would be rad, especially with Kevin," Erin said, swooning.

"Gag, barf, splash," Lashell responded. "You better give up on that boy! You know he's gay."

"He is not."

"Girl, that boy dress better than you–he gay."

Doug laughed.

"You're asking for it, Shell," Erin said, raising her free fist. "I will defend Kevin's hetero honor to my last breath."

"Speak of the devil," Doug said, pointing.

"Ha-ha! How would you even know what Kevin—oh, my god! You're right!" She lowered her sunglasses. 'He's not alone. But, who's that with him? It's a girl! I can't make out who it is, but definitely not Kathy. Maybe that's his girlfriend. Maybe he's not gay!"

"What you mean 'maybe'? Wasn't you sure?"

"Maybe it's a guy in drag," Doug said.

"Shut up, Doug. I've got to get closer." Erin knew eventually they would all cross paths, but she also knew she couldn't perform as well with Doug and Lashell standing behind her thinking wisecracks. "I know!" She pointed the dog toward the two travelers. "Sic 'em, Buster!" He started barking and charged. Erin ran close, as though the medium-sized dog was dragging her along. When her dog got within eight feet of the now-alert couple, Erin pulled the leash. "Stop, Buster! Heel! I am so sorry. He wa…oh, hi, Kevin!"

"Hi! Your name's Erin, right?"

Erin felt a little pissed but held it back. *By now you should know my name.* "Yes! How's it going?"

"Pretty cool. We're just cruising around the park."

"Me too!" She gestured at Lashell and Doug, who had slowed. "We had the day off and decided to do the park thing. But what are you doing here? I thought it was a school day?"

"It is, but Graham here wanted us to play hooky!"

"Hey! Who wanted to stay home and draw?" Graham said.

What kind of name is Graham? Well, let's take a better look at you, Graham: cute, slender, you could be a model or an actress with a little more makeup, flawless legs, decent—wait, Graham said the word 'home' as if they were living together. I gotta dig deeper. "Are you guys, like, roommates?"

"Yep." Graham said with stern affirmation.

"How many bedrooms do you have?"

"Just one," Kevin answered.

Graham raised a 'who-is-this-girl-asking-these-questions ?' eyebrow, which tweaked Erin's anxiety, already elevated at the prospect they might be dating, still higher. *Gotta find a good cover.* "The reason I'm asking's 'cause I'm looking for a new place to live."

"Well, since I have the bedroom and Graham has the living room, there's nowhere left to sleep."

Okay, God, thank you for that. Stay with me while I finally test the gay theory. "I don't know if I could live with a guy; it would make me feel funny." Erin couldn't read Kevin's face. He'd bent down to pet Buster. "I mean, it doesn't make you nervous that she might see you naked?"

"No problem, she's use to it." Kevin stood up, reached for Graham's cut-off shirt and faked trying to lift it up. She laughed while fending him off. Buster barked happily.

This horseplay is awfully casual. Are they dating but just keep separate spaces?

Lashell and Doug arrived. Erin was too busy interrogating to bother introducing them. "Are you a nudist?"

"No, I'm just comfortable with my body."

"What does your girlfriend think?"

"I don't have one."

Great—you're still with me. Don't go away yet. "How about her boyfriend?"

"Oh, he doesn't mind."

"Why not?"

" 'Cause I'm gay."

The short pause felt like an hour. Everything she had worked for, all of her hopes and dreams, and all the fending off of critics, all that was now a pile of broken ornaments on the ground. She turned to Lashell and Doug, who kept a polite silence. "Are you guys ready to go?" she said through clenched teeth.

#

An hour after the Reality Bomb had hit ground zero, Erin and Lashell stood on the West Side Bridge gazing into the river. *How did we end up here? I don't remember asking to come here, but it makes sense. I want to be as far as I can from Kevin. Maybe my memory's a little fuzzy from smoking that joint. Well, Mary Jo left her stash lying unattended in the living room and wasn't there to ask. Anyway, that ounce was payment for leaving out her drug-dealing hobby. Now we're a little more even.* "Goodbye cruel world," she said to the flowing green water.

"Girl, don't even joke like that."

"Might as well jump. Kevin will never be mine."

"Forget about him. He ain't the only cute boy in Neopolitan."

"It's not just because he was cute. We liked the same movies, the same music."

"C'mon. You think you're the only one that likes Eastern-bloc animated cartoons?"

"Well...yeah."

"True, but face it: even in these dirty-ass waters, there's more than one fish."

Erin looked down at her shadow on the water. She waved to confirm it was hers and not Lashell's or some maniac sneaking up behind them. "Just a bunch of guppies."

"Maybe you can find a guppy with a big dick?"

Erin burst out laughing. "Girl, you're so sick!" Laughing made her feel better. *It's silly to pine after a man who's announced that he's gay. I have so many other things to worry about: my drug dealer roommate, my relationship with my mom, my lack of interest in my second job, and my new credit card.* Erin heard the bell of an ice cream cart. She located it emerging from under the bridge on the shoreline trail. "Let's go get some snow cones."

"I ain't got no money."

"My treat."

Lashell shook her head. "Shit. You must be feeling happy."

The girls walked toward the steps. *I don't feel good, but I do feel better. Instead of focusing on Kevin, I should concentrate on what to wear to the concert with Donna and how to skip out on the Acid Pit without being fired. Maybe I can show up long enough so people will know I was there, then leave.*

"Hey, check that fool out."

Erin followed Lashell's finger to a man climbing onto the guardrail. "What's that dude doing? Holy shit, he's not gonna jump, is he?"

"He better not. 'Cause I ain't gonna save his ass."

She watched the man spread his arms, balancing. *Please, just be praying or meditating in a weird way.* Her hope became despair as he leaned forward, in slow motion, and his feet left the rail as he started a swan dive.

"Oh shit! Oh shit! Oh shit! Oh shit!" Erin yelled. Her feet automatically started running without being commanded. Lashell, in spite her pledge, followed close behind.

The man's body disappeared from sight. *What do I do? Even if I jump after him, neither of us would survive the impact. And if we did, the only thing I remember from classes at the Y is avoiding the clogged toilets.* Erin ran to the edge, dreading peeking over and seeing just the river or worst, a broken, twisted body on the trail. *My only option is seeing if he's alive and running for help.*

Lashell grabbed Erin's arm. "Wait! What's that?"

Erin saw what appeared to be a big white snake unraveling and following the jumper to his death. Erin's thoughts flashed the word 'rope', which led to 'elastic', which led finally to 'bungee'. She laughed. "He's a bungee jumper!" Lashell joined her in laughter. They leaned over the edge just in time to see the extreme sportsman finish the last recoil of his bouncing.

"I knew it all the time," Lashell said so unconvincingly, Erin had no need to point it out.

The guy swung back and forth until he grabbed a knotted rope fastened about forty feet from where he'd jumped. He started pulling himself up, his upper body strength impressing Erin despite her jangled nerves.

As soon as he was on the bridge, she started scolding him. "You butt-nugget! Are you crazy? You shouldn't be doing this alone!"

"Sorry. I usually come with my 'rads, but I was feeling a little awkward. I guess this was sort of a suicide leap."

"Why would you want to kill yourself?" Erin realized this was ironic for someone who'd joked about jumping earlier.

"Hello. Erin," Lashell whispered, "cute boy."

Erin ignored her, but not the long black dreads under the boy's headscarf.

"I was feeling a little down because my girlfriend left me."

"That's not enough to kill yourself!"

"Hello. Erin. No girlfriend" Lashell muttered and elbowed her. Erin noticed his blue eyes and his dimples.

"But I wasn't feeling bad enough to off myself completely."

"You should talk to someone."

"Like who? You?"

"Sorry, me and Lashell have plans."

"HELLO! Erin!" Lashell yelled.

"What? What?"

"I gotta go see my sister, so you're totally free."

"But, I thought we were gonna get snow cones?"

"I looove snow cones," the guy said.

Lashell yanked Erin aside. "Listen: he's cute, available, and dressed all grungy so he's probably straight. If you don't get snow cones with that boy I swear to God I'll throw your whiny White ass over this bridge."

"But, what if he's a serial killer?"

"What if Spiderman fought Batman? Who cares? Neither of them is real. Serial killers wouldn't be bungie-jump'n off no bridge, they be throw'n prostitutes off them. Take a chance. Look at that ass!"

The man was bent over, shoving his equipment into a bike messenger's bag. *He's definitely athletic and dresses similar to me, and I know I have to move on because Kevin's a lost dream, but it feels like cheating—not on Kevin but on my ideals. How can I go from clean-cut hipster to grungy X-Gamer?*

Lashell slapped Erin on the butt. "Go get 'em!" she growled, and then walked away.

#

Under the bridge, on the Shoreline trail, they leaned against a giant rusty boat propeller sculpture.

"So, what's your real name?" she asked, balling up her snow cone wrapper.

"What's wrong with Steiner? My friends all like it, and it reminds me of Germany."

"You've been to Europe?"

"Army brat—lived a big chunk of my life in Frankfort. Went all over the place."

"I've been to France, and—"

"Paris was cool the first couple of times. Better than London. Now, Italy—you been there?"

"No, but…" Erin started listing the places she had visited in Europe. Steiner, having lived there for so long, looked as impressed as if she were recounting her adventures walking down the street. *Well, good for you, international boy. On the plus side, you're an attractive vegetarian who remembers my name.* Erin noticed how low the sun was dipping. "I better head home and change. I'm supposed to see some band at Psychicmondo tonight."

"Oh, the Ron Jeremy Experience?"

"Say what?"

"The Ron Jeremy Experience. They're aight. Kinda got ass. I would have gone but my Ex will be there."

"That would be bad. Don't want you back here."

"Naw. Maybe we can hook up afterwards? Or tomorrow?"

"Afterwards we're going to Bistro Alley..." Erin recalled Donna's fascination with meeting strangers. "Hey, why don't you join me there?"

"I'm not a big fan of all those yuppie troughs."

"No, it's fine; the people I'm going with are totally cool. Last time they knew the waiter so we got all this food cheap as hell."

"Cheap food? I'm down. I'll meet you at the bar in Le Clochard."

"Cool, I'll—how do you know one of the yuppie feed bags restaurants?"

"Friend of mine's a bartender there."

"Oh, see you there, then."

As Erin and Steiner separated, she felt an impulse to kiss him. *That's strange, to be so open so soon after Kevin. Good sign.*

#

After lighting up a cigarette, Erin bathed, shaved her armpits, painted her toe nails, and chose an outfit to show off her cleavage and new tattoo. She was saving the apparel for snaring Kevin, but it could still be put to good use. She felt a little sad and embarrassed about the whole Kevin thing. *What does he think about this odd girl always acting like a clown around him? Did he not notice my flirtations? Is he so used to straight women falling for him that he just ignored it? Either I'm a bad flirt or he's an egotistical idiot.* Makeup made her feel better; a reason to spruce up offered a spark of hope that things were okay for now.

Mary Jo came home, cleaned up her illegal clutter, and left to work on her giant penis. Erin camped out in the bathroom the entire time, putting herself behind schedule.

Someone had run out of gas on the bridge, creating a traffic jam, and she arrived fifteen minutes late for work, further hindering her plan. Now, instead of sneaking away from one person who knew her, she ran the risk of numerous others accosting her to do jobs for them. Her fear was well-founded: as soon as she walked in Buddha, asked her to clean up some trash at the back exit; after she'd finished, Riff Raff needed help carrying crates of records; and then Bebe wanted a hand photocopying some kind of employee manual.

All these people bossing me around is really pissing me off.

Toad waved to her. "Hey, Erin. Can you empty the trash bins? Thanks."

Great. I've missed half of the concert by now. I better call Donna's cel phone.

Paul intercepted her on the way to the pay phone. "Erin, I need you to polish the disco ball."

"Are you serious?"

He looked puzzled. "Yeah, why do you ask?"

"Buddha said that was like a joke."

"I assure you it's quite real and someone has to do it." He handed her a spray bottle and a rag and then walked away.

"Someone has to do it?" *I'm just a generic hired hand. Anyone could do my job. And no one seems to notice or care that I'm a little dressed up. Maybe they're just used to fancy clothes or wild makeup, but at F.J. Pizza even Ed comments on my outfits—negatively, but he does.*

At the supply room, where she had come to get the extra-long ladder, she paused. Right next to it was an exit door. A force, like pure, concentrated id, filled her, a delicious feeling reached her legs and took her through the exit. *The last stunt didn't get me fired, but this one surely will.* She took a deep breath. In spite of the surrounding factories, the air outside felt fresher.

Fear began creeping into her exhilaration. *How will I pay rent? Will I fall into another boarding house situation?* A part of her said: "never again" and she believed it. She dashed across the parking lot. Her car started after three cranks. She breathed out and realized she had been holding her breath. At the exit, Toad was hanging a poster on a pole. They locked glances as Erin drove past. She wasn't sure what Toad was thinking, but Erin's message was simple: "Whatever."

The euphoria lasted the entire drive to the bridge. Rather than panicking about the future, she was excited about seeing her new friends, half of a concert, and eating a fancy meal.

Another traffic jam, this time caused by a BMW rear-ending a SUV, delayed Erin. *The concert will surely be over by now, Donna and friends won't be waiting on me, I should go straight to Bistro Alley. Even if they didn't show up, maybe Steiner will.* She remembered him climbing the rope and imagined him, hot and sweaty, climbing toward her naked body on a high platform. When she almost killed a guy on a bike, she took a break from fantasy land.

The difficult search for parking kept her grounded in reality. She walked eight blocks from a space near a construction site. She cleared her mind of the Steiner scenario and the ones she'd clung to with Kevin. *Interesting that most of my fantasies with Kevin were non-sexual: going to movies, museums, clubs, and other cultural activities. Like sex was just a bonus dream.*

The Alley was a place she wouldn't go to without being invited: fourteen restaurants strung along a narrow walkway made narrower by outdoor tables overflowing with loud-talking, drunk-laughing, passerby insulting Neo yuppies, guppies, buppies and hipsters. Erin was used to people thinking she was weird just because of her hair, and she ignored their comments as she read the restaurants' names: The Velvet Curtain, E, 103 Bistro Alley, Canard, Red, and, finally, Le Clochard.

How will I find Donna and her friends if they're not outside or up front? She scanned the sea of blondes in animal-carcass jackets. *Where do these people hide during the day? None of them look like anyone I know or serve.* "Ooh, this Champagne's fifty dollars a glass—let's try it!" she heard someone say. *Holy crap! Does it come with heroin?*

She checked out Le Clochard first. Its vocal wall hit her. *Whoa! A noise meter here would register in the jet plane range. What the hell does everybody think is so important that they have to shout it?* She surveyed the room. Most of the patrons stood around the bar, and the rest squeezed around tiny tables which were too small to hold anything bigger than two salad plates. A woman Erin edged past, scanned her from top to bottom with the expression of an aristocrat discovering a servant in the wrong part of the house. "Fucking skank," Erin sneered, knowing the woman couldn't hear her.

Steiner was talking to a redheaded bartender. *That guy looks kinda Irish to be working in a French Bistro.* She poked Steiner under the arms. "Points for actually showing up." He jumped a little and Erin laughed.

"Hey! You, too." He gave her a side-hug "You find your friends?"

"Not yet. I just got here. I missed the concert because of work."

"They wouldn't let you leave early?"

"I don't think they were going to let me leave at <u>all</u>. I snuck out."

"Cool."

"Maybe not. Some girl saw me, so I guess I'm gonna get busted."

"Oh, well. You wanna beer?"

"Sure, why not?"

Steiner gestured to the bartender, who filled two mugs with draft Olden Town. *No introductions?* His friend didn't tilt the glasses enough, and their drinks had too much foam. Steiner blew on his, sending a bit into Erin's eye.

"Oh shit! Sorry," he said, laughing.

Erin blew some of her foam onto his shirt. "Me, too!" As she drank, she looked around the room for Donna.

"See your friends?"

"Naw, and I have no idea if they're even coming."

"You wanna get something to eat?"

"Not yet. Let's see if they show up."

"Cool. This place is too pricey anyway."

"What do they serve here?"

"Little plates of French food."

"Like tapas?"

"Yeah but like coq au vin chicken wings and shit like that."

"I had tapas for the first time the other night."

"Cool." Steiner started bopping his head to the music.

"So, you were jumping off a bridge because you broke up with a girl?"

"Yeah, that's right."

"Can I ask why?"

"Age."

"What?"

"Age. She said I was too young for her."

"That sucks."

"It's not like a Liz Taylor thing. Only five years."

"That's not so bad. How old are you?"

"Twenty-eight."

Shit! I thought you were twenty-three at the most. That's seven years difference between us. "How long were you going out?"

"Hey, too much me, not enough you. I'm all open-out. Your last boyfriend—why'd you break up?"

"Assholeism."

Steiner laughed. "Which particular strain?"

He's interested in me. More points. "I guess I'll name it... Fisheritis. Anyway, Peter and I—"

"Peter Fisher?"

"Yeah, know him?"

"He was in my illustration class."

"You go to the Academy?"

"Used to. Too expensive. Besides, I wasn't learning anything I couldn't pick up from the school of life."

"You know a girl named Tawnee?"

"Tawnee Fitzgerald?" They both shrieked at finding a common thread. "Oh my God, that's cool! We use to be friends

"Use to be?"

"Yeah, during school. But I just got so sick of her mood swings. I couldn't deal with it. She was such a psycho."

"Psycho? Hey! She's one of my favorite people. I love her."

"Don't get me wrong, I think she's great, but before the Prozac she was a nutcase."

"What Prozac? She's not a nutcase." Erin was getting angry.

"She's a manic-depressive, or she used to be. I guess the meds keep her stable. I thought you knew?"

"She's probably not comfortable with blabbing it out to everybody."

"My foul. I figured everybody knew. Don't get me wrong, I think she's got ass, but I'm glad she's calmed down. She used to hide in her room or disappear without telling anybody where she was going. It was pretty scary. 'Nother beer?"

"No, I should be looking for my friends."

"Cool, let me finish mine and I'll join you."

"Right." Erin worked her way through the crowd. Starting at one end of the Alley, she searched each bistro. After the fifth, she gave up and headed back towards Le Clochard. *I'll call Donna tomorrow and explain—Hey! That's Donna's friend.* She patted Art on the back of his Led Zeppelin shirt. "Hey you!" she said, forgetting his name.

He turned and acted as if he knew it was her. "You made it."

His tone sounds like he's been saying bad things about me for not showing up "Yeah, I missed the concert because of work. Where's the gang?"

"They're at E, one of the outside tables."

Right across from Le Clochard. Good sleuthing, Erin. "Cool, I'll be right there."

Steiner was talking to his bartender friend. She grabbed his arm and started to lead him out. "Hey, my friends are here."

Steiner stopped at the door. "Hey, I know that guy."

Erin followed his gaze to Art, who was struggling to get past two oblivious guys.

"Me, too. I think his name is Bart or something. We can follow him to Donna." She tugged but he didn't move.

"Her name's not Donna Etcheverria, is it?"

"Yeah…Oh, shit! She's not your ex girlfriend is she? No, wait, she's around my age."

"No, but her sister's thirty-three."

"Holy shit! You dated Tamara Etcheverria? Whoa! Ain't she like 40?"

"Thirty-three! I told you it was only a 5 years difference."

"Oh man, is Donna mad at you for breaking it off with her sis?"

"Don't know. I think she had a crush on me before I started dating her sister. If anything, she'd probably like to hook up with me."

"Not <u>too much</u> of an ego, eh?"

"I'm serious. At this rave, she was all over me."

"And you avoided it? Are you gay?"

Steiner lowered his eyes at Erin. "No! I'm very picky about who I hook up with. Donna's cute and all, but she's kinda shallow. I would just be like her trophy bitch or something."

Well, shit, Lashell was right. Donna is a friend collector. "Bart's going to tell her I'm here, so I have to make an appearance, but there's no reason for you to feel uncomfortable. Wait here, I'll be back."

"Okay, thanks."

Erin found Donna surrounded by Art, Kim, and Duncan. Donna held up her pink cocktail. "There you are!" she said. She immediately made Erin feel as though she had done something wrong.

Erin waved. "Sorry I didn't make the concert. I got trapped at work."

"We waited for you, for-ever."

"Sorry. I actually snuck out of work to come here. I'm probably gonna be fired."

"We almost couldn't get a seat here because we were waiting on you at the café."

Again, sorry! Guess I'm not apologizing enough. She reluctantly sat down. "So, how was the concert?"

"You missed out. They were grey…great."

She's slurring. I wonder how many pink drinks she's had?

"Well, I guess you're not the only one late. Where's Monroe?" she asked Kim.

Monroe...that name sounds familiar. Holy shit! I gave a drunken hand job to a Monroe. What are the odds—of course the world would do this to me. "What does Monroe look like?"

"Interested? You know, Duncan really liked Lashell. What's her problem? He's cute and smart." Donna grabbed Duncan's cheeks and squeezed like a grandmother. "What's her problem?"

"Don't know—so, Monroe, what's he look like?"

"He's kinda cute. Listen, why didn't you call me on my phone if you were going to be late?"

"They wanted me to polish the disco ball," Erin said, almost through clenched teeth. "So, Monroe?"

"He's blond, wears glasses. He's nice. You'll like him."

Erin started her panic attack. *This sounds exactly like the guy. There's a chance that I'm wrong, but if I'm right? Monroe will show up, and either he'll explain how we know each other or we'll both sit there feeling awkward. I have to get out of—no, I'm sick of running away from bad situations. This time, I stay and fight. Anyway, Monroe's not going to blab about the whole hand job scenario right in front of Donna.* She looked back at La Clochard. *I have to set Steiner free. No reason to suffer along with me if Monroe drags me down.*

Erin stood. "Excuse me, I have to use the bathroom."

"You're not going to flake out on me again, are you?"

Erin stopped for a second and then continued. *That last statement was a plain insult. Donna's not acting like a bitch because of the alcohol, she's saying what's on her mind.* Erin reached the bar and stood there brooding.

"What's wrong?" Steiner asked.

"Nothing." She finished his beer and lit up a cigarette. "I have to go to the john." Erin joined the long line. *I wonder what Donna's saying behind my back. When did I go from an interesting new friend in Donna's eclectic collection to some kind of punching bag?* She felt she didn't have the patience to deal with waiting in line or anything else at that moment and walked back to the bar to rejoin Steiner.

"Did you go already?"

"No, I can hold it." When she looked outside, she saw Monroe heading toward E. "Fucking hell."

"What?"

"Whelp, you have a girl outside that you want to avoid. I just saw a guy who I'd rather not see for the rest of my life."

"Ex-boyfriend?"

"He wishes." Erin craned her neck. A large party was leaving, creating a clear view. Monroe made it to Donna and kissed her on the cheek. As they talked, Donna pointed toward Le Clochard. "Fuck!"

"What now?"

"I gotta get the hell out of here!"

"Why is she looking in here? Does she know I'm in here?"

"No, they're talking about me. Hell! Is there a back exit to this place?"

Steiner turned to the bartender. "Any way out besides the front?"

His friend looked deeply suspicious. "Only an emergency exit with an alarm—don't use that."

She grabbed Steiner's shoulder. "I don't want to draw that kind of attention. What about a window in the rest room? Is there one big enough to crawl through?"

"I think so, but wouldn't it be easier just to walk out and face the music?"

"Sure. I'll do it if you will?"

Steiner thought for a few seconds. "Fine, but we go out through the men's room."

"Why?"

"Because if guys see a woman in the men's room, they think it's no big deal, but if a guy's in the girls room it'll cause a riot. Believe me, I know."

As the two hurried past the queue, one man grabbed Steiner.

"Line, buddy."

"She's gotta puke, dude."

The man let go and they burst in. A couple of guys turned, and then went back to peeing. Steiner moved the garbage can under the window, lifted the sash, and hoisted himself out. He reached back inside to pull Erin up. Not being as much of an athlete, it took her three tries just to balance on the garbage can. Getting through the window was a slow and sloppy process until some guy grabbed her legs and helped push her out. It would have been a kindly act if he hadn't squeezed her butt at the last minute.

"Pervert!" she complained, confusing Steiner, helping her down from the garbage can outside. "Not you."

They jogged alongside the filthy backsides of the fancy bistros. When they reached the main street, Erin realized they were still holding hands. She felt excited. The thrill of hiding from Monroe and being with a man Donna wanted, made her feel like she was in an adventure. "What now?" she asked, as if Steiner would answer: "Now we steal the diamonds!"

"I rode my bike here. I'd offer you a ride but, you know, the riding on the handlebar thing."

Erin laughed. "It's all right, my car's down the street."

"Right on."

There was an awkward pause. *Is this when we're supposed to kiss?* "Too bad we didn't get a chance to talk more."

"Night's still young."

"True, true." Another pause. "You wanna do anything?"

"Like what?" A few more seconds of thinking followed.

"We could talk somewhere?"

"Okay, another bar?"

"I don't feel like risking us running into our past again."

"So, what's your plan?"

Well, the whole purpose of this conversation is a proposal to have sex. You don't seem like the shy type, so why aren't you saying, 'I want to go home with you'? Dancing around the issue because you're a gentleman? A coward? Let's find out. "We could get some snacks and find a place to hang out? There's a Super K near my house."

"That'll work."

They awkwardly released each others hands and headed to their respective transportations.

"What to do?" she asked herself as she drove. *I'm physically attracted, but the only thing we seem to have in common is a talent for running away from problems. It'll be like being out on a date with a male version of me.*

At Super K, Erin considered tortilla chips, but instead chose cigarettes, while Steiner picked out chocolate chip cookies. He hooted joyously when they reached the wine aisle.

"What is it?"

"They carry Liebfraumilch!"

"Leeb-what?"

He waved a bottle with a Madonna and Child on the label. "Liebfraumilch. It's a light wine I used to 45-degree back in my German teen days. Means virgin milk."

"So, it's like a wine cooler?"

"No, it's a wine for lightweights; awesome!"

They took their dinner of cookies, awesome wine, and cigarettes back to Erin's apartment. As Erin introduced Mary Jo and Steiner, he became distracted by the video she was watching.

"What's this?"

"My Fist, Your Face. The box claims it's an homage to Battleship Potemkin, but I don't see it yet."

Erin didn't want to watch it because she was horny and the current scene involved a guy punching the inside of a supposedly occupied baby carriage. She could tell Steiner wanted to see it, so she sat down. Near the end, as the hero punched a nun so hard her head exploded, Mary Jo had fallen asleep. The beer, wine, and lack of nutrition were taking their toll on Erin, and she contentedly let her head melt onto the arm Steiner had draped around her. The credits began to roll over a still of the hero's knuckles aimed at the camera.

"You want me to go?" he asked.

"No, it's cool. Man, that lightweight wine packs a wallop."

"Only when you drink half a bottle and smoke a joint."

"I smoked pot?" She noticed her pipe on the coffee table. "Man, I don't remember doing that, I gotta cut that shit out. I will have more wine, though." She 45 degreed the bottle. "I really shouldn't be drinking in front of you."

"Why not?"

"Cause every time I drink around boys, I get horny and do stupid things."

"Like what?"

Erin killed the wine. *I wish I hadn't told him that booze makes me horny, like I'm some frat boy's fantasy.* "Like that guy we ran away from." She broke out laughing. "That was so funny—we were running away from those guys like they could hurt us. We should've just walked past them holding hands, or made out in front of Donna. That would've killed her."

He chuckled. "Probably."

"She totally O.J.ed me about being late. Like, chill out, bitch! Damn."

"That's Donna. She's a control freak. You do one thing wrong and she's all flip-out city. That's why I liked Tamara better. They had the same upbringing, but you'd never see her at Bistro Alley."

He's obviously still in love with her. That's okay. I have no desire for a relationship with him—we'd both be 'in-betweens'—I'm just wine-horny.

"Awesome," Steiner said. Erin turned her head. Mary Jo had recorded another movie onto the same tape. Currently, a shopping cart full of flaming bowling balls and a taxidermy cat on a crucifix was rolling down a hill in what appeared to be San Francisco, while the artist explained in voice-over, what this particular performance piece was all about. *I don't think I can compete with that for attention.*

She shifted until the back of her head lay on his lap. He started stroking her hair. *Even my time with Peter started when we got drunk at a concert and ended up in the back of someone's pickup truck. I wanted to hook up with Pat, but he was chasing Mimi. Things sure would have been different.* She wanted to chanced it. *Nice guy or not, he's still a guy. All I need to do is get the blood transferred from his brain to his dick.* She ground her head as though shifting to get more comfortable. Her lap-pillow became more firm. She smiled. *Compete with that, flaming bowling balls.*

Steiner's next "awesome" startled Mary Jo awake, and she got up and staggered off to bed. Steiner stopped the tape. "Oh, man, I'm sorry. It's three o'clock. I shouldn't be keeping you guys up. You probably got to go to work in the morning, right?"

"Not until ten, I'm cool. You gotta work early?"

"Naw, I got this gig at Copy Cow. I don't go in until noon."

"Sounds good." Erin twisted until she was looking at him. If he wanted, he could lean down and kiss her, but now he was interested in a woman singing a ballad on the Spanish channel's variety show. A sequined dress accentuated a pair of breast, larger than two human heads. Steiner's lap got even firmer. *Ah, a breast man, eh?* She sat up. "You think those are real?"

He considered. "Maybe. She's a little chunky, so could be natural."

She laughed and settled back into his lap. "One time, I was so desperate for cash I thought about becoming a stripper."

"Right on. I have a friend who's a stripper. Hard work. Good pay, though."

How can a man have a boner, a girl's head in his lap, and huge boobs on TV and be talking about the mundane aspects of stripping? She pushed her breasts together to form more of a bust line. "I guess I'd have to get a boob job."

As if an invisible alarm had announced breast are being touched, he looked down at Erin. "Why? Your breasts are fine."

"I don't know…do guys like strippers with fat nipples?"

"Wha-what?"

"You never seen women with puffy nipples?"

"Oh, yeah, yeah. I've seen those."

"Live or on stage?"

"A website, I think."

"You into the cyber-porn thing?"

"You ask a lot of direct questions."

"Must be the Labe frog milk." They both laughed. "But seriously, I don't own a computer—what do guys do on those cyber sex sites?"

"I guess they work like those 900 numbers, you know, talk to someone while they get you off? I've never done that."

"Then where did you see the puffy nipples?"

"On a porn website."

"A site for nipples?"

"You can put in anything you want and find a site just for that."

"So, if I put in 'big fat butts'…."

"You'll get a site for that."

"Male or females?"

"More likely female."

My lap pillow is softening. He must find this conversation more informative than stimulating. "What if I put in….girls that like getting their big tits oiled up?" *That came out harsher than I intended, but it's out now.*

"I'm sure there's a site for it. Many."

"From the women's perspective or the man's?"

"Mostly guys'."

"So there's nothing on the internet for women to get off to?"

"I'm sure there is, but I can't imagine getting a boob oil massage is a fetish for women."

"I don't know, I'd like it." Steiner's lap pillow throbbed.

"That's your fetish?"

"Not that one, but you know, I can see a women out there who lives to just have some guy oil up her tits and that makes her come."

"But more likely she'd want some guy to do it in person, not look at pictures of it."

"Perhaps. I love to look at pictures of guys doing the stuff I like to have done to me." Erin waited for the two words she knew would seal the deal.

"Me, too."

What? You're supposed to say: "like what?" which would lead to a demo. Wait, did you just say— "You like to watch <u>guys</u>?"

"No! I meant I could watch women doing stuff to a guy; same as you, in reverse."

I could ask "like what?", but you deserve payback "I think I'll just stick to my imagination."

"Some things are better in there anyway."

Was that a hint for, 'Keep your thoughts to yourself?' Screw that. "If I designed a web site, it'd be guys pleasuring women."

"They sorta have that, but it's always a part of the same old step-by-step porno."

"You talk like you look at a lot of that stuff."

"It's unavoidable. Every time you do a search for anything like, say, canned beans, you'll get links for women with beans all over their cans."

"Women and sausage links?"

Steiner laughed. "No, links to websites." He regarded her puzzled expression. "Search engine links? No? Maybe you should come over to my house for some internet lessons."

"I don't know, if I can't find women-directed porn, why bother?"

"You'll just have to make your own."

"I guess. I'd need to get actors and shit."

"I know this guy that makes pornos."

"You've seen a porno movie being made?"

"No, his rule is if you're not fucking in the movie, get the fuck off the set."

"You seem to have a lot of sex friends."

"I guess I do."

"You ever have sex with them?"

"No. I only know them 'cause I used to be a bike messenger."

"What the hell do they get delivered? Dildos?"

"Nothing dirty. It was all forms and letters."

"Ha! That sounds just like a movie: sexy bike messenger shows up on the set of a porno movie, gets dragged into it."

Steiner laughed. "I can see that. You should direct it, so it's all women-oriented."

"Would you do one?"

"Probably not."

"I thought guys liked to fuck beautiful women with big implants?"

"Not me. I like natural women."

"You're sweet."

Even though it wasn't directed at her, Erin took it as a compliment. She stretched out her arms as if trying to crack her back. "Oh, man, is my neck stiff. Could you—"

"Can I use your bathroom? Two beers and half a bottle of wine…" Steiner slid Erin's head to the couch and race-walked away.

What now? When he comes out, there's a thirty percent chance he'll say it's late and has to go. Is he's masturbating into the toilet to avoid having sex with me? This thought angered her. *Okay, no more fucking around: if he wants me, he should be a man and go for it. I'm wide open, damn it!* She heard the toilet flush and the faucet run, but Steiner didn't come out for at least seven minutes. When he did, he still had a hard-on. *Yes! I have no earthly idea what you were doing for those seven minutes—maybe you were deciding what to do next —but I won!* He sat in his former place and she was about to lay back on his hard crotch but changed her mind. *If I draw attention to the hard-on, then it would be letting him off the hook. Acknowledging it would be the same as unzipping his pants and going down on him, but as much as that appeals to me, I'm not going to let him off easy. Either he makes the first move, or, after he leaves, I'm quite prepared to masturbate my way into the Guinness Book of World Records.* She placed her legs on his lap. He started rubbing her calves.

"That's nice," she cooed, smelling victory.

"Man, when I ride I totally feel it here." He grabbed her other calve and shook it.

That wasn't a very sexy move. Still, he moved a game piece and it's my turn. "Speaking of bikes… I remember this guy they caught going around smelling girls bicycle seats. What the hell was that about?" *You probably heard that news story, but I'll bet you had no idea I was going to start talking about it.*

"I…I don't know."

"I mean, you remember that guy, right? Why girls' bikes?"

"The smell, I guess."

"What? Estrogen?"

"No, you know, girl-smell."

"Oh, all right. I guess sweaty girl crotches leave behind a musky odor, huh?"

"Y…yes."

Erin wiped her hand across her jeans crotch and smelled her fingers.

"I don't know, how a girl's smell can travel through panties and a pair of pants to a seat. I guess she'd have to be wearing spandex, or thin cotton panties and maybe a miniskirt." Before she finished the last word, Steiner's hand slid from her calf to her crotch. He smelled his fingers.

I win.

"Not really."

"Really? I didn't smell anything," she lied.

He returned his hand to her crotch again and rubbed more. He brought his hand back to her nose. "Well?"

"I can see what he was aiming for, but can you imagine being addicted to that?"

"Maybe you can make a movie about him?" Steiner slowly rubbed his knuckles on her crotch.

Her accelerating blood, racing heart, and moisture buildup were making it hard to concentrate on a strategy. Feeling ruthless, she refused to draw attention to it.

"Girls on bikes could sell, but maybe if the guy was more... active?" She spread her legs wider. He started using his thumb and index finger. She swallowed a moan and breathed deeply. *Steiner's finally becoming the aggressor I wanted, but now what do I do? At this point, we've skipped over first base; I could do or say anything I wanted without losing the game. It's almost like he's working for me.*

"What else could be in your movie?"

His thumb started making circles. A jolt of energy ran through her and she let out a moan. Erin ran her hand up his shirt to feel his chest. She stopped. "What's this?"

"It's just my nipple ring. You want me to take it out?"

"No." She moved in closer to get a better look. There was nothing particularly interesting about it, but his not mentioning it was like finding a prize in Cracker Jack box. *What else does he have?*

"Does it hurt?"

"No."

"Even if I pulled on it?"

"As long as you don't go nuts."

Erin moved in and kissed it, and then tugged slightly with her teeth. *He's undoing my bra. We should probably kiss before moving on.* She started kissing up, her fingers still toying with his nipple ring, until their lips met.

"You sure that doesn't hurt?"

He took advantage of her disengaging his lips to lift off her shirt and bra. He became immediately absorbed in her puffy nipples. His hands began undoing her zipper. Erin stood up. *My pants are staying on as long as your pants stay on. This is what I want: sex on my terms on my ground. No cars, no coke, no inhibitions.* "Condom?" she said.

Steiner looked surprised. "I'm sorry, I wasn't expecting this."

"Me neither."

"We could always..."

"No, no, no." Erin slipped her shirt on and fast walked to Mary Jo's bedroom.

She knocked on the door several times. A tired-sounding Mary Jo told her to come in. Erin tried not to step on anything important in the dark, cluttered room. "Mary Jo?"

"Erin?"

"Do you have any condoms?"

"Top drawer."

Erin opened the dresser and rummaged through a surprisingly large amount of condoms. "Damn! You must have a hundred in here!"

"I give 'em away to kids too embarrassed to buy them."

"Aw, you must have prevented so many unwanted pregnancies and diseas—"

"I also have eight lovers."

"Er-ah, thanks, we'll talk again."

"Have fun."

Steiner was gone. *What? He chickened out and left? Now? For fuck's sake, why?* Erin almost ran after him, but pride won out and she stomped towards her bedroom. Then she noticed light seeping from under the door. Steiner sat on her bed in nothing but white boxer-briefs. *All right! He's leveled the playing field.*

She put the condom on her nightstand, stuck a Nick Cave disc in the CD player, pushed Steiner over and straddled him. They started kissing again. *He's bigger than the last two...and more patient.* She drew down his briefs and grabbed him. Now he was the one making the most noise. He pulled away from her and rolled her onto the bed. With one smooth motion he pulled her underwear off, and then stopped.

"What? Yes, I know, I'm actually more of a redhead."

"No, it'll be great, like eating strawberries."

"Say what?"

This was a first for her—all her past boyfriends had focused on getting to penetration and skipped any kind of oral sex. Even Kenneth, the great English lover, called it a "nasty habit." But Steiner went at it as if it really were a strawberry patch. Erin felt like her eyes were going to explode. She grabbed his braided hair, and as a convulsing wave of tension built, she began yelling "Oh, God!" over and over. After her dramatic climax she figured he'd jump to penetration, but he licked Erin to yet another milestone: a second orgasm with another person at the helm. She shook and cried out like a howling wolf on a roller coaster.

Now she wanted penetration. As he moved up and started sucking on her breast, she felt something small enter her. *That can't be his dick, can it? Wait, it felt at least eight inches—it's his finger!* This time she sounded like a wolf losing its balance on a high-wire. *I don't know the downstairs neighbors, but now they definitely know me as that loud girl yelling "oh god yes fuck!" at 3AM.* She stopped fretting as her brain left her head and crashed through the roof. She clawed his shoulder, and though he said: "ouch!" kept at it. *This is it. If I don't take a break my legs won't work anymore.*

She twisted out and guided him to a receiving position. She started her infamous hand-pumping technique, and while Steiner seemed to enjoy it, she could tell it was nowhere near as pleasurable as what he had just given. *Well, I guess it's a night for firsts—my penetration fan exes never pressed for head. I want him to feel as good as I did, but what if I'm terrible at this?* She began by licking. When he moaned encouragingly, she added stroking, which brought more approval. She discovered she got the most reaction around the tip, and his sounds and gyrations increased with her pace. *I should go down on him, but it just doesn't feel right. Why? The idea doesn't repulse me. What is it?*

Steiner seemed to pick up her discomfort. He sat up and directed her onto her back. *If he goes down on me again, I'll die of pleasure overload.* He reached over to the nightstand and grabbed the condom. He had it on in the time it took most of her lovers just to unwrap. Still patient, he rubbed around every part of her genitalia as if he were using a handheld sex toy. He nibbled on her neck, ear, and nipples. *Who is this guy? Does he watch porn for the techniques?*

Erin felt the edge of another orgasm, but she held back. *I do want to come, dammit, but I want him inside me right now. Is this his game? To make me so crazy in the lead-up that I'll beg him for the main attraction? Not gonna happen*—"Fuck me now!" she commanded.

Steiner lost his rhythm for a second, and then, grinning, entered her. Erin tried to hold off coming. Soon, a jolt of energy ran from her toes up her spine and into her head and shot out her mouth as "I'm coming again!" This seemed to excite Steiner even more, causing him to accelerate towards ejaculation. This pushed Erin into her fourth orgasm and she howled like a wolf's ghost inside a dryer.

#

Erin woke up at 7AM to the morning light illuminating the crisscrosses on Steiner's bare back. She remembered him rolling off of her and going to the bathroom but not his returning. She started through her 'day after' test to see if she had done anything wrong: she hadn't been drunk enough to blame alcohol, she'd told him to fuck her and meant it, so there was definitely no unwillingness involved, and she'd done it out of desire, not from pity or desperation. *So why do I feel bad about it? He's cute. I don't feel dirty, or in any way embarrassed. But, there is a lot of guilt present.*

She slid carefully out of bed and walked to the bathroom. *Dating Steiner isn't what I want. I want that morning-bathed back in bed to be Kevin's. Yes, he's now officially out of the picture, but I'm still in love with the fantasy.* She wiped carefully, still tender, and checked herself in the mirror. *Steiner's a great lover and I like him, but outside the sex, we're too similar. What can we learn from each other? Perhaps if*

I had the least bit of interest in riding a bike, computers, or jumping off of bridges it could work. But if we get into a fight both of us will flake out and hide from each other like we did from Monroe and Donna last night. I need at least one person in a relationship to be stable. She took a deep breath and went back to the bedroom. She stroked Steiner's arm.

"You have to go."

Steiner rolled over, confused. "What?"

"Get out!"

"What?"

"You heard me. Get out!"

"And what, pray tell did I do?"

"You...took advantage of me."

"I what?" he yelled.

"I told you wine makes me horny, and you brought some over knowing full well what your plans were."

"It was Liebfraumilch! And hey! Just say no! All right?"

"Whatever...just get out."

Steiner slid out of bed. "Fine! God! What a psycho!" He hurried off to the bathroom as Erin tried her best not to feel like a bitch.

#

Erin was so desperate to talk to Lashell, she drove across the bridge and picked her up. Filling her in on all the events leading up to the arrival at her apartment took a while, especially through all of Lashell's questions and comments. At F.J. Pizza they took over a table and Erin continued with what had happened after Mary Jo had gone to bed. Lashell got quieter as the action got sexier.

"...And then I told him to get out."

Lashell's jaw dropped. "You what? Are you crazy? Girl, that guy's perfect for you! He's cute, he's weird, and how many orgasms did you have?"

"Three or four."

Brenda, eavesdropping from the cash register, inclined her head to hear more.

"What?" Lashell yelled. "Girl, if you don't take him, I will!"

Erin slumped down on the table. "You don't understand, Shell. I'm in love with Kevin, not Steiner." She put her head into her arms. "…And now I feel like I've cheated on him."

Erin's head was down, so she didn't see Lashell's hands. Ed came out from the back and noticed one of his workers reaching across a table as if she were going to choke her coworker.

"Hell-lo! Can you two cut the chitchat and get to work?"

"Hey! We're discussing matters of the heart here," Lashell answered, completely unfazed.

"Then discuss them behind the counter!"

"Anyway…" Lashell continued as they put on their aprons, "…You can't cheat on someone if you're not dating them."

"True. But I'm not in love with Steiner, so I can't just use him for sex."

"Why not? Brenda does all the time."

"Quelle? Putain boudin!" Brenda muttered.

"I can't do that, Shell. It's not fair to Steiner."

"What if you just explain it to him? Maybe that's all he wants."

Well, that's an option. If we had an understanding, then my feelings for Kevin are irrelevant. I could be happy with a purely physical relationship with him. Remembering last night's sex made her horny. Ed was hovering like a hawk, so she couldn't just sneak off like the Acid Pit, and he probably wouldn't see hot sex as a valid excuse for leaving early. As she helped customers and made pizza and sandwiches, she felt she needed to apologize to Steiner for kicking him out. When Ed left to pester the people hanging out in the break room for too long, she leapt for the phone. *Wait, I don't even know his last name. How can I even begin to track him down? Hey, he said he worked at Copy Cow.* She flipped through the Yellow Pages and started calling the first of Neo's five locations. As luck would have it, he answered at the first try.

"Steiner?"

"Yes?"

"It's me, Erin." Steiner said nothing. "Listen, I was stupid, and I'm sorry. I didn't mean to kick you out. I...I was in a panic."

" 'Bout what? You felt guilty? Are you and that guy still dating?"

"What? Who?"

"That guy at E?"

"No! We never dated. That was an accident. But it's not him."

"Oh, you have another boyfriend?"

"Not exactly?"

"You're a lesbian?"

"No! What made you think of that?" *Maybe I shouldn't have held off on the dick-sucking.*

"No reason. Just throwing it out there."

"Well, throw it back. I'm quite straight."

"So, why the freak out?"

"Steiner. There's this guy that I was in love with...well I think I may still be in love with him and..."

"Oh, so I messed things up between you and him?"

"No. He's...he's gay." During the pause Erin could picture little wheels turning in Steiner's brain as he tried to figure out what was going on.

"Wha?"

"That's why he and I couldn't be together."

"Oh, he came out of the closet?"

"Not exactly, there was no closet to come out of. He was always gay. I fell in love with him and then I discovered it."

"But shouldn't that make it easier to get over him?"

"You would think, but this morning I felt like I cheated on him even though I've never even been out on a date with him. Does that sound stupid?"

"Don't know. I'm still in love with Tamara."

"You are? But what about last night?"

"Erin, you're a biscuit. I tried not to let anything happen 'cause I'm still trying to get over Tam, but last night, baby, I just could hold it in."

"Really? I'm a biscuit?" Erin twisted one of her dreds.

"Totally! I didn't want to hurt you and you think we were in a serious relationship or something."

"Me too! I just wanted...well, you know."

"For sure. We were just having fun."

"Definitely. So, we're square?"

"Of course. But, we can hang out and stuff?"

"I'd like that, too."

"Cool. You wanna go bike riding sometime?"

"Not much of a physical fitness type. I know I should be, but walking is enough."

"Oh."

"You wanna see a movie? There's a killer animation section at Jolly Roger's?"

"I don't like watching cartoons. They give me a headache."

"Oh..."

"What time do you get off?"

"Six. Why?"

"I could come over to your place, and we could just hang out?"

I know what you're thinking: there will be no hanging out, just two horny people using each other for sex. At least this time I can send him home pleasantly so there'll be another time. Or perhaps I'll let him stick around to regain his energy and try to beat my orgasm record. This goal made her cross her legs and take a deep breath.

"Okay. My place, 6:30."

#

Later, in her bed, Erin was thinking about how wrong this was. Both of them were in love with other people and probably fantasizing about them during sex. When Steiner squeezed her breast, she imagined it was a straight version of Kevin; when he entered her, Kevin did; and when she yelled, "I'm coming again!" it was for Steiner to keep them coming.

Part Two
Liquor up Front,
Poker in the Rear

What is the first thing you do in the morning in Neopolitan? You go home!

Erin was neither home nor dry. After opening her eyes, she immediately checked to see if she had peed herself. The liquid her fingers brought back didn't feel or smell like urine, or any other body fluid. She was glad, but still didn't know what it was or why it was there. She heard rushing water behind her. "Where am I?" she tried to mumble through a cotton-balls mouth at the big, moving, white, blurry thing behind her, on the chance it was human. Her arm slipped and she felt herself falling, falling towards the blur. As soon as the water reached her elbows she was awake.

She pushed off, out of the shallow pool, and righted herself on the concrete edge where she'd been sleeping. *What? Wake up! Wake up!* She scooped some of the water onto her face, which helped clear her head. *What the fuck?*

Another splash to the mouth "Where the fuck?"

Okay, I can see I'm sitting on the edge of a fountain. Her bare feet touched concrete. *My shoes are gone! Wait, I didn't feel any underwear earlier. Oh my God! I've been raped!* She dug under her black skirt. As far as she could tell there had been no recent sex, or at least not intercourse.

"Where the fuck are my shoes and my panties?"

She looked around. A man, probably passed out and not dead, lay on the ground near her feet. To the left she spotted people on benches. Everywhere she looked she saw bodies.

One person lay half in the fountain. *Oh My God, they're dead!* The body in the fountain began to shake off the water falling on this head; a body on the bench got up and started throwing up into the fountain; and a girl lying on the concrete ground near a fast food wrapper, who may or may not have been Chelsea, took a drag on a cigarette. They were all alive. *But where are we?* Another splash to the eyes cleared up her depth perception. Buildings came into focus: Vêtements, Shoe Fly, Coffee Barn. *Somewhere downtown. That's the Pan Handle leading into Central City Park, which should put me in the Piazza near the Clock Tower.* She looked behind her and there it was, lumbering over them as if they had soiled the name of the city by their drunken public display: 125 stories of respectable businesses crowned with a stern face of Roman numerals declaring 9:15 AM.

More people started making morning noises, some perhaps going through the same disorientation she'd just experienced. She attempted walking and felt like her legs had coat hangers for bones. Even holding onto the fountain's edge, she found standing, hard. *But how did I get here? And why would I hang out with Chelsea?* She looked around for anyone else she knew. She spotted some of Steiner's bike messenger buddies sprawled in various positions of unconsciousness across the fountain. On one bench, a blonde Asian girl lay on Steiner's chest and his left arm, along with her right, was up her black tank top. *When did this happen? When did I run into Steiner? Why didn't I wake up with his hand on my tit? Hey, don't I know her?*

Erin staggered over and tried to shake him awake. "Steiner?" She shook him again. The Chinese girl sat up and wiped drool off her mouth with her shirt, flashing a bare tit.

"Hi, Erin," she said.

"Hi...I have no memory for names right now." She shook Steiner some more.

"Whaat?" he whined, like a spoiled child.

"Hey! What the fuck is going on?"

"Huh? Wa? Who's that?" he said looking around.

"It's me, Erin."

"Erin? Eh-where the fuck are we?"

"Downtown, somewhere. Wake up we gotta go before the cops show up."

"Fuck da police!" He flipped two birds at unspecified targets. Two little old ladies going into Coffee Barn received them.

Erin took a wider scan of the area. *We are definitely not the night's only casualties. I see more bodies passed out in the park across the street, and some on the sidewalk next to that yuppie jewelry store. Wow, and some are in costume.* "Hey," she said to no one in particular, "I don't remember coming here. How did we get——?" She spotted Mary Jo, wearing a ball gown made out of bubble wrap, exiting Coffee Barn holding a cardboard tray with four cups of coffee. "Mary Jo!" Erin called out, her voice cracking.

Mary Jo stopped and smiled. "Hi, Erin. You look like shit," she said as if it were a complement.

"Thanks. What are you doing here? Who's all that coffee for?"

"My friends in the park." She gestured with the tray to a group sitting on the grass.

"Oh, shit! That one's my Uncle Howard." She waved. Waving back seemed to be as much as he could manage. *Good. I have no desire to walk that far yet.* "I don't even remember coming here Mary Jo, do you?"

"I remember sweet music and a cool breeze on the faces of teddy bears."

"What the f——"

"I gotta take this coffee over. See you later."

As she walked away Erin's confusion level skyrocketed. She turned back. More of Steiner's 'rads were awakening, like zombies with brain munchies. Erin slapped her skirt as if it would have pockets.

"Shit! Where are my keys? Where's my purse? Did I even drive?" She caught up with Steiner, who was washing his face in a stream of water from a stone cherub's penis. "Steiner? Do you know how I got here?"

"I don't know—hey, Wolf!" he yelled to a big guy with long black hair and beard. "You guys going to the nooner?" The guy shook his head, no. "Aight, bro."

"What's a nooner?"

"Afternoon rave over in the Cannery. Wanna go?"

"What? No! How can you even <u>think</u> of going when you know about as much as I do about last night?"

"Oh, I know—I just choose to ignore it."

"Whatever. And who's that girl you woke up with?"

"Debbie? You should know her. You did gin shots off of her."

"What? Oh, God, no. Please don't tell me I licked salt off of a girl's neck?"

"Belly, and then the lime out her mouth thing. You did shots off everybody. It was great." Erin hunched down and buried her face in her hands.

"God! Why didn't you stop me?"

"You were having a blast."

"But you're supposed to look out for me!"

"Why?"

Because you're my boyfriend, but that wouldn't be true. "Because you're my friend."

"So, Big Dog's my friend, and he's fuck'n over there pissing into that Mercedes convertible."

Oh…He really is. "But I'm not just one of your drinking buddies."

"What are you saying? Are we dating now? Because someone should tell me."

"No."

"All right, then. It's no big deal."

"It <u>is</u> a big deal Steiner. We're a little more than friends and you know it."

"Again, are you saying we're dating? Because we talked about this: sex, whenever we want as long as it's convenient for the other; no relationship, other than being friends; and if we hook up with someone else it's over. Now, if you hang out with me, you gotta expect the occasional gin shots and pissing into a Mercedes." He started walking away to join his friends.

Erin felt abandoned and stupid. *I remembered the talk we had being more than just a guide for a booty call. I definitely don't remember giving him permission to have his hands on Asian girl's boob.* "But, where's my purse and keys? And my shoes? And my underwear?"

He kept walking as he turned his head. "You didn't have a purse after the parade." He resumed talking to the group.

"Where are you going?"

"24 Hour Cafe, the nooner. You wanna come?"

"It's Sunday! I have to help open at work before ten!"

"Skip out."

"I can't afford to."

"Suit yourself. Later." The departing party animals laughed and talked until they were out of sight.

Erin's tired brain was at a loss. *What do I do? F.J. Pizza is walking distance, but not home.* She glanced around. *Mary Jo and Uncle Howard are gone—maybe to the rave? Okay, I could walk to work, wait on Lashell or Pat, and somehow they will help me get possession of underwear and shoes. The keys will have to wait until I remember what I was doing before I met up with Steiner.*

She started walking, and quickly changed from the concrete to the cool grass. At the Oak Grove the booze and whatever else she'd had started making her woozy, so she sat down and rested under one of the trees. It felt nice, like a sanctuary. Others apparently saw it that way, as the grove was littered with illegal substance-filled bodies. Next to Erin a blonde girl dressed as a mime cradled a half-filled bottle of Jack Daniel's. Erin fell asleep while reading the label. She dreamt of a hammer-wielding baby smashing holes into the walls of a house. Erin tried to stop it, but it ran too fast. When, finally, she got close enough to grab it, it turned around and swung at her kneecap. She woke up before the hammer hit.

"Shit! How long was I out?" Most of the people she'd seen earlier were gone. She was cold and sweaty, but she felt better. "God, what time is it?" She spotted an old man walking a small dog. "Excuse me? You have the time?"

"10:15."

"Thanks." She started walking again, trying not to step on any rocks. "I'm screwed. Steiner, you asshole! See if your ass gets some, anymore!"

\#

Brenda was smoking a cigarette in front of F.J. Pizza. Erin braced for the negative comment, but Brenda merely looked her up and down and continued smoking.

"Finally!" Lashell called out. "Where've you been?"

"I wish I knew."

"And where are your shoes?"

"<u>Again</u>, I wish I knew."

"Girl, you look like Death's big brother."

"Whatever. If any one wants me, I'll be washing up in the bathroom."

"I want you," Jeannie said, peering out of the office.

Fucking hell. Erin slumped and shuffled in. Jeannie closed the door behind her. They both sat down. Erin looked at Ed's neat and orderly part of the office. His desk had no pictures of anyone, except the one of him shaking hands with the mayor. Jeannie's side was cluttered with papers, toys from Happy Meals, and numerous photos of her and Velma Flum, her lover, on rafting trips, nude on Greek cliffs, and kissing under a sprig of Christmas mistletoe.

"Rough night?"

"I feel like shit."

"I'm glad you came in instead of calling in sick."

"It was tough."

"I can imagine. I barely made it in myself."

"I just wish I could remember everything."

"I'm sure you will, then you'll really be sorry."

"Great. Looking forward to it."

Jeannie laughed and then she got serious. "Erin, you've been late a lot this month."

"I know, I've been having problems and–"

Jeannie held up her hand. "It's cool. You don't have to tell me anything. It's just that if you're as late as you've been, the policy is to write you up. You do know what three write-ups mean, right?"

"Yeah."

"It means letting you go, and believe me, I don't want to see that happen."

"I'm sorry Jeannie. I'll try to be better."

"You have to. Did you know that Evan is leaving?"

"No, why?"

"School. But since he's leaving, you and Pat could be considered to be supervisors."

"Oh! You should give it to Pat. He's been here longer and everyone likes him."

"I know. Thing is, he doesn't want it."

"What?"

"I know, I'm working on it. But my point is, I like you enough to consider you for a promotion, too. But the thing is, Ed doesn't like any of you guys. You know that, right?"

"Of course."

"I'm not crushing you with that information, am I?"

Erin laughed. "No."

"Good. I mean, he hates me too, so fuck it. If he had his way we'd all be replaced with minimum wage high school students."

"He's such a nugget."

"I know. So, it's like, if Pat backs out and you have one or two strikes, then an outsider gets put over the staff, and I know from being in that position, nobody likes it."

"We like you."

"I like you guys, too, but at first, you guys were a little assholeish. That's why I try not to bust balls too much. But Ed didn't hire me, Sal did. If we need a new person, Ed'll hire them, and with his taste, you know he's gonna hire some tool…" Jeannie took out a tardy form. "…So, you see this?"

"Yes."

"For now, pretend you never saw it." She put it back in the drawer.

"Thanks, Jeannie"

"Hey, thank me by coming in on time."

"I will."

"All right, so now that that's out of the way, what did you do last night?"

"I don't remember, but I know it involved gin shots."

"Cool. What happened to your shoes?"

"Don't know. I also lost my underwear, but you didn't need to know that."

"No, too much information—Get out!" She laughed and touched Erin's arm. "Just kidding! No, we can't have you working without shoes for health and safety reasons, and underwear because–actually there is no underwear rule." She reached into a drawer and pulled out a metal box, took ten dollars out, and gave it to Erin. "Here, Go to that dollar store around the corner, I'm sure they'll have something you can use. Erin took the money and departed. Lashell's expression looked like she was waiting to see if Erin had been fired.

"How'd it go?"

"Fine. I have to go to the dollar store. I'll be back."

"Oh, by the way..." She handed over Erin's keys and purse."

"Thank God!" She looked inside, she had no cash. 'Shit!"

"Also, I love you too, but if you call my house again at 3AM, I'll kick you and AT&T's ass!"

"What are you talking about?"

"Last night?"

Erin didn't comprehend.

"Last night you called my house and told me how you loved me and some shit."

"Omigod. I'm not one of those drunks, am I?" Erin covered her face with her hands.

"You were last night. You don't remember calling my house?"

"No."

"How about, 'I love Jews?'"

"What the fuck are you talking about?"

Lashell reached for a cup, filled it with water and handed it to Erin. "Here, drink this, go get your damn shoes, and I'll fill you in."

Erin drank it and started walking. The more she walked, the more she remembered. Like having sex with Steiner before she went to work.

"Turn over," Steiner said.

Erin rolled, expecting him to enter her from behind. He spanked her left buttock, which usually felt good, but this time he did it kind of hard. "Ow!" she complained. When he grabbed her butt cheeks and spread them, an alert went off in her head. When she felt the tip of the condom on her anus She immediately twisted away. "Hey! I don't go for that crap!"

"Why not just try it?"

"No!" she said sternly.

Steiner looked mad, as if she'd dashed a fantasy of his. "Come on, just try it."

"Hey, I don't know who you were dating before me, but not in my ass!"

"We're not dating."

"You know what I mean. I just like the regular stuff."

"Fine, whatever, missionary it is," he said sarcastically. He grabbed his penis and aimed for a frontal entry.

Erin closed her legs and moved to the side. "Hold on a minute, what was that about?"

"Come on, why'd we stop?"

"'Cause you're complaining about me like I'm a prude or something."

"You're not a prude. Now open up."

"No. What, am I boring now because I don't want to be fucked in the ass?"

"You're not boring. Let's go before I lose my erection, damn it!"

"I don't think so. Why the sudden interest in triple-X positions? I never told you I liked that."

Steiner pulled away from her. "Jee-zus. You pick the worst times to fight, you know that?"

"That's because we never talk. You've never asked me what I like in bed."

"Those multiple orgasms you keep having, tell me I don't have to ask!"

"Then why the change? If I come when you do something, then just stick to the program."

"Hey, what about me? Maybe I'd like to try something new?"

"If you want something new, you should just ask me, first."

"Fine. I guess I should say: Hey, Erin, do you mind if I fuck you in the ass or bring a girlfriend over for a threesome or maybe you give me some head for once!"

She rolled out of bed, stormed into the bathroom, and slammed the door. She sat seething on the toilet seat lid, waiting for him, at any moment to knock on the door and apologize. More time passed than she'd expected. She heard a door closing. She walked quickly to the living room, where Mary Jo sat on the sofa watching the 700 Club with the sound turned off. Erin, remembering she was naked, quickly grabbed a T-shirt that was on the floor and covered up. "Did he just leave?"

"Yep. Man, that was the worst sex I've ever heard."

Erin walked back to the bedroom.

At work, she managed to make Pat turn a shade of red.

"W-what?" he stammered.

"Have you ever fucked anyone in the ass?"

"Jesus Christ, Erin! What the hell kind of question is that?"

"I'm just asking. Is this what all men want?"

"You're asking me what men want in bed?"

"Sure."

"Erin, all men are different. Some guy's like anal, some guys like having their ears tickled."

"You like your ears tickled?"

"Hey! Not about me now, okay? I'm just saying everyone's different."

"I guess," she admitted gloomily.

"Why do you ask? Trouble with your boyfriend?"

"He's not my boyfriend."

"Then why do you want to know what he wants in bed?"

"Just to be fair. I just think sex should be a tradeoff, am I right?"

"Of course. Unless…"

"Unless what?"

"Well, unless there's something you really don't like or it's illegal or involves kids or animals. Your boyfriend doesn't want to fuck underaged goats does he?"

"He's not my boyfriend!"

Pat pointed at her. "Oh my God! You're more upset with the boyfriend statement then him wanting to fuck goats!" He burst into laughter. Erin threw a used rag at his face.

"You're an idiot."

Ashlee, who had been eavesdropping, interrupted. "You know what I like in bed?"

"I'm pretty sure I don't know."

"When a guy bites my toes really hard."

"Eww, too much information!"

"Ah, what's the big deal. Everybody has something freaky that they want to do."

"Not me. I just like the plain ol' vanilla sex, with just a little hot fudge on top."

"I find that hard to believe."

"Whatever, it's true. There are over thirty positions you can do, and that's plenty for me. Call me a prude but I seem to enjoy myself just fine."

"C'mon Erin, there's not a little part of you that want's to try something dangerous or sick?"

"If a guy wants to get all freaky-deaky, then he should go find someone else."

"Yep. That's what they always do." Ashlee went back to the register.

Would Steiner cheat on me, and is it cheating if you're not dating? Would I be jealous if he did sleep with someone else? I guess my only problem with that is risking an S.T.D. Or losing my regular sex sessions. The second threat panicked her, especially after the fight they'd just had, because not having Kevin was one thing, but losing Steiner would be like losing the second half of a relationship. She picked up the phone and dialed the Copy Cow print shop.

After a long wait while someone fetched him, he picked up the phone.

"Yeah?"

"Hey, Steiner, it's me."

"I know."

She wasn't sure how to respond. She had planned to start the conversation by apologizing, but changed her mind. "So, you wanna get together after work?"

"What for?"

"You know, maybe erase the morning we had."

"I don't know. We were going to check out the Screw the N.E.A.! Show, then try to catch the tail-end of the Monster's Day parade."

"Sounds like a full day."

"Yep."

I want him to invite me along, but that would be something a boyfriend would do. "Well, maybe I'll see you at the show."

"<u>You're</u> going?"

Erin felt a little insulted. "Of course."

"Right. See you then."

They hung up. Erin had no idea what the Screw the N.E.A.! Show was. She asked Pat.

"How could you NOT know? Mary Jo has some paintings in it. The flyer has been on the bulletin board for a month."

"I've been busy, okay."

"Get'n busy more like it."

"What-ever, Baldy." She went into the break room, where Lashell sat eating a sub sandwich while studying. Erin looked at the poster. On top was the National Endowments for the Arts logo with a screw through it, and below a crude woodcut of a dancing man holding a paint brush in one hand and a microphone in the other.

"How come no one told me about this? Are you going?"

"Hell naw."

"Why not?"

"Look who the band is."

Erin read through the list of artists and performers. One name jumped out. "Feces? Yuck!–no, wait, ain't that Pepe's band?"

"Same one."

"Oh, my God, are those assholes back in town? I'm amazed they stayed together. You think Pepe'll try to come back to work?"

"Who cares? The only reason I would even <u>consider</u> going would be to see Mary Jo's giant bronze cock."

"We probably should go then, for support."

"...Of course, support the arts and all that shit" She broke a smile at Erin's giggle. "You wanna invite your Bo-friend?"

"He's not my boyfriend." Erin returned to the front. *If he were my boyfriend, then I wouldn't always be the one to calling to get together. We would also eat together or see movies together before sex, and I would know his real name. Though I guess without things like restaurants, gifts, or movies, it's affordable. I just wish he was Kevin. Since Tawnee told me that he went out with a girl in their class, he might be bisexual instead of gay. Maybe his girlfriend broke up because that freaked her out and I have a chance. If I'm gonna be a booty-call, I'd rather do it with Kevin.* Her thoughts then drifted to an ultimate fantasy of sex with Kevin and Steiner at the same time, the very idea making her ecstatic.

#

On the walk back from the dollar store, wearing her new kung-fu shoes, she saw more day-after party victims walking the streets. *I've never seen it this bad before—a lot more than last year, and a lot more underage kids.* Two passing youths mentioned the 'nooner' that Steiner had mentioned. *How could they have the energy to keep going? Don't they have jobs or school?* I'm only twenty-one, younger than Steiner's crowd, but I feel like partying about as much as the old lady at the 99-cent store.

Back at work Roger was sitting at his usual table, waiting for a delivery. He smiled at Erin.

"What?" she asked suspiciously.

"I love Jews?"

"What the fuck does that mean? Why does everyone keep saying that?"

"You don't remember saying that?"

"Why would I say that?"

"Do you remember calling my house and telling Tawnee you loved her?"

"Shit! Tawnee too? Man, I must have been totally faced last night."

"Do you remember running naked down Broadway?"

"Oh, my God! No!"

"Just kidding." Roger started laughing until she punched him in arm. "Ow, you psycho! Watch it."

"I'm very vulnerable right now. Tell me, did I run naked down Broadway?"

"I don't know nor care. I didn't see you after the art show."

"So, 'I Love Jews' was at the art show?

"What, did you smoke crack last night?"

"Shut up, Roger." *What kind of drugs did I take? Crack or cocaine wouldn't make me forget so much detail.* She put on her apron and started prep ingredients for calzones. She remembered going to the Screw the N.E.A.! Show and tried to figure out how the 'I love Jews' statement fit.

The event, held at the 10th Street Gallery, showcased artists denied funding because their work was deemed too weird or controversial for the general public. Like most things in their second year, this one was a lot more organized and had received more media attention, and was thus more crowded. After thirty minutes in line, Erin and Lashell were three car lengths from the entry. Erin had recognized plenty of people she wanted to avoid—the Etcheverria sisters; Chelsea, Pepe, and Gregg; Judith, Jeff, Monroe—along with some she wanted to talk to, such as Tracy, J.J., April and Spike.

"Are you guys sneaking in?" Erin asked them.

"Not this time." Tracy answered. "Gotta support the arts."

"I need a drink," said Spike, crossing her arms.

J.J. Lifted her black leather miniskirt and removed a silver flask strapped to her fish netted thigh.

"Whoa! Cool," Spike praised. She took a sip and passed it along.

Lashell skipped out and handed it to Erin. "Try to take it easy, we have to go to the parade after this," she warned.

Erin took a sip and coughed as the whiskey burned her throat. She managed to get out the word, "Smooth."

The girls kept downing the flask, talking about guy's butts and inching their way inside the gallery. Erin's empty stomach started to feel a little warm. When, during a lively discussion of what made a guy's butt superior, she mentioned Steiner. J.J. told her that she knew him.

"You do? From where?"

"I think I slept with him."

"You think?" Erin asked.

"She lost track after 300 men," Spike added.

J.J. laughed. "It's funny because it's true." They all laughed. "Yeah, I'm not sure. He have long skinny dreads like mine?"

"Yes."

"Yeah, I did him."

"I thought you were a lesbian?"

"Bisexual, sweetie."

"Really? Do you think you could spot another bisexual?"

"Like who?"

"Oh, Lord," Lashell groaned, "you're more concerned with that, than the fact that she slept with yo' man? Wait! This isn't about Kevin, isn't it?"

"You're dating Steiner?" J.J. asked.

"He's not my man!"

"Are you still chasing after that guy?" Tracy asked.

"No...I mean, yes."

"But he's gay!" Lashell complained, causing Brenda, who was far in front of them, to turn slightly for better eavesdropping.

"He's not gay...I think."

"Who's gay?" April asked.

"This boy she was after a month or so ago," Lashell complained. "He came out and actually said: 'I-am-gay!', and she's still Pollyanna chasing after him."

"Darling, I know from experience, even if you sleep with them, they still go back to boys," said J.J.

"You slept with a gay man?"

"She's slept with everything," April said.

J.J. Laughed. "Again, funny because it's true."

"What about AIDS?" Erin asked

"Anybody can have AIDS, Erin. I always use protection and I get tested regularly."

"This health message, bought to you by the National Association of Nymphomaniacs," April joked.

"Getting back to my original question: Can a gay man actually be a bisexual?"

"I use to be a straight girl, then I discovered women. But every now and then I like a flesh dildo." A guy standing behind J.J. who had been listening seemed both uncomfortable and a little excited. She smiled at him.

Erin turned to Lashell. "You see, Shell, I know for a fact that Kevin was dating a girl a while back. I kinda suspect that it's that girl we saw him with, 'cause they're living together."

"That tall-ass model-looking girl? Erin, if that boy goes back in the closet, who you think he'll hook up with, you or that model?"

"Er, well…" *She's right. What do I have to offer over a sexpot?* She took another hit on the flask.

The girls made it inside and split into their two groups. Erin and Lashell, following the flow of the crowd, worked their way clockwise around the room. Some art actually did appear too controversial for the N.E.A.'s taste: one had multiple panels of vaginas of different colors, shapes, races and age; another, titled 'Merry Fucking Christmas', showed Santa Claus fisting a reindeer.

"Is that art?" Erin asked.

The girls skipped over the paintings apparently made by a guy who drank some paint and vomited it on the canvas, as they did the sculpture of a barbed wire-wrapped Christ.

"Why's all this shit so violent?" Lashell asked

"Not all of it..." Erin pointed to an 8 foot by a 6-foot black and white close-up photo of a laughing clown called 'What are you afraid of?' "...Some are just creepy."

"Well, it is Halloween."

"I like this one," Erin said, pointing at a painting of a can of beans sitting on the stove. "I feel it represents a bachelor or divorced man coming home and now he has to cook his own dinner. He probably eats it over the sink, wearing nothing but a tank top and some boxer shorts..."

"It's called Fart.

"Ugh."

"Mary Jo!" Lashell yelled.

Mary Jo's face lit up when she saw them, and she ran over and hugged them both. "Hey, guys! Great! You made it!"

"Of course," Erin replied. "Free wine and food? We're there, dude."

"Isn't that your boyfriend?"

Erin turned. Steiner stood by himself and looking around. He saw Erin and walked over. *No greeting? I wonder if he's still mad about this morning.* "Er-ah, well, sort of," she answered Mary Jo."

"I thought you liked that gay guy? He's here you know." Mary Jo pointed off to the side.

"Er-ah, uh." Erin looked at Steiner. *He seems angry, but if it were about this morning, he'd have looked mad coming over. Is there something else? And why is he alone?*

"Go ahead," he said "we've already discussed this."

Was he was hoping to spend some alone time with me? Like a real date? Does he want to go official? Shit—if he does, should I stay behind and see what happens, or should I pursue the impossible? "But, Steiner, I don't want to leave you here..." *C'mon, show me a sign of jealousy, some indication that an almost-normal relationship is possible.*

"Erin, it's not like we're dating or something," he sneered.

"Yeah…I guess we're not." *You know what's awful, Steiner—I just realized that I don't love you, but with some work I could have, if only you'd shown me you wanted to talk about it.*

"C'mon guys!" Mary Jo yelled "Let me show you my new painting!" Jogging excitedly, she lead Erin and Lashell away from Steiner, who didn't follow. "Hey! Tracy!" she yelled and waved at the gang of four who were already admiring Mary Jo's eight-foot bronze cock statue. It was a lot more abstract than Erin thought it would be: phallic-shaped, yes, complete with testes, but a lot smoother and curved, and with a hole in it like a randy sewing needle. People admired it, and women especially rubbed their hands over it.

"Yo! Like your work, M.J.!" Tracy yelled back.

Mary Jo's painting was of a field under a moonlit sky with three cows stretched out and so warped, they almost reached the moon.

"Thanks! I call it The Relationship Between Cow and Moon." Mary Jo said proudly.

"Neat," Lashell commented.

"I like it," Erin agreed, baffled. "Where's the booze?"

"Over there, near that guy you like."

Kevin was standing near the reception table talking with Graham and Chelsea. Graham put her arm around him.

"Oh, God! He's with Graham!" Erin whinnied. "Oh, God, he's a bisexual! He's not gay. I wasted my time with Steiner!"

Lashell sighed. "You don't know that! Anyway, if you're smart, you'll forget the whole thing and stick to Steiner."

"Erin," Kevin called out, waving.

Oh shit! He called me over! And he remembers my name! He's never remembered my name! "Oh shit! Oh shit!" she mumbled as she left her friends. He gave her a quick shoulder hug, which made her tingly all over.

"So, how's my favorite pizza girl?"

"Fine. How's it going?" she answered, soaking in the fact he was touching her.

"We're doing well."

A blond guy with multiple earrings and tattoos covering both arms approached Graham and kissed her on the mouth. "Hey, Graham. Sorry I'm late."

"Hey! Baby!" she responded

"Who's that?" Erin whispered to Kevin

"That's Geo, Graham's Bo-friend." Kevin answered.

'But...I thought you guys were dating—Had dated. Or—actually, I thought you were gay"

"I am. That's why we're not dating anymore."

"But..."

"But what?"

The second time around, this statement crushed her more. *He's a 'came-out-of-closet' gay. I should be relieved. The Kevin quest is officially over. I can move on with my life. Not with Steiner, because he's acting weird, but with someone less complicated.* She scanned the room. Lots of perhaps straight guys were looking at art and flirting with girls. *This gives me a little hope. But I'm not finished with Kevin. I want to tell him about my crush, just to get everything out of the way. Where is some confidence-builder?* "But, ah...I gotta get some wine."

Erin cut into the long refreshment line in front of Lashell. "Whelp. He's definitely no bisexual."

"What? You saw him tongue kissing a guy?"

"No. He came out of the closet. I doubt he'll go back in."

"Well, that's good in a way. Now you can move on to Steiner."

"I don't think so. We had sort of a fight this morning and he was kind of a jerk. Plus, what's up with him sleeping with J.J.?"

"<u>Now</u> that bothers you? That girl fucks anybody. Who knows when that happened? I doubt it happened when he was dating Tamara...unless."

"Unless what?"

"Unless that's why they broke up."

"Wow, I never thought of that. I kinda been wondering if he actually does sleep around. I mean, he seemed like the kind who sticks to one girl at a time, but who knows?"

"I know P.J. wasn't."

"You think he was cheating?"

"According to him, it was only when we were broken up, but we sure as hell broke up a lot."

"Men suck."

"Girls suck, men lick." They laughed.

The self-serve table held multiple snack items and lots of box wine. "Eh," Erin said, "I'm not a big fan of cube crap. Back when I was 12 I got drunk on some at my cousin's wedding and threw up in the back of my grandmother's Oldsmobile; very embarrassing." She looked around for anything else alcoholic and saw Spike holding an actual bottle of white wine. Erin grabbed a red plastic cup and walked over. "Hey! Where did you get that?"

"Some asshole had it behind the table hidden in a cooler. I guess he was saving it for a better crowd," Spike said pouring herself a glass.

"Can I have some? I hate that box shit."

"Sure."

As Spike poured, Erin saw the thirty-dollar price tag. "Holy crap!"

"I know, right?"

They drank and watched as the asshole in question, music critic Quincy Zeitheit, approached the table leading Donna, Monroe, and Art, all holding empty glasses. Quincy rummaged through the cooler and started cursing. Before he thought to look around and discover which riffraff had taken his bottle, Spike took Erin's arm and they snuck off to another part of the gallery and hid behind a group of Neo hipsters. The girls laughed and toasted to the success of the mission.

After the first cup Erin thought: *I should tell Kevin I had a crush on him.* After the second: *I should confess that I loved him.* The third: *I want to hug Spike.* To erase that, she had a fourth, which brought: *I want to fuck Kevin.*

A hardcore grime band started playing some live music. *Wow, is that Feces? How can those Riverview boarding house assholes be making music I like?* Pepe's vocals had grown sharper and more controlled, Greg's guitar less flawed, the Hispanic bassist, a friend of Roger's named Stephanie Martinez, was playing to the audience, and the drummer, who Erin didn't know, drove the band so well, she had to dance. Others reacted the same way, and she felt great: the music, the art, the wine, and both the men in her life in the one place. She spied Steiner thrusting his arms as if he were in his own mosh pit. She wanted to join him but didn't feel comfortable doing it in front of Kevin, who was watching from the side. *Perhaps he's not as innovative as I wished he were. Perhaps he's not many of the things I thought.* She danced over to him.

"Come on out!" she yelled.

"No, thanks," he yelled back.

"Why not?"

"Cause those guys are assholes."

Erin laughed. "They treated you like shit, too?"

"Not me, my friend Kathy. You know Kathy?"

It took Erin a second to remember his over weight friend with the big boobs. "Sure."

"When they all went on tour, Kathy wanted to go because school was out and stuff. And they totally left without her."

"That was mean."

"Yeah."

"So, is there another band?"

"No, that's it."

Erin thought. "Oh, well. I guess after they finish I'll go to the parade, then."

"We went earlier. That thing is so long this year. They're not gonna finish before ten."

"That's what I'm hoping."

"You have a costume?"

"I don't know. Maybe I'll go as Ian Svankmajer's Alice."

His eyes widened. "Oh, my God! You know Svankmajer?"

"Sure. I love that kind of animation."

"Me, too! Did you see "Faust?""

"In Prague."

"Holy shit!" He touched her arm. "I bet that was so cool."

"It was." *Wow, he's never been so friendly before.* As they talked, he touched her arm whenever he wanted to make a point. The conversation switched from animation to soundtracks to music. *With the exception of his sexual preference, everything I've fantasized about him is true.* The subjects began to get more informative, and she told him how she had been fired from the Acid Pit.

"Yeah, I did the same kind of job at Club Gothica. Good riddance!"

Her excitement and a wine-influenced brain began lowering her superego's panties. "I'm in love you."

The band's volume suddenly swelled, burying her confession.

"What?"

"I love you!" she yelled as Pepe screamed into the mike.

"What?" he repeated, coning his hand over his ear.

Fuck! I finally confessed my love and he didn't hear it. Fine. One more, then leave it alone. The band ended their song right as she put her whole lungs behind "I love..." The sudden sea of everyone's attention slapped her superego awake. To avoid the embarrassment of including the crowd in her personal business, her brain tried to quickly find a substitute for 'you'. Rather than something logical, like 'wine' or 'your taste in clothes', her pressured and tipsy brain just threw out the first rhyme that popped up. "...Jews."

There was a second of silence, and then some laughter.

"We love Jews, too," Pepe announced.

"I'm Jewish," someone yelled to more laughter.

"I'm half!" shouted someone near the back.

Erin backed away from Kevin, who looked both puzzled and amused. He began to say something, but the band launched into their next conversation-destroyer. Most of the crowd began dancing again, and the music was too loud for Erin to hear the diehard hecklers as she pushed through to the gallery exit.

#

Reliving the 'I love Jews' incident made Erin almost burn a customer's pizza "Gee, what a dork."

"Who?" Lashell asked.

"Me. I totally ruined things with Kevin."

"There was nothing to ruin."

"I'm not talking about the dating thing. I'm talking about a friendship. I can't even be friends with him."

"Why not? We're friends and you do stupid-ass shit all the time."

"He knows I have a crush on him. How can I look him in the eye after that?"

"I say drop it and move on."

"To what? When we all woke up this morning, Steiner had his hand on some girl's tit."

"Really?"

"I can't even be friends with him."

"Again, drop it and move on."

Erin rung up a customer and gave him his change.

"You're right. If last night wasn't the big hint to let them both go, I don't know what was."

"Atta girl!" Lashell patted Erin's back.

As Erin started making a list of all the disposable utensils they were running short of, she tried to remember more about the previous night

There was no longer a line to get into the gallery, and some of people who had come early were now leaving to catch the parade. Erin leaned on the wall and watched their shoes as they walked past.

"Erin!"

She looked up. Lashell was trotting over "Where you going?"

"I just had to get out. You know, after making a dumb-ass of myself and all."

"Oh, big deal. We all do shit in front of people."

"I couldn't care less about other people. I made an ass out of myself in front of Kevin. The fact that his last name is Goldberg didn't help either!" She started tearing. Lashell gave her a shoulder hug.

"Why do you torture yourself with that boy?"

"I don't know. We have so much in common."

"You gotta stop torturing yourself!"

"I can't help it. Everything I have has a fucked-up angle to it; I get an apartment, oops!—my roommate's a drug dealer. I find a man, oops!—he's a Homo. I get some dick, oops!—he wants to fuck me in the ass!"

"Hold up, who wants to do who in the what?"

"Long story. Let's just say he thinks I'm a prude. Maybe that's why he nailed J.J." Erin wiped a tear away. "God knows what Tamara was into." Someone grabbed her butt. She spun, prepared to pummel. It was Steiner. "Speak of the Devil. You didn't tell me you slept with J.J."

"You never told me you loved Jews," he chuckled. Lashell turned her laugh into a cough. "Just kidding." He put his arm on her shoulder.

He's acting a lot happier than earlier. She sniffed. *No smell of pot.* "Well, my life is ruined," she told Lashell. "I'm heading. You staying?"

"You going to the parade?"

"Sure, my life's a fucking circus, bring on the parade."

"Hey! We should get some costumes," Steiner suggested.

"We? Are you going?" Erin asked

"Yeah, let's go! Wooo!" he yelled

"Are you on speed or coke?"

"Speed of life, baby!"

"I have no idea what that means."

"It means his cranked ass ain't driving," Lashell clarified.

They rummaged through Erin's closet. Her more interesting clothes had been left behind after the fire at the boarding house. The best she could manage for herself was a black mini skirt with red pumps and a pink feather boa; for Steiner a white blouse with ruffled collar and sleeves, and a red headscarf for a vaguely pirate-y effect; and for Lashell a tie-dyed shirt, sandals, and a big pair of sunglasses won at the county fair. Erin called Lashell's look 'Funky Reggae' but Lashell called it 'Smelly Hippie Begging for Spare Change on 10th Street.' While Lashell was in the bathroom, Steiner grabbed Erin's breasts from behind while kissing her neck. He moved away when Lashell reappeared. *What the hell was that about?*

They trotted down to the NRT station. The trains were packed but would be faster than driving downtown on Monster's Day. Erin grew claustrophobic as more people crushed on board at each stop. At Grandview Station a hand lighted upon her thigh, and then rose until it was under her skirt and heading toward her crotch. Steiner smiled coyly. Erin looked around, but no one else appeared to notice what was happening. The hand entered her panties. The risk of being caught intensified Erin's excitement. When the hand started fondling her vulva she wanted to pull Steiner's pants down and go at it in front of everybody. Then she panicked: *What if it isn't his hand? What if it's that old Black man, or the woman with dyed green hair?* She pulled the hand away and Steiner laughed. *It must have been him.* The doubt still creeped her out.

At Broadway Station the group and eighty percent of the passengers shuffled off the train and up the stairs, towards the sound of Dixieland Jazz. A normal day in Neopolitan was already Halloween: people dressed weird, had parties, pulled pranks, vandalized, and reveled into the night as if they were juvenile delinquent vampires; but as soon as October hit, people ramped it up, as if Halloween was a national holiday they had invented. The Monster's Day parade—miles of locals walking or riding elaborate floats down Broadway and wearing elaborate costumes assembled over months, or in some cases, ten minutes ago—used to be on Halloween day, but even with mandatory overtime the police and fire departments couldn't cover both the parade and the gin-soaked tomfoolery elsewhere, and the city separated the events by a week.

When the group made it to ground level all they could see was a wall of backs blocking the parade. Several blocks down, away from the heaviest concentrations of people, they found a space big enough to see through. The Dixieland float had been replaced by a large silver flatbed truck with a DJ spinning heavy drumbeats, while shirtless guys in silver shorts tossed plastic sample bottles of vodka to, what Erin hoped, were adults of legal drinking age. Steiner almost knocked a teenage boy over intercepting one. He downed it in one swallow.

"Thanks for sharing," Erin complained.

Steiner didn't apologize. He started dancing.

"Man, people went all out this year," Lashell yelled, pointing to the oncoming float. Against a backdrop, colored like an Edvard Munch landscape, the riders waved weapons and wore masks, bloody clothes, and identifying signs: Lizzie Borden, Jack the Ripper, Vlad Teppes, and other famous mass murderers, though, Erin noticed, no one modern, like Jeffrey Dahmer, or the Unabomber.

"Yeah, how are they gonna top that for Halloween?" Erin replied.

Most of the passing floats had corporate sponsors. When a condom manufacturer's float approached, blaring outdated House music while sexy girls in bikinis threw samples at the crowd, Erin scowled. Then she noticed the green bumpy monster with 'HIV' on its chest in a cage topped by a sign proclaiming: 'Monster Savings!'.

"This is too much! I feel like I'm watching TV commercials. Did we miss the non-corporate stuff?"

"I heard all that was at the front," Steiner answered.

"I guess that's why the parade's bigger this year," Lashell said. "Corporate sponsors have taken over."

After the condom rain was a big black float covered with large papier-mâché skulls. Topless girls danced in cages while others, dressed in leather S&M outfits, danced around whipping one other.

"So much for a family parade," Lashell complained.

"At least they're not selling anything."

"Don't be too sure," Lashell said pointing to the sign reading, 'Neopolitan Absinthe Co.—Monster Savings!'

"What the hell is that, Steiner?"

"Hey! I know that girl!" he yelled. He ran out into the street, and one of the girls stopped dancing when she saw him. She bent down and kissed him.

"I recognize her. She's from Tawnee's birthday party."

"Whoa! Girl's making a play for your man," Lashell said.

"He ain't my man."

"Long as you're cool with it."

"I'm fine." *Okay, I'm angry. But it's not a feeling of jealousy, more of abandonment.*

The girl gave Steiner something and he ran back over to Erin. "Man, I didn't know she was back in town!"

"Who?"

"Debbie Chan. She got a job at that bar."

"Did you sleep with her too?"

"Whoaaa! Is this a jealous thing?"

"No. Just curious."

"Surrrre it is."

"Steiner…" *I don't love you.* "…it was only a question."

"All right. Matter of fact, I did sleep with her. Does that bother you?"

"No." *Am I just another number?*

"Okay, whatever."

Erin rolled her eyes at him. "I'll be back." She walked into the Crow's Nest bar. Lashell followed.

"It bother you that he slept with that girl?"

"Not really, not in the way you think it would."

"What can I get ya?" Asked a woman behind the bar, dressed like a pirate wench.

"Black and Tan, please," Erin answered.

"Coke for me…." Shell requested "…Sure you're not bothered a little, Miss Boozehound?"

"Hey, I'm drinking to forget."

"I have to say, that boy sure seems to get around a lot."

"Yep. We need to find men who are cute but aren't just male sluts."

A table next to the window emptied and they sat down to watch what they could through the crowd of backs. More booze floats passed, and each time they could see Steiner jumping high to get free samples.

"See, if you do what he do, then you wouldn't have to buy anything."

"That's the thing about him. He takes whatever is thrown at him—he never works for it. Like, everything he wants: booze, jobs, pussy—it's all given to him.

Lashell laughed.

"What?"

"Sorry. Just the word 'pussy' coming out of your mouth."

"Grow up, you know what I mean. He makes me look mature. I think I should tell him we can't hang out anymore."

"What? Right after Kevin dumped you, you're going to dump Steiner?"

"There's been no dumping; no one's dating."

"You know what I mean. I think you got your ass kicked and you want to project it onto his ass."

"Whatever. I don't have time for someone like that." Erin pointed at him. "He's dancing in the street with some stranger in a Frankenstein costume. I mean, fuck, why isn't his ass in here dancing with me?"

"Oh, I see. You have attention jealousy."

"Okay, Doctor Freud, that's enough of that shit."

"I'm just saying."

"Just say it to yourself." Erin chugged her ale and lit up a cigarette.

"You gonna stay to the end of the parade?"

"Naw. Maybe there's a party somewhere I can drive to. Wanna come?"

"Unless you have a specific goal, I'll have to pass. Tell you what, though, I don't want your drunk ass on the streets. You better hand over the keys."

"Whatever, Mom!" Erin grabbed her cash and handed her purse to Lashell."

"Just the car keys."

"Keep them together. I'll get them from you tomorrow morning."

"What, you ain't going home? We gotta work tomorrow, party girl."

"Nope. I'm gonna stay out until I forget Kevin Goldberg's name and 'I love Jews', and then find me a normal man."

"Maybe you should just go home now and sleep it off?"

"Shell, I'll be fine. I'm sure Mr. Wonderful out there won't let anything happen to me."

"You mean that guy who just hopped onto the Pink Pony float with those devil girls?"

Erin turned. Topless women painted red, with horns and tails, surrounded Satan on an elaborate throne, and Steiner started dancing with them.

"Fuuuuck! What's with him?"

"Maybe he's trying to make you jealous?"

"You think he has a crush on me?"

"That would explain why he was so happy after you fucked up with Kevin."

"Sympathy would have worked better. How come men just can't be honest with their emotions? They feel horny, they act like assholes; they feel scared, they act like assholes and start wars." Erin finished her cigarette and stubbed it out. When she looked outside again, a large group of people with jack-o'-lanterns on their heads were walking by. "Where's Steiner?"

Lashell shrugged.

"I guess Mr. Wonderful took off with those strippers," Erin said with little concern.

"You gonna chase after him?"

She took a gulp of ale and lit up another cigarette. "He knows where to find me."

#

Erin sat smoking a cigarette and drinking water in the break room. *If Monster's Day was that crazy, Halloween will be a zoo. I pray that I didn't do anything else stupid besides calling Lashell, Tawnee, and Fabrianne. Wait, if I said that I loved them, which is true, who else might I have called?* "Pat!" she yelled as she exited the break room.

"Yo!"

"Did I call you and Mimi last night?"

"That was you?"

"Shit! What did I say?"

"I don't know. I just picked it up and hung up."

"Pat! What if I was in trouble?"

"You never ask for help."

"I guess that's true." *But I bet you just said that to cover your mistake.* After Pat left, she ran down the list of people she loved whose phone numbers she has memorized. *Dave is the only one I know by heart, so there's no chance of Dad or Josh. Mom is the only person I would have called in a drunken state.* Shit! *What mean things might I have said? What would she have said back? There's only one way to find out.*

She picked up the break room phone and dialed. *I have no idea what to say after two and a half months of not speaking. I should be direct and handle it like a business call.* The phone rang twice. *One more, the voice mail kicks in, and no way I'm leaving a mess...*

"Hello?"

Erin almost hung up, but forced herself to continue. "Hi, it's me."

There was an uncomfortable pause. "Hi, how are you?"

"I'm okay. A little hungover." Erin wished she could take the information back.

"Monster's Day, eh?"

"Yeah." Erin waited, to give her mom time to bring up any late-night conversations. She also seemed to be waiting. "So, did I call you last night?"

"No."

"What? Really?" Erin was shocked and a little ashamed. Of course she was mad at her mom, but even she knew a part of her still loved her.

"Yes, why? Did you want to tell me something?"

"No—well, yes, I mean—I called some people last night, and you know how stupid people can get when drinking."

"Oh, I see. So did you want to tell me anything now that you're sober?"

"No, I mean—no, I'm fine."

"Okay. Well, I guess you're at work so I should let you go—"

"Yeah-er-no, I'm good. I'm just running up the clock. Anything new with you?"

"You mean with my life?"

"Sure."

"That's a lot to talk about in one phone call."

"You're right, I guess."

"I was thinking of going up to the cabin, you know, to see how it is and stuff. I think next year we could rent it out, get some extra cash for you, me, and your Uncle Howard.

"Yeah. That's a good idea. I guess it needs to be dusted. So– I guess you and Dan are going up, eh?"

"No, not Dan. I was thinking of going up sometime this week. You can come. You're off on Wednesdays, right?"

"Y-yes."

"Okay—so you wanna spend a couple of nights up there? We could go to the hot when it's cheap and it won't be crowded."

"Uh–sure. That sounds rad."

"Great. I'll call you later for a confirmation."

She sounds like she's in business mode. "All right. Bye...Mom."

"Bye sweetheart."

The minute she hung up, Erin felt warmth, as if the months of avoiding her mother didn't exist. *She mentioned the hot springs. Whenever we get into bad arguments, we go to a sauna to relax. Mom must have been planning this conversation for a while. That's cool— she never gave up hope on working things out.* She carried this feeling back to the front.

The customers increased, as an invasion of Party Zombies who had all been sleeping off hangovers, hungrily awakened. Erin overhead someone talking about the infamous 'nooner' party. She imagined the professional partiers like Steiner, still dancing without eating or sleeping or perhaps having sex with girls like Debbie Chan. *Am I feeling a bit disgusted with Steiner, or is it jealousy? He has more energy, more friends and more sex than I do. Hey, if he left Lashell and me at the bar, how did we get hooked up later?* She remembered Lashell had left her at the bar.

After finishing her ale, Erin went back outside to watch the end of the parade. Just like at the Thanksgiving Day parade ends when Santa Claus shows up, the Monster's Day parade ends with Dracula riding in the back of a black Cadillac convertible. Viewers from the sidewalks filled in behind him and walked behind the car. Some were banging on drums, coffee cans, or anything else, creating a rhythmic marching beat for their own parade. Erin joined in as well. *I have no idea where the parade ends up, but with so many drunken people in costumes, it ought-to be interesting.* Erin danced around with her feather boa, waving and shimmying for the introverts still watching on the sidewalk.

As the crowds got denser, the sounds grew more interesting: plastic buckets; cheap toy horns, even jangling car keys. *This isn't just a bunch of noise, this is the beat of Neopolitan, a bunch of people of different makes coming together to get off the sidelines and make some music.* Eventually the noisemakers caught up with real instruments and DJs on floats. It took a little while, but they managed to sync up and the sound became even richer. *I can't believe that corporate-sponsored sounds could blend so well with Bohemian ones. If only the groups could mix so well socially.* The parade was over but the music continued. Dancers tossed the last of their liquor samples and people danced, some topless, in the street; the end of Broadway became a big club. The police ignored anything that wasn't dangerous or too blatantly criminal: a group of guys sharing a pot pipe was ignored, but the drunkard trying to climb a light pole was told to cool it. Eventually the professional DJ's sound became too loud and fast for the amateurs and it was the only music. *Ah, mainstream takes over again.* Erin wandered from float to float until familiar faces started to appear in the makeshift clubs. Toad, Bebe, and Ashlee were in DJ Slam's area; Jeff and Brenda in Anne D' Beher's; and Steiner, Debbie Chan, and Lisa Ann, whom Erin remembered from Tawnee's birthday party, danced in DJ Sexy

Party's block. Erin danced over to Lisa Ann and tapped her on the back. It took her a second to recognize Erin.

"Holy shit! Oh, my God! Hi, Girl!" she yelled while hugging Erin. "How the fuck are you?"

"Drunk…and happy, right now."

"I hear you. This is wild!" She gestured at Steiner. "Do you know Steiner?"

"Yes, we were hanging out earlier until he ditched me."

"Whoa! That's not very nice."

"No, it wasn't. But that's Steiner."

"Definitely."

The two started dancing. "Have you seen Tawnee or Fabrianne?" Erin asked

"Earlier, at the Farmer's Market, but not since."

"Cool. So, how are you doing?"

"I'm good. School's good. I'm still into metalworking. Me and Tawnee are still selling our junk at the Market."

"That's great! I've always wanted to see your booth, but I work on weekends."

"That sucks ass. It's doing pretty well. How about you? Still at that pizza place?"

"Yep, and living with Mary Jo."

"Who's that? I don't know her."

"Oh, she works with me, she's an artist, and she also sells pot."

"Wow! Really? Is it good stuff?"

"Yes, but you know what? I don't wanna be around that kind of shit."

"I can imagine, after what Tawnee, Ro, and Fabe went through with Hanna."

"How did that turn out?"

"Fast. It turned out fast. I heard after some guys killed her pusher she stopped being social. Took all her shit and disappeared. They haven't heard from her since. The police came by and everything. That's been like…three months?"

"Three months! Have they thought of a new roommate?"

They never even considered asking me to move in.

"It's Roger. He's the master tenant in that house, so he'd rather they pay more rent then get another basket case in there." The dance area was getting increasingly crowded and people started bumping into the girls. "Can we go somewhere else?"

"Definitely."

They wove out through the crowd and sat on the first store's stoop that didn't smell of urine.

"Anyway, I think Ro was still hoping that Hanna would come back."

"But three months?"

"Yeah, I know. He's like that. I mean, he may act like an asshole, but when it comes to friend loyalty, he's pretty tight."

"That's cool. Thing is, I wish I could have moved in there instead of Kenwood."

"Oh, I'm there with you, I wanted to live there, too, but Roger said no."

"Wow. So he hasn't given up hope, yet?"

"Here's the thing: Tawnee and Fabe are tired of him calling all the shots..." Lisa Ann looked around for eavesdroppers. "...and there's this three-bedroom house opening up near the park next month. It's owned by a teacher of ours and she said she'd give us first pick."

"That's great for you guys. Doesn't do me any good."

"Well, I'm not moving in with them—I live in a great place on 10th now." She looked around again, and then waved at a blond guy dressed in a red and black Star Trek, the Next Generation outfit. "Tony! Come here!" she yelled. "That's Tony, my yuppie roommate."

"Yuppie?"

"Yeah, I kid him about it. He's one of those Techno yuppies working in Dot Com Alley. He used to live in Upper Heights, but moved into the city because he still thinks he's one of us."

"You mean he's a dabbler?"

"Yeah, but he's cool."

Tony came over. "I remember you—from F.J.P., right?"

"Yes. People only remember me from there. Just once I'd like to hear, 'didn't you work at the Acid Pit?'"

"You worked at the Acid Pit?"

Lisa Ann put her arm around him: "Ah, Mr. Holmes, amazing how you followed her trail of clues, starting with the words, 'I worked at the Acid Pit.'"

Erin laughed.

"That's it!" Tony complained. "I think you need a dose of —body slam!" He grabbed Lisa Ann and picked her up. She giggled and squirmed while yelling for him to stop. He eventually put her down.

"Yuppie bastard!" she laughed

"Gutter punk!" he responded.

They're flirting with each other but not admitting it.

"I was just telling Erin how you're trying to be cool and live in 10th Street and all," Lisa Ann said, catching her breath.

"You tell her how your punk-ass sponges off of me?"

She elbowed him in the ribs.

Get a room! "So…if Fabe is thinking about moving, then what about Roger?"

"What about him? If she's not tired of the way he treats her like shit, I think she should be."

"Is Roger's abusing her?"

"Not in that white trash, wife beater, Jerry Springer way, but more like a mental thing." They sat back down. "I mean, Roger flirts with girls, he's disrespectful. I mean, I love the guy, but he's an asshole."

Steiner joined them, dancing around the girls as if he were coaxing them to join him.

"So, should I call them about this, or is this hush-hush?" Erin asked

"I think it's hush-hush until Fabe talks to Roger…" Steiner started shaking his butt in Lisa Ann's face. She pushed him away. "Get that thing away. Gawd damn, that just screams of attention!"

Steiner ignored the insult and tried to dance the same way in front of Erin. She stood up and turned to Tony. "Where on 10th Street do you live?"

He didn't answer, he was too busy laughing at Steiner, shaking his butt in front of Debbie. Unlike the others, she hooted and grabbed as if she were in a strip club.

"He's such a jerk," Erin informed everybody.

#

At the end of Erin's shift, Lashell lent her train fare. Again, she cut through Central City Park, now void of rubbish and drunks sleeping off their hangovers. Now there were yuppie joggers, parents with kids, and some hippie-dippies selling their wares. Erin felt very awake and alert. She held onto this feeling even as she boarded the train.

I wonder if I'd put as much effort into forming a real relationship with a straight decent guy as I did with Kevin, where would that have lead? And what was Steiner's problem? The way he hung all over other women and acted like a big baby when I questioned anything he did. Maybe he doesn't like the ground rules I set up, especially the rule that the first hint that Kevin would be mine I'd break it off. How else was he was supposed to treat me after that? Maybe his sudden happiness after I made an ass out of myself with the 'I love Jews' incident was ...what's that German word? For a shameful joy? By the time she reached her stop, she realized he was in love with her.

When she exited the Kenwood station, she did what she and Mary Jo called the 'Two-Block Sprint' through the circumference of drug dealers, prostitutes, addicts, and transients who hung around doing what they did best. In the future, when the yuppies, lofts, and Coffee Barns were more established and the calls to the police become more frequent, this part of Kenwood would change almost overnight. But for now, Erin walked as fast as she could without running until she'd reached the less active area, near Mary Jo's apartment.

Mary Jo was out, perhaps still dancing at the nooner. Erin wrinkled her nose. The toll of caring for four cats had apparently become unbearable for Mary Jo, who changed their box less and less. Erin moved it from the bathroom to the hallway, right next to Mary Jo's bedroom. She then took Buster out for a short walk. It didn't take long for him to go to the bathroom, which pleased her, because her dearest goal in life right then was to return to the apartment and take a very long hot bath.

Erin poured lavender bath soap from the bottle she had bought at Bathe Her and Bring Her to Me and settled into the suds, expecting that by relaxing, she would forget all about her weird night, but like bubbles in the tub, more memories bobbed to the surface.

"Where are we going?" Annette Dean asked.

I'm just drunk enough to punch her if she asks that question one more time.

Annette was twenty, with blonde hair in a pixie-cut. She was Steiner's friend from his old job at Van Go's Art Supply, and had latched onto the group around the time the police lost their patience and started harassing people. They took the hint, it was a good time to find something else to do. *I wonder if he ever slept with her.* Steiner seemed more interested in Debbie Chan, who showed more interest in the half bottle of vodka she was nursing. They were walking along the boundary between Chinatown and Little Italy. Tony had mentioned a big party somewhere in the Banking District, and that had lead them on what so far had been a forty-minute, block-by-block wild goose chase, as they searched for somewhere someone else had taken Tony one time, when he was already wasted.

"If we turn into another blind alley," Erin grumbled, "I am prepared to bail."

"Tony, do you even know where we are?" a pissed off Lisa Ann complained.

"Yes, I think this is it, near that fabric store."

"It better be, cause I'm tired."

They went to the end of the alley. Tony spun around and slapped his hands on his legs. "Fuck!"

"This ain't it?" Steiner asked.

Erin looked around. The writing on the doors and signs was in Chinese. A pair of battered green steel basement doors had stenciled red dragon designs. Steiner slopped a drunken arm around her shoulder. She wiggled away from him as if he were a wet stranger. "How do we get back to Broadway?"

"Damn it, yuppie, we're lost!" Lisa Ann snapped.

We're not lost, we just need to—"

"Wait! I hear music!" Annette called out. They all went silent, pricked up their ears like radars and creeped around like the ground contained land mines. They tried to pinpoint the muffled, thumping bass. Erin realized where the noise was coming from, but Debbie beat her to the revelation.

"The basement! It's coming from that basement!" She pointed at the double doors. Erin noticed while the paint was old and worn, a fresh, white ribbon had been tied to one of the handles. The group had approached to within three feet when the doors flew open with a loud crash. Everyone screamed and jumped back.

A guy wearing a black suit with a red shirt stumbling up the stairs, supporting what could be a Hispanic transsexual in a red sequin dress.

"Heeeeey! Whatsup?" the one not in a dress slurred.

"Hey, is this Vampire Ball?" Tony asked.

"Naw man, this is Hallow-X."

"Shit! Damn it, yuppie! Lisa Ann yelled. Erin was about to tell her to shut up when Tony jumped in.

"No! No, this is better. This is an alphabet party!"

The stranger shushed him while glancing around for cops. "Not so loud, dude. My deaf grandmother in Russia could hear you."

Tony lowered his voice to a low whisper. "This is great! These things are rarely advertised. It's all word of mouth!"

"Wait, is this that thing where you take drugs from A to Z?" Annette asked.

"That's right—say, how far are you two up to?" Tony asked the man.

As if counting numbers on his fingers, he did the alphabet. "F."

"What's 'F'?" Steiner asked.

"Fags, Fosters, or Forty-ounce."

"Fags?" Annette asked.

"English slang for cigarettes," Erin answered.

Steiner looked at her, surprised. "How'd you know that?" Tony clapped his hands. "All right, it's still early, let's go."

"Wait, they charge for those things," Erin said. "How much is it to get into this?"

"Don't worry about it, I'll cover everyone," Tony suggested.

Erin's eyes widened. *I have no idea how much it's going to be, but if the cover is anything like the Acid Pit on a special event night, it's gonna cost at least thirty bucks each. How much money is Tony making where a hundred and eighty bucks is nothing?* Tony took a swig of Debbie Chan's vodka. *Maybe he's just one of those people that buy you free drinks when they get drunk, trying to fit in with the hip crowd.*

At the bottom of the steps was a badly lit, concrete hallway painted lime green. Rusty metal pipes lined its low ceiling. Debbie held into Steiner's arm as if they were in a haunted house. Erin walked ahead of everyone to show her impatience and to demonstrate her bravery and independence. At the end, in front of a set of black metal doors, stood a large, bald Black man in a leather jacket. Next to him, sitting at a card table covered in club flyers, sat a White guy with spiky purple hair and thick, red glasses.

What an odd pair.

"Hi!" Purple Hair said to Erin. He looked at the group behind her. "How many?"

Erin started extending fingers as she ran through names in her head while Steiner began pointing to people and counting out loud. "...four, five!"

"Six, actually," Erin corrected.

"Alrighty, that'll be sixty dollars."

Erin's eyes bulged out. "Sixty dollars? Is that it?" *How can they charge only ten dollars to get into a rave?*

Tony seemed unsurprised and casually pulled out his wallet and paid. *Did he know how much it would be? Is that why he volunteered to pay for us?* The spiky-haired guy handed them some flyers. Each advertised future events: Transporter, Light

Wave, and Phantasm Orgasm. The Black guy opened one door; music hit them like a solid wave of sound. At the end of a second narrow hallway they passed through a curtain of man-made fog into the main room. Wall-mounted strobe lights assaulted their vision as an air canon fired silver confetti onto their heads.

I feel like we've just boarded a space ship.

Her eyes adjusted to the lights. The space was wide, but the low ceiling made it claustrophobic. Colored lasers and disco lights danced across every surface. Circles of dancers appeared and disappeared in the pandaemonium of a psychedelic slide show. Black lights intensified neon-colored paint, splattered on the floor, as well as the highs of the drugged-out, sitting on glowing pink beanbag chairs in the room's corners. Shadows of laughing, screaming people swirled all around them. *What the fuck am I getting into?* She reached out and grabbed Lisa Ann, the closest person to her. Lisa Ann held Erin's hand like a parent and lead her through the chaos.

"Where are we?" Steiner asked.

"Under Chinatown," Tony yelled. "This used to be where people came for opium, cock fights, hookers, and other black market shit back in the good old days. They must have cleaned it up for this thing,"

Cleaned it up? As far as I'm concerned, it's the 1800s again: women are acting like prostitutes, everyone is on drugs, and any moment now, there's going to be a cock fight.

"How do you know all that?" Annette asked.

"Library?" he said as if it were the obvious answer.

They managed to find what appeared to be a bar, though Erin couldn't see any alcohol behind it. Tony, who had now officially become the leader, gave the woman behind the counter fifty dollars and said something. She handed him a lanyard with a shiny badge reading 'G-I'.

"What the fuck?" Erin asked.

"No idea," Lisa Ann responded. Both went up to Tony and examined the glittery tag he now wore around his neck, like a back stage pass.

"You need one of these," he said, "for stuff."

"G-I?" Lisa Ann asked, smelling the tag to see if it were made of drugs.

"Ganja through Ice, I guess." He smiled at the girls' confusion. "You pay for the drugs you want, in batches of three. But forget X-Z—nobody ever makes it that far."

Erin pondered: *J-L would be my choice. I'm not sure what K is, but L has to be LSD.* She went up to the counter.

"What's your pleasure, luv?"

What a terrible fake British accent. "J-K-L?" The woman gave her a tag and said something Erin couldn't hear because of the loud music and screaming. It could have been a warning or just the price. She handed the woman the last of her money and took the tag. *This is where they make their money. With so many sets of letters at fifty a pop, someone could easily spend over a hundred before they passed out.* Erin looked around for where people got their drugs. She spied no other booths, but she did notice costumed people wandering around with glowing neon trays. She approached a guy dressed like the Pope, complete with miter hat. He gave her a what-do-you-want stare, and she returned a give-me-fifty-dollar's-worth-of-drugs-now! Look.

He read her tag. "Not yet, sweetheart. We're still on G through I."

"G through I?"

"G through I," he repeated as he walked away.

*G? Could be Ganja, or...*she searched her brain's drug encyclopedia...*glass? I should skip cocaine and speed mixed together— I don't really feel like taking anything mixed. The booze is still swirling around in my head. Anything stronger than pot's gonna be dangerous on so many levels. Whatever I get, I'll take just one and stash the rest away for another day.* She turned to see where everyone else had gone, and found herself face-to-face with her old boyfriend, Peter Fisher.

For a second they regarded each another, Erin in complete shock and Peter in dazed apathy, as if she were just someone in his way. Erin fast-walked away to some of the glowing beanbag chairs. Once in the shadows she slowed her heartbeat. Peter wasn't looking in her direction. *Is he avoiding a confrontation, or is he just that out of it? Did he not recognize me? The last time he saw me,*

my hair wasn't in blonde dreads. He looks exactly the same: hasn't changed his crew cut hair with a duck's ass flip on top—and is that the same Sex Pistols shirt?
She sank onto one of the chair. *He has an M-O card. Marijuana, Nicotine, Opium? Looks like he's taken at least two cards' worth already.* Seeing him so out of it pleased her, in a way. *I could walk up and trip him or kick his balls, and he wouldn't know what was going on or who did it or why.* She saw Steiner and Debbie Chan approach him and start talking. "God Damn it!" she yelled, safely drowned out by the music. "Do they know everybody? What could they have in common?" The conversation was short, like a greeting. Debbie patted Peter on the back and he walked away and joined a group of guys. *If they know him, either it's not very well or Peter can't talk.*
Steiner and Debbie started dancing near a large, six-foot devil's head. *Am I really seeing that? Wasn't that on the dancing devil girl float from the parade? How the hell did they get that down here?* Checking on Peter, she saw two people she recognized joining his group: Chelsea from the boarding house, and a guy who usually hung out with Kevin. *Knowing what I know now about Kevin, this guy is probably gay and maybe even Kevin's boyfriend.* Chelsea was a G-I and the guy was a J-L. *Joints, Special K? LSD? Fuck! Why do I know so many drug names? Why don't I know as much about chemistry?* As she stewed, she glanced around impatiently. *The strange thing is, I haven't seen any sign of drugs anywhere. There's guys going around with trays, but I don't see any pills or smell pot. Are they somewhere else I haven't been, or maybe the alphabet thing is some kind of symbolic thing? For fifty damn dollars, it better be real!* Peter put his arm around a frat boy type and they laughed like best friends. *Disgusting. Peter, best buds with a yuppie! I'm glad that everything Peter does I dislike.* Her contempt led to embarrassment, as if she had wasted her time with him. She saw Steiner dancing under a black light with Debbie. "Ass-wipe!" she yelled.
She looked around for a regular bar. *Maybe the booze is free. If I can't have drugs, I can at least keep my buzz going.* Amid the visual clutter, she hadn't noticed before, but on the wall near where she had bought her tag there was a sports stadium-like

scoreboard displaying the letter F. It switched over to G, right when the music switched tempo to another song. The costume guys with the trays were now carrying clear plastic shot glasses. The little cups looked like they were filled with water but she imagined it must have been vodka. When the guy dressed as the Pope came by, she grabbed a shot glass and downed it. It tasted like some type of energy drink instead of alcohol. *Why put that in the shot glass?* The Pope grabbed her tag.

"No! You're J-L. This is G.–Geeeee!" He took her card exchanged it for a G-I card, and then hole-punched it with a star shape.

"What? Why did you do that? She asked?"

"G," he said, as if she had asked a stupid question.

"G? G? What the fuck is G? Why was it in a shot glass? I didn't want G! I wanted pot! If It's not Ganja, should I be mixing G with alcohol?" The guy rolled his eyes and walked away. "Fuck!" She ran over to Chelsea. "Chelsea!" she yelled.

Chelsea reacted as if she had spotted her grandmother in a porno movie. "What are you doing here?"

"Whatever—Chelsea! What's G?"

"What are you talking…"

"The drug! Letter G! What is it?"

"Ganja?" she answered, unsure.

"No! It was a liquid."

"GHB, maybe?" Answered the gay guy.

"What does it do? How much did they give me?"

"No idea. They dilute the fuck out of everything at these parties so people don't go ape-shit. If you ask me, for fifty they should give us the full Monty."

"But I'm drunk already. What's that shit gonna do to me?"

"Last time I took it, I woke up in the men's room with a condom up my ass." He started laughing, as did Chelsea.

"Oh, God! Oh, fuck!" Erin felt a wave of panic.

"Don't worry, just go dance it off. The small amount they gave you, it ain't gonna do nothing but relax you."

Erin grabbed her shoulders as if she were about to explode. She returned to the bean bag chair and sat down. *Oh shit! What if that stuff's like heroin?* She waited for something horrible to happen. Five minutes passed, and then fifteen. Finally, after twenty, she relaxed. *That asshole's right about how much they dilute things.*

The letters on the scoreboard switched from G to H. Erin waved over a girl dressed like a devil carrying one of the trays. She looked at Erin's tag, gave her another shot glass and punched the H.

"This isn't heroin, is it?"

The girl shrugged and continued on. Erin was mad. *You're serving this stuff and yet you don't know what it is?* She sniffed it, which didn't give her a clue. *Well, maybe I'll just skip this one.*

"Erin!" Peter said. He was standing right next to her. In a panic, like trying to hide evidence from a cop kicking in your door, she quickly downed the liquid in one gulp.

#

Mary Jo came home at around 8PM. She didn't say a word to Erin, completely ignored the litter box, and went straight to bed. Though Erin felt wiped out, she chose to lie in bed listening to Jesus Swept. As the female vocalist droned over slow, industrial-like art rock rhythms about death, depression, and teddy bears on fire, Erin's mind began to drift.

Peter. How the hell did I forget about seeing him? I swear to God, I'm never doing drugs again. Even as she finished that thought she knew that it was a lie. *Wow. Steiner, Kevin, and Peter—my past, present, and future in one day. Good ol' Peter. Since when did Mr. 'Disco Sucks' start going to raves? And my Mom? I have to go to Mountain Springs on Wednesday. I should have just said: What? You think we're okay now—after not speaking and shit?' Too much going on, I need to step back from all this crazy shit!*

Buster stirred and started cleaning himself. "Buster, I gotta step back and figure out what's going on. Is it me? I didn't ask anyone if they wanted to butt-fuck me, or leave my ass at the airport right before I went to Europe. Or deal with Dan." She covered her eyes to block out the streetlight, then slowly spread her fingers so the light seeped through. *Like turning invisible and reappearing. I wish I could teleport far away.* An old, cheap car playing a booming rap song on an expensive stereo rumbled down the street. *But I'm still here.*

Erin picked up the phone and dialed. *Mary Jo's gonna be hard to take for another month. I like her free spirit and shit, but it rubbed me the wrong way how she dissed me this morning. I thought she cared about me, but she treats everyone the same, like one big art project. And I sure won't miss seeing her naked, pimply ass, walking through the living room, or that stinky-ass litter box.*

"Hello," Fabrianne said.

"Hey, Fabe! It's Erin."

"Oh, cool. What's up?"

"I'm calling to ask about something I heard through the grapevine."

"What's that?"

"Is it true that you and Tawnee are thinking of moving out?"

"Sure. I got that homework assignment."

"What?"

"Yeah, I'll go look it up in my notebook. Hold on."

"What the…oh."

After a minute, Fabrianne returned to the phone. "Sorry about that. Ro was in earshot."

"Yeah, I figured. So it's true."

"Yeah, we're working on it. My teacher has a place in an awesome location near Grandview."

"Grandview? Holy shit! That's a nice 'hood."

"I know. It's a three bed-roomer near the park, and since my teacher is like a communist-slash-socialist-slash-whatever, she ain't gonna overprice it."

"So, it's gonna be you two guys?"

"No, we want you to move in, too, but we weren't sure what your situation was now with that weird girl—what's her name?"

"Mary Jo. Well, I'm not on a leash or anything."

"Leash?"

"I mean lease—Freudian slip. Feeling a little trapped right now. I can leave whenever I want." Erin began feeling a little pissed. "But why didn't you guys talk to me about this? Mary Jo doesn't sound like much of a reason."

There was a short pause. Fabrianne lowered her voice almost to a whisper. "Erin, I'm not just moving out. I'm gonna break up with Roger at the same time."

Erin was astonished. "Oh, my gosh, are you sure? That's major."

"Yes. It has to be done."

"So what was the final straw?"

There was a pause and then the sound of a door closing. Fabrianne raised her voice again. "Besides him being a jerk?"

"Yeah, what made you say, 'that's it?'"

"I had been thinking about it for a long time, but it hit ground zero when we went to a concert at The Hole in Da Wall. They had the usual metal hair bands making the usual noise, and during Death Maggot's set I told Roger that I thought that the guitars were too loud."

"And?"

"And he acted as if I'd missed the point of rock and roll completely and I was the stupidest girl in the world. Like, I mean, I like rock and I like loud music, but not to the point where you can't hear the singer."

"Of course. So you punched him?"

"No. Then we went to have coffee at the 24 Hour Café."

"Then you punched him?"

Fabrianne laughed. "No. But I had to work the next day and he was keeping me out later than I wanted. He didn't care; it was all about him. He's sitting there ranting about 'those fucking Republicans' and 'those fucking Democrats' and 'the fuck'n communists' and 'that fucking Green party' and how they should all be put in a flaming school bus and driven off a cliff. And then that woman who owns Psychicmondo-grooverama, who was sitting behind us—"

"Tamara Etcheverria?"

"Yeah, that's her. She interrupts and starts telling him that it would do no good to kill a bunch of people just because you didn't agree with their political views, and if he didn't like

Democracy or Communism or Socialism, that left only dictators, monarchs or fascists."

"Yeah." *What is she talking about? The only thing I know about politics is that if someone tried to take away my booze, cigarettes, or right to abortions, I'd register and vote against them.*

"And she was making some <u>total</u> logic points. And I was thinking, 'Yeah. This chick is right on.' And Roger starts ranting about how great anarchy would be, and she calls him on that, saying without order, the ones with guns always take over the weak and stuff."

"Right, right. She's deep. So SHE punched him?"

"No. My point is..." There was a pause, as if she had forgotten what she was talking about. "...my point is, later, Roger went on about how stupid the woman was and totally discounted her opinion. This was a chick who I thought was totally right on and wished I could be as successful a business owner and as sharp and popular, and Roger dissed her! He dissed my aspiration just like he disses me. It's like, it's hopeless with him. He's always treating me like I'm stupid, and runs around with his female friends."

"He cheats on you?"

"You know, I actually don't think he has, but it doesn't matter. He knows that hanging out all night with some girl isn't right. But it's not like I'm a jealous person or anything. It's his lack of respect that pisses me off." Fabrianne voice raised. "I've put up with this shit for over a year–I'm done, Erin! As soon as we get the word, I'm out!"

"Good for you. But why didn't you tell me about this earlier?"

" 'Cause you work with him. I didn't want to put you in the middle off all this."

"Fabe, it's not like me and Roger are 'rads or anything. You can tell me anything and I won't tell him."

"I know. You're right. I just wanted everything to be in place before I made a move. If it fell through, it'd be like swinging a bat at Roger's head behind his back and missing, and when he turns around, you're like, 'What?'"

"Interesting analogy."

"So…who did you hear about the move from?"

"Sorry, can't reveal my sources."

"Lisa Ann. That girl has a big mouth. I'm so afraid she'll tell Roger."

"Naw. She knows what's going on."

"Where did you see her?"

"Monster's Day parade. Then we went to some Alphabet party."

'How was it?"

"I remember the parade, but the Alphabet party is a little fuzzy after I had something that starts with a G or H. I think G wasn't ganja, 'cause it fucked me up bad."

"GHB?"

"What?"

"Sorta like roofies."

"Date rape drug?"

"Yeah. You have memory loss? Loss of motor control? Pass out?"

"Yep. That's the one. I didn't really pass out that fast. Then again, some guy told me that they use really low doses of everything. But what about H? I took that right when I ran into my ex."

"You ran into Fisher?"

"Yep."

"Peter!" she said as if surprised. She stood, but she wasn't sure why. *I'm not going to hug or kiss him hello.* When her legs hit vertical, the first liquid took effect: she felt like she had been holding her breath for five minutes in a crouched position and suddenly jumped up really fast while going backwards, downhill on a bicycle without a handle bar. "Whooooooooaa!"

She steadied herself and tried to tell Peter what a fucking butt-faced douche bag he was, but only managed a bunch of garbled gibberish. She then tried to hit him, but was so sloppy and ungraceful it turned into a lumbering hug. Peter, surprised, hugged her back.

"How are you doing? You look great," he said.

"Why?"

"What?"

"Wha-poht?" she blurted in place of 'Why did you leave me at the airport?' She pointed a finger. "You fudged."

"Fudged?" He'd misunderstood 'fucking bastard coward.' "I didn't expect to see you here."

To Erin, his face looked like a marshmallow. She laughed at the talking marshmallow, then tried to rip off a piece. Peter didn't know what to make of Erin pinching his cheek and laughing.

"Erin, are you too wasted to recognize me?"

His voice registered, and she remembered who the marshmallow was. As she bent over and slid sideways from a wave of vertigo, she tried to punch him in the stomach. This time she really did punch someone—Jeff from work, and it wasn't in the stomach but the left testicle. He doubled over and vomited whatever pharmaceuticals he had taken earlier.

Before she crumpled to the ground she was suddenly flying through the air like a butterfly, through the room and into a bathroom. Steiner had carried her there.

"What the fuck are you doing?" he asked.

Erin grabbed his face and laughed at his cat whiskers. "Meow!" To keep from falling, she grabbed his butt.

He pulled her hands away. "Not a good place or time for that. Man, you're fried. Did you take the drugs? Don't you know you can't mix drugs and booze?"

"Martha!" she answered.

"What?"

"Martha-can't-make-bubbles!" she said carefully, confusing even herself.

Steiner's eyes widened as he looked up. "Shit, ladies, sorry. Ran into the wrong bathroom." The two girls making out in the corner didn't react.

"Camper door cam!" Erin said, pointing to a toilet.

Steiner got the hint and guided her into the stall. He closed the door and stood guard. Erin squinted at the toilet. It was crawling with purple bugs and green, pulsating slime. "No way I'm going to sit on you." She pulled down her panties and stood over the opening. Suddenly, she had a penis. She pantomimed holding and aiming it. "Regular or s-ssuper?" she blurted out. She could see the pee shoot out from her imaginary dick but felt it pouring down her leg. A slight bit of reality kicked in, enough for her to figure out what was going on. She pulled down her panties, which apparently were still on, and moved closer to the toilet. She still didn't manage to hit it, but at least more got on the floor than her legs. She took off her panties and tried to flush them down the toilet. It got clogged and overflowed.

Steiner heard the sound of water hitting the floor and opened the door. "Holy Shit!" He lifted Erin over the spreading puddle and set her down outside of the stall and began to laugh very loud and hard. He put his hands over his eyes. "The toilet's overflowing! The toilet! Man, the toilets!"

Erin had always believed, when she was drunk, she could find all the other drunk people in a room. She now felt she could see the drugs hitting Steiner. He was turning as incomprehensible and as lacking in motor control as she was.

"Goddamn!" he yelled, scaring Erin. The pure anger behind it frightened her.

"Why are you so mad?" she asked in all vowels.

"Fucking, fucking, no!" He kicked the wastepaper basket. "Why are you all like that? Like Mom!" He took on a blurry, shapeless red form. Another shapeless form entered the room. This one was green. It joined the red one and they mixed, creating a mud color. Erin's vision became clear again. Steiner was kissing Debbie Chan.

#

"Holy hell!" Fabrianne said. "He cheated on you? In the ladies' room?"

"Well, technically we aren't dating, and I already knew they were doing it."

"But not in front of your face. That's mean."

"Mean is right. He was very mean on drugs. Actually, he's a real asshole just on booze."

"I always thought that when you get drunk your sub conscience comes out and all those things you have buried, rise to the surface. How do you act?"

"Me? Confused and horny—no surprise."

"And he was all angry and rude. What is he so angry about?"

"I don't know. He's good-looking, has lots of friends, and apparently can get ass whenever he wants."

"Maybe there's more to him then you think."

"Maybe. He's two people. He can be really nice, but then it's like he hates you."

"Weird. But it didn't bother you that he was making out with that other girl?"

"I actually left."

"The bathroom or the club?"

"Both…"

After running into numerous people and staggering down the hallway, she crawled up the stairs. She wasn't angry, she just needed to get outside into the fresher air. Emerging from the entrance, she spotted Chelsea and the gay guy.

"Hello!" she yelled.

"Erin?" Chelsea looked at Erin's feet. "Where are your shoes?"

"I left them in the bathroom. They were wet."

"Gross. T.M.I!" said the gay guy.

Erin leaned on Chelsea as if they were old friends.

"Chelsea—fucking wasted—Help me!"

"Help you what?"

"Help me!"

"She needs to sober up or something," said the guy.

"Well, Gary, what do you wanna do?"

"Let's help her walk it off."

Gary and Chelsea each draped one of Erin's arms over their shoulders and began walking her down the street.

"We're not going to miss his party are we?" Chelsea asked.

"No. Kevin said it's an all-nighter."

"Kevin!" Erin yelled. "I love Jews! What-the-fuck?"

"What is she talking about?" Chelsea asked.

Erin turned to her. "You're nice."

"She IS drunk," Gary commented.

"No. You're helping me. But you're all mean." Erin tried to keep Chelsea's face from morphing into a banana. "Why are you so mean?"

"I'm not mean. I'm just...I just don't like people fucking with me."

"She's heavy...And she smells like piss," Gary said. "Here!"

He guided them to a wall and leaned Erin against it so she wouldn't fall.

She didn't know what was going on or where she was, she just felt like curling inside a giant ball and disappearing.

A lot of laughter swelled from the entrance to the rave. Steiner wobbled up the stairs, followed by some guys dressed like pirates Erin didn't recognize, all yelling and screaming as if trying to wake up the whole neighborhood. Erin transformed them into wolves howling at the moon, vicious creatures ready to devour any small animal. She felt like she was a terrified rabbit, and wanted to run away, but her legs had given up.

The Black bouncer appeared. "Keep it the fuck down!" he yelled at Steiner and the guys.

Slurred words were said, and the only one Erin understood was "You shut the fuck up!" Someone tried to push the enormous bouncer and went crashing into a garbage can. Another pirate lumbered at the angry bouncer and landed on concrete. Erin's legs began to work and she started running away from the violence. She saw a gum wrapper floating in front of her and realized she was actually crawling along the ground. She heard a woman scream, "Leave him alone!" and a guy yelling, "I'm calling the cops, motherfu—" before suddenly falling quiet.

The voices grew fainter as Erin fled. She bumped into a pile of boxes with pictures of fruit and Chinese writing on them; she was still crawling, then suddenly she was flying again

She looked up. "Peter. Why are you helping me?"

"I know. After you tried to punch me, even."

"Tried?"

She heard the fading cries of the wolves, one of whom was yelling about what a blast it was seeing his friend get his ass kicked by that Black guy. Her feet were not touching the ground. She still felt like a rabbit, but now being carried in the mouth of a wolf. The rest of the pack hooted and yelled indistinctly.

She felt grass, first on her bare knees, then her face. The grass felt good, like a kiss of coolness and well being. She lifted her eyes and recognized Grandview park. Someone laughed. She lifted herself until she was kneeling. There were colors all around her—lots of reds and blues; bright lights, flashing on and off.

"Got out just in time, man," Peter said to Steiner before they high-fived one other.

Police cars. The lights are police cars. The wet grass, the dead, crunchy leaves and the crescent moon—which was actually a streetlight—felt so pure after the technology and cold hardness of the Alphabet party. Steiner and Peter were talking and laughing. *I hate them.* She was able to stand up and walk. She used the grass to tell her where to go. Whenever she stepped on anything hard, she moved back to the grass. Several times she hit a tree.

"Erin?" Peter yelled, grabbing her arm.

"Get the fuck away from me!"

"What? What did I do to you?"

"Dumb-ass! Airport! Hello! Stupid dumb-ass!"

"I know! I was stupid."

"No, you said I was the one stupid enough to believe we were going to Europe."

"I know. I just couldn't do it."

"You stupid! Stupid jerk! Stupid money! Damn comic books!" Erin turned and started walking away from him.

"I know. I should have said something. But I...I don't know why I didn't say anything."

"Fuck'n coward! Hate you!"

"You're right," He said, turning into an oak tree. She realized she had been talking to a tree. When she had thought it was him grabbing her arm, it was probably a branch. She finally located Peter. He was getting into the back of Donna Etcheverria's BMW convertible. Erin sloppily ran over and grabbed the door handle before the car pulled away. Donna looked at Erin like a homeless person had grabbed her purse and barfed in it.

"Hey! Donna," Erin slurred. She got in and sat on Peter's lap. "Where the fuck are we going?"

"Erin? What are you doing?" Peter asked.

"I'm not finished with you!"

"Yes, you are. What do you want? You smell like piss!"

Steiner ran over and jumped into the front seat with Donna and her Korean friend, Kim. "Let's go!"

"Steiner?" Donna asked. "Where did you come from?"

"Alphabet par-tay, bay-bay." He leaned over Kim and tried to kiss Donna, but she moved and he ended up kissing her shoulder. Art, Kim and the fourth person Erin realized was Quincy Zeitheit, didn't look too happy with the hitchhikers. "What do you guys want?" Donna asked.

"Where are we going?" Steiner asked.

"What do you want? Steiner? You think I'm going take you with us?" She pointed at Erin. "And her?" Erin was too buzzed to follow the conversation. She looked at Art's balding head, offset by being long in the back.

"Hi Art. How's it hanging, baby?"

Art seemed overwhelmed by her attention.

"Go on, get out!" Donna commanded.

"Let 'em stay," Art said.

He thinks he has a chance with me because I'm wasted. "Yeah, let us stay," Erin pleaded. "Where are you guys going?"

"Gothica, Vamp Party," said Art, smiling at Erin.

"Yes, and you guys are making us late," Donna complained.

"No, it's fine. Let 'em come," Peter said, defeated. Donna looked surprised. The expression on her face was one of betrayal. "After what he did to me! And what she did to you?"

This surprised Erin. *I remember ditching Donna at Bistro Alley, but if Peter had told Donna about our relationship, what could I have done that was worse than being left at the airport and forced to travel to Europe, alone?* "Wait, wait," Erin interrupted, taking her hand off of Arts leg. "What did I do to him? He left me at the airport. I had to go to fuck'n Europe! No French, no Spanish —fuck'n nothing!"

"Yeah, of course you went alone, after you treated him like crap!" Donna sneered.

"What are you talking about? I treated him great!" She tried to remember their relationship. All she could conjure up were memories of bliss that came to a sudden harsh ending, thanks to him.

"Oh, please. He said you always put him down, telling him what a loser he was, how you were never satisfied…"

"Donna! STOP!" Peter yelled.

Erin stared in blank silence. "No, it's not true. He was always–he use to say–I was always the one…" She tried to come up with an argument to contradict Donna's statement, but an example escaped her. *Was it true? Was I really a horrible bitch to him?*

"Maybe you guys should leave?" Kim suggested.

"Wha-what! No," Art said.

Erin bolted out of the car and into a nearby bar. She kept thinking, *It's not true. It's not true. It's not true. It's not true.*

Steiner's 'rads had already staked out a table and were doing body shots off of some drunk college fraternity girls. Erin ignored the alcohol games and sat down at her own table near an old jukebox machine. Steiner entered. *Is he coming to comfort me?*

Steiner saw one of his friends lick salt off of the belly of a girl leaning back on the bar, take a shot of tequila, and then suck a lemon out of her mouth. On the way to join them, he patted Erin on the back like an encouraging football player after his teammate misses a field goal. Erin looked closer at one of the loud college girls. *That's Ed's daughter, Courtney, whoring it up with a gang of strange, rowdy guys. I guess if Ed were my father, I'd be sucking a hundred dicks in a porno by now. Ugh.*

She started thinking about her own dad. *I should call him. Maybe have a cigarette first to calm down.* She waved her hand around. "Where the fuck's my purse?" She slapped the table. "What a shitty fucking night!" *I should call everyone I'm pissed at and let them have it, starting with Peter!* She slumped. *Peter. What if he's right and the only reason he didn't go to Europe with me was because I was being a bitch to him? And if I was, what if I'm being an asshole to my mom and dad? I have to find out. I should call them, now.* Patting her sides reminded her she had spent all her money. She walked over to the horny huddle.

"Anyone got some change for the phone?"

Only two guys had noticed her. The first said no, the second stared silently at her chest.

She tapped the guy Steiner called Big Dog.

"You have any change I can use to make some calls?"

"No. But you can borrow my phone." He pulled a cell phone from his back pocket, but before Erin could take it Steiner snatched it. "Hey, Steiner! What da fuck, man?"

"What, are you making a callllllll?" Steiner teased.

"No, she wants to."

Steiner smiled coyly at Erin. "Really? Well, I think she should work for it."

"Give me the fucking phone," Erin commanded, reaching for it.

He moved it out of reach. "No way. Work for it."

"Steiner!"

"No. Hey, everybody! Erin wants the phone. Should I give it to her?"

"No!" they all yelled in unison.

"Should she do something for it?"

"Yeah!" the drunken crowd roared.

"Take it off!" a voice yelled.

"To get the phone back, you have to…you have to…." He looked around the room. "…you have to take a body shot off of one of these girls!"

The crowd hooted agreement. Steiner grinned at Erin as if this task would to be the ultimate breaking point for her dignity and will.

I am not in the mood for your mind games! She grabbed a lemon slice off the table and stuck it in the closest girl's mouth, who happened to be Debbie Chan. In one smooth action Erin took a shot of gin and took the lemon out of Debbie's mouth. The whole performance took less than 10 seconds. Some hooted but most booed.

"That wasn't right," Steiner complained. "You did it wrong. You should—"

"Just give me the goddamn phone!" Erin tried to grab it, but he pulled it out of reach again.

"Steiner!"

He started bringing it close to her and then yanking it away. She elbowed him in the chest and grabbed the phone. "Asshole!" She yelled and walked away.

Outside was quieter. "Okay, how do you work a cell phone?" *I'll try it out on a number I know by heart.* After punching the buttons and pressing 'send' it dialed.

"Hello?" Lashell answered four rings later.

Erin stood wordless as the adrenalin from fighting Steiner and the gin and the 'G' and the 'H' all interacted in new and interesting ways. She felt like her brain had been tied to a rotating helicopter blade.

"Hello?" Lashell tried again, now less friendly.

Words escaped her. Finally, her mind found the three simplest ones in the English language: "I love you." Then she hung up. She started laughing, imagining what Lashell must be thinking. She punched in Pat's number, then her brother's in New Jersey, followed by Tawnee and Fabrianne's. Each time she said "I love you" and hung up.

She started feeling like she was going to throw up, and then started thinking about the word 'throw' and then she threw Big Dog's cel phone at a passing car. The driver stopped. The head poking out the window looked worried. Erin laughed. He drove on without investigating what had hit his fender. Still laughing, she wandered into the busy street. To her luck, the light had just turned green. On the other side of the street, on grass again, she slowly lowered her head and raised her arms into a position like Jesus, crucified on the cross.

#

After agreeing to get together on Thursday to talk about the housing prospect, Erin and Fabrianne said goodbye. Though it was 12:35AM, she couldn't sleep. *Probably an effect of the chemical smorgasbord still in my veins.* The city was very peaceful: the parties were done, no bottles were breaking, nobody was yelling, Techno music and sirens had been silenced, and even the most hardcore party people were either in bed or dead of an overdose.

Her thoughts wandered to Peter. *In spite of me trying to hit him and my desire to kill him, he helped me out and didn't try to take advantage of me. He seemed more of an adult now, grown up. But what am I? Still a child that has to be rescued? Was I really his reason for not going to Europe? Probably not, the asshole. If the best revenge is living well, I need to work on my vengeance. The next time I see Peter Fisher, I'll be living in a better neighborhood with a better job and a better boyfriend.*

Erin heard Mary Jo kick the plastic garbage bag of pot as she stumbled into the hall, then the sound of the litter box getting stepped on followed by granules spilling onto the floor. Erin could not see her, but knew she'd be nude. Mary Jo went to the bathroom with the door open and left without flushing.

"Mary Jo?" Erin called out as her roommate crunched across the litter box mess.

There was a long pause. "Yes?"

"I think I'm going to be moving out."

There was another pause. "Oh, okay. But can you clean the litter box first? It's your turn."

"Mary Jo, I don't have a cat."

"But, Buster uses it, right?"

"Dogs go outside, Honey."

"Oh right…goodnight." Mary Jo closed her door.

Erin put her hands over her eyes. *How fast can I pack?*

#

Erin looked out the car window. The green hills were getting bigger and bigger. Soon they would turn into mountains. The trees around them were vibrant and stood out like confetti.

"Just look at those colors. Ain't they pretty?" her mom said. "You know, sometimes I forget how pretty it is outside the city."

"Hmmm, I guess."

Carolyn reached over and pinched Erin's shoulder. "Oh cheer up. It's not the end of the world."

"Ow! Yes it is. Mom. I embarrassed the shi—er, ah, heck out of myself in front of the man I love, who now thinks I'm a total weirdo."

"So, how did you get to the fountain?"

She staggered through Grandview park until she fell. She began to cry and hit at the ground, and then, continuing to cry, crawled until the grass turned into concrete again. She heard water. *Water is a pure thing. It can cleanse me of everything and everyone. I have to reach it.* She grabbed onto a bench and, as if using it as some sort of launching pad, pushed away from it to a lamppost. Then she pushed from it to another bench, each time getting closer to the sound. Someone yelled and she heard a bottle breaking, then police sirens and cars blowing their horns. She ignored everything and focused on reaching her goal. Finally her palms touched what felt like the edge of the world, a cold stone ledge, smooth and curved. She slid her fingers into the splashing water. *How did my tears create so much water? And why are things so cold?*

"Hey, look!" Steiner yelled, "...A fountain!" He and his friends joined her at the Plaza fountain, some dancing around it, a few jumping into it, and others laying down around it.

They're dancing around my tears. Why are they dancing around my tears?

#

"...And then I passed out."

"Wow," Carolyn said. "That's some story. I'm amazed you remember all of that."

"Yeah, I know."

"So, Peter was Mr. Nice guy and this Kevin guy is wonderful to talk to but he's gay."

"Yet I still hate one and love the other."

Carolyn looked out Erin's window. "There's a vineyard near here that makes a nice dessert wine I like."

"No, thanks. No more drugs or alcohol for me."

"Oh, right, sorry. But what's wrong with the other boy, Steiner? He seems like a nice person."

"He is, kinda, but..."

"But what? Is he bad in bed?"

"Mom!" Erin turned beet red.

"Oh, pish! You just told me about taking a night's worth of illegal drugs. I'd rather you be having group sex than that."

"Oh, my God, Mom!"

Carolyn laughed.

Erin tried to hold it in but giggled anyway. *Might as well be happy now. Telling her about my weekend was easy, but in one hour we'll be at the cabin, and after dinner and the hot springs, at some point, we'll have to discuss what had happened between us.*

Erin wasn't looking forward to that part, but she was looking forward to getting her friend back.

Part Three
Mixed Messages

"My penis is pierced."

"That's nice." Erin had forgotten the staggering guy's name —not from consuming alcohol, she was just not interested. She took a sip of her strawberry soda water. *If this were a beer, would his strange pick-up line have worked?*

"I'd never suck a guy who's dick was pierced, because of AIDS," Tawnee added.

The man now wore the face an Olympic skater who'd shown off a quintuple lutz and been booed.

Well, even a person who's smoked pot and is drinking her second Olden Town beer isn't impressed, so maybe not. Erin peered down from the balcony. Leftover guests occupied the small back yard, some sitting at the tile-covered patio table, and others hanging out by the barren little garden area. In spring, the girls had decided, they'd grow their own vegetables. *I am so goddamn lucky.* Her landlord, Katrina "Neon" Butler, sat enjoying the housewarming party with everyone else. Beyond the high wooden fence, in a formerly empty upstairs room in the Victorian, Erin noticed new baby furniture. *I guess our neighbors are probably a yuppie family that can afford to buy the kind of large, beautiful house that me and my roommates never could. Bunch of...You know, Neon owns this house, and she's super-cool. I guess I should have more faith in humanity.*

"I also have a tattoo on my anus," the guy tried again.

Erin departed and entered Tawnee's bedroom. She stopped, as she had done several times, to diminish her jealousy. Fabrianne and Tawnee had taken the two large upstairs bedrooms with balconies and a view of downtown and park. *My room downstairs is nice; I no longer have to share a bedroom with*

Buster, since he's happy in the backyard; I have a half-bath to myself; and my creativity is stoked since Neon gave us permission to do anything to our bedrooms that could be painted over. Feeling better, she sidestepped three of Tawnee's Goth friends sitting on the floor and bed, smoking pot and discussing art school. *It is so damn tempting to join in all the drinking and drugs here, but I've been good for almost a month: no drugs, no meat, no alcohol, and down to two cigarettes per day. Living close to work lets me walk everywhere and get some exercise. Project Get My Life Together is going great, if you don't count my skyrocketing masturbation rate.* Carolyn had given her daughter a computer the hospital planned to throw away. Not the most cutting edge model, but good enough for e-mail and porn. *So much free porno.*

Erin crossed the landing. For the third time tonight, she heard a girl yell: "Oh, my God! This house is awesome!" *Don't I know it.* Downstairs she joined the cluster from F.J. Pizza: Pat and his girlfriend, Mimi; Lashell, Jeannie and her girlfriend, Velma; and Evan, whom she hadn't seen since he quit to go back to school.

"Great digs," Pat said.

"Don't I know it. But how long will it last?"

"Gads, think positive! You're here. Enjoy it now." He put his arm around her.

Mimi took a sip of beer. "Really, baby. Enjoy it while you can. Take it for all it's worth."

"I'm trying, but the back of my head is saying, 'don't get too attached'."

Lashell put her hand on Erin's shoulder. "You treat this house like your men."

Erin sighed. *That's rather insulting. I've been as good staying away from man problems as any other vice. I even moved without informing Steiner, and contact with Kevin ended at the N.E.A. show.*

"Hey, don't look all pissed off," Lashell said. "You doing good, though."

"Thanks."

"We're gonna blow this popsicle stand. Love the space," said a very drunk, wobbly Jeannie, putting her arm around a sober, designated-driving Velma.

"This place rocks and or rolls, Erin," Velma added. "Much better than the sock drawer me and Jeannie have to live in."

"And hey!" Jeannie continued. "Congrats on the supervisor thing."

"I'm not a supervisor, yet."

"Big deal. Just a week of training and you'll be in." Jeannie waved her hand around as if to say don't worry about it. The couple said their farewells and left. Evan followed with no goodbye.

"I guess we should go, too," Pat said, rubbing Mimi's head. She had let it grow out into a dyed it orange buzz cut *I like her hair, I should do that next time*. "We gotta get up early tomorrow so she can catch the plane to jolly ol' England. Then I fly out after work; fuck'n discount fares."

"Man, everybody's going overseas," Erin complained. "I could have sworn you were just on vacation."

"I was in Oregon, what, five months ago? I only used one of my two weeks. Perfect time to get yourself promoted to supervisor, by the way."

"I guess, but you know how Ed feels about me."

"Shove a squirrel in Ed's ass to kill the bug he's got up there. You're the best candidate. Next to Lashell, of course."

"Hey, soon as I graduate next month, I'm so fuck'n out of there," Lashell re-informed them."

"Exactly. So he has no choice."

"I guess. I just don't trust him."

Mimi hugged Erin. "Don't worry about it, baby. It's only a job. You'll do fine."

She hugged Pat and kissed him on the cheek. "You guys say hello to Mr. Humphrey for me."

"We will. Thanks for hooking us up with him."

"I'm just glad he remembers me. And remember, if you go to the Toad in the Hole club and see a Black Rasta guy named Kenneth working there..."

"We know, we know, kick his ass," Pat interrupted.

"No, just tell him hi. I have no ill will at him."

"Those too are gonna come back married," Erin said after they'd left.

"Really?" Lashell asked. "Why you say that?"

"The look in their eyes. It's like pure love." Erin sighed again.

Lashell looked at her watch. "I gotta go."

"You want me to take you home?"

"No need. You guys are close to the station. I'll catch the all-nighter and get my sister to pick me up."

"It's almost two o'clock. She ain't gonna want to pick you up."

"She will if she wants me to keep babysitting her damn kid."

"Well, at least let me walk you to the station."

"Ain't nobody gonna mess with me in this White neighborhood."

"I know, but I also want to step out for a second. All the booze and pot in here is making me antsy."

"Fine, whatever."

The converted gaslights made Grandview even prettier than in the daytime. One side of Chestnut Street was Queen Anne-style houses, the other cafes and cute, small businesses you'd never find outside a $100K-a-year neighborhood. The lights were still on in Penny's Books and Wine Bar, and people were actually browsing at 2AM.

"Try to keep a bar or bookstore open that late somewhere else," Lashell complained.

"Yeah, the only people who'd be in it would be homeless and perverts."

"Still, a nice 'hood, though."

"I know."

"That didn't sound too enthusiastic."

"I'm still a little cautious."

"Don't worry about it. You doing good. Get your sorry ass in school and you'll be all set."

"Maybe. I talked to Neon about that. She thinks I'd have no problem getting student loans and stuff."

"All right, then. Next phase: go to art school and get out of F.J.P."

"You can say that because you're almost there. But this may be the only time I'll be able to make supervisor at any job. If I go to school and reduce my hours, I'll have to be a floater for two more years."

At the station, Lashell grabbed Erin's shoulders and looked her in the eyes. "Fuck F.J. Pizza. It's only a job. Look at Mary Jo. She been there twice as long as you, and she said, 'Oh, I think I'll go to Tibet. Bye.'"

"She also has forty-five grand in the bank."

"...Yeaaah, but still, she gave up her drug-dealing alibi. My point is: don't make your decisions off some shitty pizza job. Ed know he needs your ass, and if he don't appreciate that it's time your ass moved on. There are a million other shitty jobs out there."

"You can say that because you can get a nice receptionist job or something."

"Administrative assistant, but yeah, if you go to school you can get something better, too."

"But look at people like Tracy. She's a supervisor, and she's happy and stuff."

"Tracy likes being a supervisor because her party ass can slack off when she wants. And that's her. I like Tracy, but I can't see her living in this neighborhood one day."

"Shell, I couldn't live in this neighborhood without renting. No matter what job I got."

"You don't know that. You could go to school, open your own jewelry store and be just like your landlord Neo Deo, whatever."

"Doubtful."

"Shove your doubts up life's ass, Erin. Nobody ever knows. Only way it definitely won't happen is your sorry ass works at F.J. Pizza forever and you end up like Ashley. Now there's your motivation: I sure as hell don't want to be a thirty-something taking orders from twenty-year olds while waitin' for my boyfriend to get out of jail or the cops to find my meth lab ass. If you still there in your thirties, girl, I'm gonna do a drive-by and put you out of your misery.

"Thanks, Shell."

She hugged Erin. "You're welcome."

Erin started walking back. *Lashell's not usually a hugger. Must be positive energy overspill from almost completing her degree. And she's not the only one. Next month Fabrianne's joining the BA-graduate job market, and Tawnee in three. I'll be the only person in the house who stopped at a high school education.* As she glanced into the boutiques she thought about how easy it would be to blow forty dollars a day in this neighborhood. *I want to get to a point in my life where forty bucks isn't such a big deal. Not rich, but the money factor removed. To be able to travel without having to quit a job to make time for it, to have weekends off to go to the flea market, work on projects with a beginning and an end instead of a constant flow of annoying, unsatisfied customers that never let up. I guess I don't hate the actual job —I could probably be quite happy working there while going to school. But Ed and the customers take up so much mental energy that focusing on school would be impossible.*

At home, the rest of the guests had left and she found Tawnee and Fabrianne in the kitchen separating the recycling and washing the dishes. Erin grabbed a towel and helped dry and put the dishes away.

"That was nice," Erin said

"It was," said Fabrianne. "I'm so glad Roger didn't show."

"You invited him?"

"No, but I'm sure he knows."

"That would have been a bad scene," Erin agreed. "He's been real quiet at work, which I've never seen before. He was even out sick for a couple of days after the bomb dropped."

Fabrianne nodded. "It was bad. And not only did he lose a girlfriend, but two roommates and their incomes."

"Yeah, I actually feel sorry for him," Erin said. "But if he'd come it would have been too emotional."

"That's why I didn't invite Steiner and Peter," Tawnee interjected.

"No. Not in the mood to see any of them. "You're lucky, Tawn, you don't have anyone to avoid."

"It's not about hiding from them, it's all about the energy it takes to do it. When I go to my favorite hangouts, I want to be able to sit down without being, like, 'will he be here?' and stuff."

"I'm not afraid of Roger," Fabrianne said, handing Erin a wet beer mug. "If anything, I'm worried about him."

"Ahh, still in love, eh?" Erin accused.

"No, it's not like that. I mean, yes, I still love him. I have to. He's a friend of mine. But at the same time, he's a soul vampire that feeds off of other people's misery. I don't have time for that shit."

"A soul vampire," Erin said. "Maybe that's what Steiner is."

"Steiner really is a nice guy," Tawnee said. "But he's not a good person to date."

"I'm sure, but I couldn't separate being friends with Steiner while I was fucking him. That was my fault. If I'm fucking you, we're dating. If we're dating, treat me like we're dating, not a bud."

"But, I'm still friends with him…" Tawnee said.

Erin's plate-drying slowed and stopped. "…I…didn't know you dated him," she said, lowering her eyelids.

"It was before you guys were dating. I shouldn't have said anything."

"Why didn't you tell me?"

"Because I didn't think you'd want to hear about it."

"Of course I'd want to know about you sleeping with a guy I was sleeping with." Erin raised her voice. "Did you know about this, Fabrianne?"

"Hey, don't bring me into this!"

"So you did!"

"Erin, I had no issue about her having slept with Roger, I don't see why you should have a problem with Stei…"

Tawnee's expression shouted "Fabrianne, shut up!", which ignited Erin's passion further. "You slept with Roger, too? When?"

"A year before he and Fabe starting going out. But only for about a week; I met her through him."

"And you're okay with that?" Erin asked Fabrianne.

"Yes, because I knew about them from day one. As I suggested to <u>Tawnee</u> that she should have done."

Tawnee stood up. "Hey! If Steiner didn't tell her, then what business is it of mine to bring that up? I'm not going to be the reason that they break up!"

"But, by keeping shit like that away from me doesn't help. It could have prevented me from wasting a month on him in the first place!" Erin yelled

"What waste? Erin, nobody's perfect! We all have shit in our past that we don't put on the table."

"But, I thought we were friends."

"We are."

"Friends should tell you stuff that could affect your relationships, or stuff like that."

"So if I said I'd slept with Peter, would that be okay too?"

Erin felt the breath leaving her. "Oh, my God! Please tell me you're joking!"

"Erin, I slept with a lot of guys. Sometimes paths cross."

"It's—it's like every guy I've dated, you've already fucked! Do you know a guy in New Jersey named Steven Burgess? Or Kenneth Lucas in England? Tell me who you're screwing now, so I know who I'm dating in the future!"

"Fuck you!" Tawnee said storming out of the room.

'Erin!" Fabrianne yelled, "That was mean!"

"She slept with two guys I slept with and didn't tell me. She has no right to be angry!"

"Erin, she didn't sleep with Peter!"

"Then why did she say she did?"

"Does it matter? You ripped into her anyway."

"Sorry, but I'm pissed! You guys are always keeping stuff from me!"

"Wha-what? You guys? What the hell did I do?"

"If I hadn't run into Lisa Ann, you would never have told me you guys were moving!"

"That is so untrue!"

"Well, you knew about Tawnee and Steiner!"

"Erin, we knew Steiner two years before we even heard of you. How are we supposed to know you guys were going to hook up one day? How is this my fault? How is this Tawnee's fault? It wasn't like you guys started going out and then decided to sleep together? You slept with him first and then tried to form a relationship around that!"

"So, what, it's my fault?"

"It's nobody's fault! Tawnee and I go to art school. Shit happens. People fuck other people who go on to fuck other people!"

"And you guys want me to take classes there? Sounds like Sodom and Gomorra!"

"Get a grip, Erin. Nobody's perfect. Tawnee's not, you're not, I'm not!"

"Oh really, what did you do? Did you fuck Steiner, Peter? Cheat on Roger? Abortion?"

"There's no way I'm going to talk to you when you're acting like this?"

"Acting like what?"

"The way you act. You get all dramatic and crazy. You make such a big deal out of little things!"

"I think sleeping with my ex is a big thing!"

"Erin! Put things into perspective. She meets Steiner at a party, they screw, relationship over. Years later, she meets Erin. Erin happens to meet Steiner and without asking Tawnee if she ever slept with this guy, Erin sleeps with guy. The end! This is not Tawnee's fault. Yes, it's a weird coincidence but that's it! Tawnee did nothing, and you practically called her a slut!"

"I did—it's not what—I didn't."

"You did. You hurt her. We fucked up by not telling you about Steiner earlier, but seriously! Would you have said anything if the situation were reversed?"

Erin was silent. Chances are she wouldn't have brought it up even at this point. "I'm just sick of secrets."

"Then learn to take the truth, for Christ sake."

Fabrianne turned and continued washing the dishes. Erin went upstairs and knocked on Tawnee's door. She knocked again.

"Go away!"

"Fine!" Erin yelled. She ran downstairs to her bedroom and slammed the door.

#

In the morning, lying in bed, Erin detected someone leave by the sounds of squeaky wood under foot. Since her bedroom was near the stairs she could hear anyone going up or down. One person had come down already, at the right time to be Fabrianne, so this had to be Tawnee. But this was earlier than usual, and instead going into the kitchen, she heard the front door open and close. Erin felt a combination of anger and sadness. *Well, I did it: in one conversation my living situation has gone from perfect to 'typical Erin.'*

Fabrianne was zipping up her portfolio when Erin entered the kitchen. She left without saying a word. *What? Now she's mad at me too? What did I do to her?* The question stayed in her head as she ate a bowl of overpriced organic cereal, showered, and walked the mile to work. Because her brain was obsessed with her roommate problems, it neglected to remember the yearly weather pattern. She had to dodge under bus huts, store awnings, and trees still covered with foliage to avoid the cold rain. By the time she made it to work, she was as damp as her spirits. Ed opened the door for her. He was always around now, because of employee shortages. Inside, an early twenties brunette girl in Neopolitan State T-shirt looked up nervously at Erin and smiled.

"Hi, I'm Barbara." Her voice was perky, like a flight attendant. They shook hands.

"Erin."

"She's taking Mary Jo's place. You have to train her," Ed commanded.

"Train her for what?"

"For whatever you do around here," he said sarcastically as he walked away.

Erin resisted the urge to flip him off. "So, the first thing we do after getting attitude from the boss is take a break. I'll be back to teach you how to make a sandwich." Erin went into the break room, clocked in, and sat down to smoke a cigarette. *Actually, if everyone's saying how I'm up for getting a promotion, this isn't the best time to be slacking off.* She got up and was putting her apron on right when Ed peeked into the room. *That was close.*

"What's taking you so long?"

"Just clocking in, Ed."

"Well, hurry up, doors are open."

After he turned to leave, Erin squatted a little, grabbed her breasts, and stuck out her tongue. The only witness to this, besides the Coke machine, was Lashell entering the break room. Because she couldn't burst out laughing, she shook and teared-up from holding it in. She grabbed a napkin and wiped the tears away.

"Oh, mercy, too funny! What was that about?"

"Ed," Erin answered. "Making me wish I'd stayed home."

"If I lived where you do, I would too."

"Believe me, things aren't very peachy, now."

"What happened?" Lashell clocked in and put her apron on, and the two slowly walked to the front.

"I found out that Tawnee slept with Steiner a long time ago."

"Shit. He cheat on you?"

"No, a long time ago. This was before they even knew me."

"Oh, Then what are ya worried about?"

"That she kept that info from me."

"That's not right; girlfriends should tell you everything."

"Thank you."

"I mean, what if she has herpes or something?"

"I'm not worried about that. I used condoms."

"Condoms, my ass."

"What?"

"Well, not in MY ass. I mean condoms ain't gonna protect you one hundred percent."

"I don't think she has AIDS or anything."

"How do you know? She hid one thing from you."

Erin's terror gland kicked in. *Tawnee probably slept with lots of guys in art school, then Steiner, who passes her STDs to me.* "You think I should get tested?"

"You've never been tested!" Lashell asked too loudly.

Surveying the room to inventory who had heard that lovely sentence, Erin realized Barbara was standing next to them. "Uh, Barbara, this is the loudmouthed Lashell." The girls shook hands. "Lashell is going to show you the register while I make pizza dough."

Kneading dough was therapeutic for Erin's nerves, though her paranoia did its level best to unravel them. *Tawnee admitted that she slept with a lot of guys. Each of those guys slept with other women first. Steiner even slept with J.J., who says she uses protection, which Lashell has pointed out is not one hundred percent safe, and she's slept with over three hundred men!*

Pat walked in late. "Hey, Mop Top!"

She jumped. "Hey, Pat!"

"What's wrong?"

"Nothing. I'm...have you ever been tested?"

"For what?"

"You know...The test."

"SAT? GED?"

"No, STD."

"Oh. Uh, no."

"Why not?"

"Cause I always use a condom."

"But those things aren't one hundred percent safe, are they?"

"No, but I've never developed anything. And it's been just Mimi and me for forever, so I just assume that everything is okay. Why? You see something this morning?"

"No, it's Steiner. He slept with a lot of girls who slept with a lot of boys, so I'm a little worried."

"If you're worried about it, why don't you go and get tested? Put your mind at ease?"

"I guess." *What is my doctor's name again? The last time I went was before my Europe trip. He was some elderly guy who's probably not too keen to talk about sex, let alone AIDS. I want a new, hip doctor that rides motorcycles and has a gum-ball machine full of condoms in his waiting room. You know, if anyone would know where to find Doctor Cool, it would be mom.*

Tracy breezed in even later than Pat, sporting a pair of sunglasses and a chauffeur's cap.

"Thanks for joining us Miss Kessler," Ed sneered. "Good example for the new employee."

Tracy nodded at Barbara and went to the back to clock in. She returned sipping coffee and smoking a cigarette.

"Man, don't ever mix booze and ditching a limo in the river," she groaned.

"Wha—what?" Erin asked.

"I'm sure the paper will tell it better than I could."

#

At 12:30 the rain clouds lifted, opening a two-hour window of clear, sunny weather. Like pigeons flying into one cage, customers started swarming into the parlor. Barbara smiled and greeted as if she were working at the Olive Garden restaurant. Erin, already finding it hard to keep her cool as she worried about AIDS, grew a little annoyed.

"How can she be so chipper?" she mumbled to Lashell.

"Oh, give her time. In a month she'll be just as grumpy as all of us."

"But, that's just it—work here for one month and you get grumpy. It's not right. Why do we have to get pissed at our job?"

"This is fast food. It's like that."

"But why? Things don't have to suck just because it's always been so. Why can't things just be good and that's the way it stays?"

" 'Cause that's life."

"Life sucks, then."

"Well, yeah. But, like you said, it doesn't have to. I think you wish this job didn't suck so you wouldn't have to find a better one."

"But, can you imagine if F.J. Pizza had real benefits? Actual insurance, good pay, a retirement program? Imagine that this was such a good job that you could retire here? Imagine that."

Lashell laughed. "This place? Retirement? Girl, that's a sad thought, you bein' here at sixty. Anyway, you wouldn't make it past forty, 'cause I already told you, I'd kill your ass."

"But, seriously, why can't this place be an actual career?"

"Erin, you need to move on, get a better job"

"But, it's…"

"Erin…move…on!"

Erin groaned. *She's right. No amount of hard work is going to turn F.J. Pizza into the Olive Garden, no matter how many Barbaras they hire.*

After the one o'clock register count, Erin calculated they had already done an entire day's business. When she told Ed they were running low on change, he chose to earn his salary in a non-yelling way by visiting the bank himself. The minute he stepped outside, Tracy switched the music station.

"What is this?" Barbara asked as the chorus shouted, 'A punch in the mouth, beats a lie in the ear.'

"Punch and Kisses by the Skid Marks," Pat answered.

"Is that appropriate?"

"It's okay, there's no foul language."

"I know, but they're talking about punching someone."

"Are you a born-again Christian?" Erin asked.

"Well, I'm a Christian, but I'm not a Fundamentalist, if that's what you mean. I just don't know if that's the right kind of music for a business."

"Maybe if we were K-Mart, but here people probably expect it."

"Then why did you guys wait until Ed left?"

"Cause he's King Asshole of Nugget Town."

As Pat and Lashell laughed, Tracy waved Erin over.

What? Surely I didn't say anything that Tracy would disagreed with. "Yes?" Erin asked, afraid of getting in trouble with Tracy for the first time ever.

"Be careful what you say in front of Barbara."

"Oh shit. What? Is she Ed's niece? Mistress?"

"Yuck! No, but I looked at her resumé. Ed had underlined some things in red, like her supervisor experience at some mall food court."

"So, you think she's gonna be the next supe?"

"Not necessarily, but he obviously hired her for something in particular. And if you give him any excuse…"

"Are you telling me I should behave myself?"

"I'm saying you should watch your ass."

Erin looked back at Barbara, who was smiling at another customer.

"Oh God, Tracy. We got to get rid of her. She'll ruin everything."

"Usually I would agree with you, but when Pat goes on vacation we're gonna be even shorter. And I don't feel like working that much extra."

Damn my luck. Not only does my home life suck, but now I have to suppress the small bit of self-expression allowed at work just to get an extra dollar per hour in a job I hate.

"Er, ah, holy shit!" Lashell said. "What is *she* doing here?"

Pepe Rubens had walked through the front door and nodded at everyone as she passed to the back.

"I thought she quit," Erin whispered.

"She did," Tracy explained. "She wants to pick up some extra cash."

"I'm not having fun, you guys," Erin complained.

#

The crowds never let up. Erin had to skip her usual 'goof off' breaks and continue to ring people up, make pizza, clean tables, and give Barbara all of the jobs everyone hated to do.

"We need you to change the toilet paper in the bathrooms, and while you're back there, could you mop the floors?"

"Sure," she answered cheerfully, deflecting Erin's morale attack. Her absence forced Erin to deal with twice as many customers.

"You see," said Tracy, "you get rid of her and we end up doing more work."

I refuse to give up. Surely there's a way to get the perky new girl to quit without causing us more stress. She broke off plotting her revenge when two people she recognized came to the counter:

Derrick, the Black gay guy from Bebe's party, and the doorman she'd exposed her breasts to at the Jelly rave. Both treated her as if she were just an anonymous fast food employee. *I embarrassed myself in front of both of them, so why am I mad they've forgotten me? And how can a guy not recognize a woman who's flashed him?*

Erin broke off from fretting about how unmemorable she must be when she glanced at the clock: her mother would be getting up for her shift at the hospital. Erin dialed and then jammed the phone's handset between her chin and shoulder so she could continue trying to ring people up while she talked. Some customers acted as if she were ignoring them, especially when they had to repeat their orders because Erin was more focused on listening and talking to her mom, but solving her health worries was worth the nasty stares and lack of tips.

"Hi, Mom, it's me," Erin said giving a man his change without thanking him.

"Hi sweetheart, how are you? Sorry I had to work during your house warming. How did it go?"

"Okay. About thirty people I didn't know showed up."

"Sounds successful. Did you-know-who show up?"

"No, thank God. I thought for sure Tawnee would invite him."

"Well, I think they know how you feel."

Although she still betrayed me.

"Pepperoncini, <u>not</u> pepperoni," said a Jewish Rabbi reading what Erin was writing on the ticket.

"Anyway, the reason I'm calling, I was wondering if you know a doctor who's not all stuffy who can give me a checkup."

"What's wrong, honey? Are you feeling all right?"

"I'm fine. I just haven't had a checkup in two years."

"Are you talking gynecologist?"

"Sure, why not?"

"Why not? Okay, I'll take that as a sign that's the kind of doctor you're talking about. Well, my OBGYN is Doctor Taylor, and he's kinda old and stuffy, so I guess I could set you up with Doctor Balboa."

By now even Tracy was signaling Erin to get off the phone. She pretended not to notice. "Is she cool?"

"I think you'd like her—writes poetry books, super liberal, husband raises the kids, they're all into saving the Earth."

"Oh god, not a hippie-dippie?"

"Sorta, but more new agey than pot. She's really smart and nice, and plus she's a woman."

"Okay. Can you set me up with that?"

"Sure. I'll call you later with your appointment time."

"Thanks, mom."

#

In spite of Barbara's objections, the music didn't seem to be affecting the heavy flow of customers. Every half hour Pat announced the remaining minutes until he would be boarding the plane for his first trip outside of the United States, which made Erin very jealous. *I would love the opportunity to go to Europe again. All I had to do was drink coffee in cafés in the morning, beer at* bistros *in the afternoon, and wine in restaurants at night. In Europe, if you hang out all day drinking it's romantic; in the States you're just a bum or alcoholic, plus, Grandview has fancy cafes and wine bars, but they cost too much.* For the tenth time that morning she resented her low salary. She distracted herself with a thorough cleaning of the sneeze guard around the sandwich display.

During Lashell's break, Erin was left ringing people up alone. Pepe proved less helpful than Tracy had predicted. She kept asking Erin questions about different tasks, as if she had been gone for years instead of just a couple of months. Erin became bored from obsessing about her problems. As a distraction, she asked Pepe about her own life.

"So, how did your tour go?"

"It sucked super ass. In Dallas, Gregg got into a fight with some bottle-throwing rednecks. Stephanie almost got raped at this rest stop in Oklahoma. When we played in Illinois, Greg cheated on Stephanie and so that was kind of awkward having them play together. In New York, the van got stolen. We lost everything, including a guitar that my dad gave me. On the trip back me and Greg hooked up, so now Stephanie's not speaking to us."

"Well, at least you got to see New York." Without waiting for a snide comeback or an offensive look, Erin turned away and continued working. *You know, that was shitty, even if it's Pepe. I should at least pretend to show a little sympathy.* She turned to Pepe and saw her pull her hand down really fast. *Was she flipping me off when my back was turned?* Erin narrowed her eyelids at Pepe, who suddenly became helpful with someone at the counter.

#

"Next!"

Erin felt as if she had been hollering that word all day. There was always another person needing to be served. *I wonder which is going to give first, the number of customers or my patience? And if so, when?* Two "next's" later, Erin had to serve someone she had no interest in seeing. *You are not an enemy, but I sure as shit have no patience for you at this point.*

"Hi, Steiner."

"So…how's it going?"

Barbara and Pepe had picked this time to know what they were doing and needed absolutely no help. *You two really are assholes.* "Pretty cool. We're busy as hell this week."

"That why you haven't called me?"

"Hey, man," said the girl behind him, "are you going to order or what?"

"Oh, okay, yeah. Give me a number five."

"The Tofu Mofo pizza?" Steiner just stood looking at her. *He expects an answer to his earlier question.* "I've had a lot of stuff to work out."

"It's been weeks."

"Well, these things take time."

"How long do you need?"

The girl behind Steiner, a gutter punk, elbowed him out of the way and stepped up front. "Excuse me!" she yelled.

"Hey!" Steiner yelled back.

"Hey, yourself! We have a line here, pal! Have some consideration! Asshole!"

Erin wanted Steiner out of the line, but this girl was shockingly rude. "Hold on, now!" she snapped. "Lose the attitude, girlie."

"Fuck you, bitch!" she screamed, flipping Erin off.

"Wha-what?" Erin said, realizing it was the second time in one hour someone had flipped her off.

Pat left the food he was preparing and reached the register. "Is there a problem over here?"

"Fuck you! White nigger!"

The minute she said that, Erin realized who the girl was: her hair had grown out over the last few months, but there was no doubt this was Suzan, one of the racist skinheads from the boarding house fiasco.

Several customers chanted "throw her ass out!"

"Your ass is 86'd, bitch!" Pat started to walk around the other side of the register. Erin grabbed an empty bottle and filed behind him. *I'm not sure what's going to happen, but if Pat calls me in to fight, I can at least be ready to hit the villain in the back of the head.* Suzan looked around. She pushed the tabletop soda fountain onto the floor. After a loud metallic crash, carbonated soda began spraying everywhere and customers began screaming. Erin and Pat were distracted enough for Suzan to push her way through the crowd.

"Call the cops!" someone yelled.

#

Erin sat on the curb, exceeding her cigarette ration. *Today was too eventful to just smoke two. I cant tell anyone I recognized Suzan, not even Lashell. Even if Suzan and her friends are following up on their threat to do something to the pizza parlor, if Ed makes a connection my chances of becoming a supervisor diminish. Or I might lose my job. Still, Suzan didn't make any personal verbal attacks. Maybe she really was there for just a pizza slice. I want to go home, but I have two mad roommates.*

"You all right?" Steiner asked as he sat beside her.

His voice actually sounds concerned But why is he even here? Is he here to try to make up with me? Does he even care? "I will be." She stared at the police car in the parking lot to avoid looking at him.

"What was that bitch's problem?"

"I've seen her before…" Erin caught herself "…hanging out at the Oi Bar."

"What were you doing at the Oi Bar?"

If you bothered to research my past, you would know why. "Me and Pat go there on Ska night."

"I didn't know that."

Erin took a drag on her cigarette. "There's a lot about me you don't know." There was a long pause, as if Erin had added, '…and you never will.'

Steiner stood and shuffled his feet for a second. "Well, I gotta go, my pizza's getting cold." He started walking back inside. "I'll see you around."

"Goodbye, Steiner." As she finished those words, the earlier dread turned to sorrow and remorse, as if she had done a bad thing. Her id told her: *"He's sorry. Give him another chance and get more orgasms!"* Her ego countered: *"He's only talking to you because something must have happened with his other booty call, not because he cares about your feelings."* Her superego said: *"Shut up and finish your cigarette."* She did so and stamped it out on the pavement.

"Erin!" Tracy called from the door.

"Yo! Is my break over?"

"No, Kevin is on the phone."

Tracy's words, separately, made sense: Kevin, the boy of her dreams, and a phone call. She froze in confusion. *Tracy had known to come outside and tell me, so it's important and must be real. But a lost romance calling, just after I said goodbye to Steiner?* She scrambled for the door, almost knocking into Tracy. Had there been no Plexiglas wall on the counter, she would have jumped over it.

"Excuse me," a customer waving an expired coupon called out as Erin picked up the phone.

"Sorry, I don't speak English or work here."

Even though Ed wasn't there to give brownie points and she had have no idea what to do, Barbara quickly tried to help the guy.

Erin ducked down behind the counter so no one else would interrupt her. "Er, h–hello?"

"Hi, Erin, it's me, Kevin. How's it going?"

"Great," she lied.

"That's good. Hey, I just saw in the paper that the 10th Street Theatre is having a Brothers Quay film fest."

"Cool. I love them." The last sentence ignited the memory of that embarrassing night she had shouted she loved Jews. She clinched her teeth.

"Me, too. I was thinking of going. You wanna come?"

She felt like ripping her hair out. *My dream man, my dream gay man I thought would never speak to me again, is asking ME out on a date!* Her id cheered: *"Go for it!"* Her ego cautioned: *"Why is he doing this?"* Her super ego said: *"Stop bothering me, I'm bad at this."*

"Uh, sure," she said with a reluctance that surprised her.

"Great. I'll see you tomorrow night around seven, at the theatre."

"Sure." She hung up and remained on the floor next to the napkins. Employees did their best not to bump her with their knees, but Lashell got sick of walking around her.

"Erin, unless you're down there to eat me, you better move your fat ass out of the damn way."

Erin stood up. "Oh, my God, Lashell!"

"What? I was joking. Even if—"

"No, not you, you idiot! Kevin!"

"Who you callin' id–what about Kevin?"

"He just asked me out on a date–and what do you mean 'even if'? If you were a lesbian, am I such a bad catch?"

"Excuse me," a man interrupted, "could I get some parmesan?"

Lashell held up her hand to silence him. "Kevin? That gay boy?"

"That's right." Erin started dancing around and singing a taunting song. "He's not gay-yea he's not gay-yea, in your fay-ace, in your fay-ace!"

"Naw! Maybe you misunderstood him. What did he say?"

"Movie, tomorrow, 10th Street Theatre."

"Did he say just the two of you or a group?"

"Well, I just assumed he meant us two."

"Ah-ha! Assume. That don't mean jack."

"Hey! At the very worst, it means he forgives me for the 'I love Jews' thing and just wants to be friends."

"But, how you get from hanging out as a friend to he's not gay and wants to date you?"

"Fuck'n-a, Lashell! Just be happy for me! Do you always have to slap all of my dreams down?"

"No, but I don't want you getting back in that same, Kevin rut that you've been in all year. You just got rid of one boy, what are you trying to do? Go back after the other?"

"Shell, I have nothing else!"

"If you think you have nothing else, then you won't have nothing else."

"Thanks, Confucius. But—"

"This is all very interesting," the customer interrupted. "but can I have some parmesan before our pizza gets any colder?"

Erin grabbed the opaque, baking soda dispenser and slammed it on the counter. The customer took it and backed away. "And where's your boyfriend, Ms. Expert?"

"What? You don't see me with a boy 'cause I ain't running around like some dumb-ass pawing over some cheating fool. Unlike you, I have self esteem."

"Whatever. At least someone wants this dumb ass, which is better than being stuck up and dateless"

"Fuck you."

"Back the fuck at you!"

"Bitch!"

"Bitch, you!"

Erin stormed to the sandwich counter.

#

The two girls didn't speak, apologize, or even acknowledge each other's existence for the remainder of the shift. The rain started up again during Erin's walk home. *I don't care if I get wet. I don't care if Lashell, Tawnee, Fabrianne and I are not speaking. I don't care if Steiner made a last ditch effort to be friends. I don't care if Kevin asked me out as part of a group.* Near the duck pond, she realized she had forgotten to say goodbye to Pat, who had been in the supply closet when she'd left. She knew at that moment he would already be on the airport shuttle, thinking about how much he hated flying. "Fuck!" she yelled. *Goddamn Lashell for making me forget about Pat.* She kicked a soda can into the pond. A few ducks approached it, expecting food.

Fabrianne was in her room with the door shut, playing music. Tawnee was nowhere to be seen. *I only have a little happiness, and no one to talk to. What good is success unless you have someone to share it with?* She went into the kitchen to heat up some take-out vegetarian Chinese food. She saw a note beside the phone in Fabrianne's handwriting. It read: Erin, phone message for you.

She pressed the play button. "Hi, this is for Erin," said her mom's voice. "Hi, sweetie. I talked to Dr. Balboa and she's booked for the next two weeks. But, because you're my daughter, she's willing to come in earlier and see you tomorrow morning at 9:30. I know that's cutting it really close to when you start work and you might be a little late, so if you don't wanna take her up on it, give me a call and I'll have her reschedule you. 'Bye now."

I should call back—I can't afford to be late for work for any reason right now. But, you know, fuck Ed for hiring that brown-noser for a job that's rightfully mine. And Lashell and Pepe for being bitches to me. And she wasn't there today, but fuck Brenda if she had been. And while I'm at it, universe, why don't you fuck Tawnee, Fabrianne, Kevin, and Steiner for ruining the good place my life seem to be heading until yesterday?

She put her food into the microwave and tried to consider things more calmly. *Doctor Balboa is booked for two weeks and I don't feel like waiting for an AIDS test. F.J. Pizza is too understaffed to go without me—fuck them!* The microwave dinged. A decision having been thoughtfully reached, Erin took her meal to her bedroom. She logged onto the internet and checked her e-mail. She had four spam credit card advertisements, a clip forwarded by her brother Dave titled 'Ouch! No Kids for Him' showing a skateboarder going from roof to handrail, and another spam, this one from a bargain airplane ticket company, advertising a deal to London, much better than what she had paid. *What would happen if I called in to work and quit and flew away to join Pat and Mimi at Mr. Humphrey's house? There were so many places in Europe I didn't go, so many towns where I wished I'd got off the train. I could go back to Paris—I had just reached the point where I could order coffee without worrying about my bad French. How did someone who had bravely traveled alone, end up in a fast food restaurant worrying about a lousy promotion?*

She logged on to a bookmarked porno site to try to forget about her day.

#

At around 4:18AM, Erin woke to boots clopping on the hardwood floor and up the stairs. *Tawnee must have gone to Vampire Night at Gothica.* Erin's bladder and sleepiness battled until she finally got out of bed. Knowing she wouldn't run into Tawnee but still cautious, she tiptoed down the hall to her private half-bathroom. A white, ghostlike figure appeared in the kitchen doorway. Erin squeaked, and an equally startled Tawnee, dressed in a white T-shirt, almost dropped her glass of water.

"Oh, my god! You scared the fuck out of me," Erin said.

"Huh? Oh, okay," Tawnee said before continuing on her way. She made it to the bottom flight of the stirs before Erin spoke again.

"Uh, hey, Tawnee?"

"Yeah?"

What would tell Tawnee that I couldn't care less what she did with Steiner, and that I'm sorry for calling her a slut? "I…"

"Yes?"

"I, I, you know."

"Know what?"

"You know, I, I like, you know…"

"No, Erin, I don't." Tawnee started to climb the stairs.

If she makes it to the top of the stairs, that will be the end of a good friendship as well as peaceful roommate situation. "I l-love you!" A 200-LB boulder lifted off her chest.

Tawnee stopped.

"I mean, not in that lesbian way, but, you know—I mean, I think you're cute and all, but—"

"I know what you meant."

"Yeah. So, I just, you know. With all the shit and stuff, I needed to tell you–gosh I just realized something."

Tawnee waited, but Erin just stood staring, lost in thought. "What?"

"I have never told anyone I loved them."

"You tell your mom and stuff."

"Yeah, but I'm talking about boyfriends. I've had three boyfriends, and I never told one of them that I loved them."

"Did you?"

"What?"

"Love them?"

"I…don't know."

"What about Kevin and the 'I love Jews' thing?"

"I was drunk. When I'm drunk, I love everyone. Like when I got drunk and called you guys at three in the morning."

Tawnee smiled and walked down the stairs.

"While sober, not once," Erin murmured.

"I've never said it, either."

"Really?"

"No. I mean, I've said it, but it was more of a goodbye thing—"goodbye, I love you.' You'd think someone like me who's been around would have said it once."

"Tawnee, I'm sooo sorry about that. I lost it. I was such a fuck'n bee-yatch."

"It's okay. I should have told you about Steiner."

"Oh, my gosh! Wait until you hear about my day–but, go on."

"I just didn't know how you'd feel about me if you found out about us."

"So you slept with a lot guys and I know one of them. B.F.D. You're still my friend. And apparently the only person I can soberly tell that I love them. Maybe I am a dyke." Tawnee laughed.

"I thought I was a lesbian once." Tawnee continued up the stairs.

"What? What happened?"

"Bedtime, Erin girl."

"Hey! What about my day?"

"It's late. We'll talk later. Goodnight."

Erin walked to the bathroom. *My god, what's wrong with me? Surely I loved Peter? Donna claimed that Peter didn't go to Europe because I was such a bitch. Would telling him I cared have changed anything?* A memory surfaced: Peter had refused to do a skateboard trick and she had jokingly called him a pussy for the rest of the day. *How did he see me, then?*

After trading waste for relief, she returned to her bedroom, but she didn't fall asleep again for hours.

\#

Erin sat in Doctor Balboa's waiting room reading an old copy of Women's Health & Business Magazine. Every page had size-12 women biking while talking on cel phones, jogging to work while pushing a baby strollers, or running Fortune 500 companies while breastfeeding. She looked up at a stressed woman rocking a baby to keep it quiet. Erin smirked as she tried to picture her talking on a cel phone while breastfeeding during a Fortune 500 company meeting. *You can have it all, my ass.*

She checked the clock. She had been waiting thirty minutes. *Mom was right about the full appointment card. Every seat is taken.* A woman in her mid-thirties with long blond hair joined the receptionist and a nurse behind the counter. *Hey, I remember her, she performed at Pyschicmondogroovearama Café's grand opening.*

"Hey, you're here early," the receptionist said to the Doctor.

"Came in to see Carolyn's daughter. Erin?" she called out.

"Yes?" Erin walked to the counter. All the workers stared, as if she was going to break into a song or dance. *This is uncomfortable.*

"Oh, so you're Carolyn's Erin," said the receptionist.

"You're so pretty," added the nurse. Erin blushed.

"Hi, Erin, I'm Dr. Balboa." They shook hands. "You can tell how much we like your Mom."

"She's great," added the nurse.

"Elsie, take Erin to room three. I'll be right there."

The nurse walked Erin to one of the back examination rooms.

"So, I understand you work at F.J. Pizza?"

"Uh, Yeah."

"I love that Vegan Supreme there. You guys still have that?"

"It didn't sell too well, so the manager put meat on it and renamed it the Vegan Scream."

"That's awful."

"That's Ed."

In the examination room, the nurse took Erin's blood pressure and weight, and ran through a list of questions, some of which Erin didn't feel like answering to anyone but the doctor.

"What is the purpose of this visit?"

I slept with a man-whore. "Because it's been a while."

Elsie reviewed the information and hung the clipboard on the wall. "You're twenty-one? Your mother looks so young. How old was she when she had you?"

"Twenty-seven."

"Oh..." Elsie looked confused. "But that would mean she must be around forty-eight."

Erin did the math in her head. "Yes."

"The month after she started working here, we had a big party and took her out to celebrate her fortieth. I guess we got the year wrong. Well, that means you must be a dream to raise, because she doesn't look it. Go ahead and change into this gown. Doctor Balboa will be with you shortly. Nice meeting you!"

As Erin put on the gown and waited, she did the math in her head: *If Mom was twenty-seven when she had me, she had to be twenty-five with David, and eighteen with Josh. Damn, just graduated from high school and then you're married with a baby. She never had the choice to travel around Europe, sneak into raves, or chase after gay boys.*

She wondered how that might affect marital happiness until, after fifteen more minutes with no Doctor Balboa, she transitioned to worrying the window was closing for her to be just a little late to work. The door opened and the doctor entered.

"Hell-lo Erin. Now, let's see what we got: You're twenty-one. You smoke—bad, bad girl." She shook her finger like a pet owner.

"I know. I'm down to two per day."

"Keep it up. Cigarette companies are evil. Okay, you're single and fun to mingle. Dating?"

"Not really."

"I take it that means nothing serious?"

"Definitely not."

"Sexually active?"

"Er-ah."

"You know what I mean, outside of masturbation?"

"I know. Uh—I'll say not in a month."

"Right. And what kind of protection do you use?"

"Condoms."

"Ever been pregnant?"

"God, no!"

"No history of disease, problems, or surgery, and your last exam was over a year ago. So, what brings you here? Something new show up?"

"Not really. I just felt it was time."

"Anything you want to tell me about?"

"No, I'm fine."

"I've seen and heard it all, Erin."

"I'm cool."

"Well, great. Okay let's get you in the saddle and have a look at ya."

Erin put her feet in the stirrups and prepared for the cold speculum. Apparently, it had been warmed which reduced the discomfort a little, but when it was spread, it was just as invasive as ever. The doctor made lots of 'hmms' and 'okays' as she moved one part around and pressed on another. Erin ignored the urge to put her legs down and get out of there. *And how comfortable would I be running away with an inserted speculum? And dressed in a paper gown?*

"You can sit up. Well, everything looks and feels normal. With the exception of the evil smoking, you seem fine. We'll get the pap smear down to the lab, and if nothing shows up, you can keep on trucking."

"That's good. I—"

"Anything else?"

"No."

"Are you sure?"

"Well, actually, I was wondering…"

"Yyeees?"

"Okay. Theoretically, if a boy slept with lots of girls, and he, like, slept with you…"

"Right."

"And we always used condoms—I mean, one always uses condoms. Is it possible to get AIDS?"

"Well, properly used and no breakage, you have a really good chance of protection. Did you use them properly?"

"Oh, yeah, of course. But let's say there was one time, like in the heat of passion, right?"

"Right."

"And he, like, tries to er-like, you know, from the back thingy…"

"Fuck you in the ass?"

"R-right. And you roll over before he has a chance to really drill it in."

"And he didn't have a condom on?"

"Oh, he had one on."

"I really wouldn't worry about it."

"Okay, what if he's giving you head and he has, like, chapped lips or he just flossed his teeth or a pierced tongue, or some crazy guy at the condom factory has been poking pinholes in every tenth condom, or—"

The doctor raised her hand. "All very interesting scenarios, but I know how to put your mind at ease." She started writing out a form. "You get dressed and meet me at the front desk. I'll give you a lab slip for a full STD blood screening."

At he registration desk, Dr. Balboa handed Erin a slip.

"And how soon will I know my results?"

"By next week. I'll call by Friday. Anything else?"

"No, I'm cool."

"Excellent. Just remember to lay off the cigarettes."

"I'll try. You really have it against tobacco, don't you?"

"Oh, God, yes. They darken your aura."

"Say what?"

"You know, the energy around you. Yours is yellow, but that cigarette stuff is kinda smudging it."

"You can see my aura?"

"Oh, yes, and your chakra."

"My what?"

"Your chakra. The spinning energy that goes into your aura. Your root chakra is over-stimulated because you feel your survival is being threatened. Try meditating or drinking some warm tea to strengthen your chi. And remember…"

"Yes, lay off the cigarettes. Well, alrighty, then. I better go get my…shots—blood thing, whatever." Erin backed out of the room. *Wow. She went from professional doctor to new age shaman in one sentence. I have no interest in something spiritual, cosmic, religious —anything unscientific—looking up my vagina.*

#

She wanted an evil cigarette really bad, but the signs in the train let the passengers know smoking was not allowed and how expensive doing so might be. *I wish they had signs for: No Tagging the Windows, No Eating Sun Flower Seeds and Leaving the Shells on the Seats, No Coughing without Covering Your Mouth, and Deodorant is Mandatory!* She was now an hour late for work, and stressed. When she'd called in after the blood test and told Ed she'd had a medical emergency, he was surprisingly dispassionate. *Why didn't he insult me, or make snide comments, like usual? What's up with that? And I have to wait a whole week to find out if I'm infected. Yeah, the doctor said there was little chance of having something, but she also believes she can see auras. If I have AIDS, would she tell me to meditate or rub crystals to feel better?*

#

Erin took the path through the park. This time she was prepared for the Neopolitan fall weather, and raindrops pattered impatiently on her blue umbrella. *I can't wait until the rain turns to snow. Then—shit! Today's my date with Kevin. The day has arrived that could prove all the other days wrong, and I'm busy thinking about snow. If he's bi, will I even have a chance? What if the wacky doctor is wrong and I have AIDS? He won't want me. Pursuing cute guys might cost me my life and my love. What will I have left?*

Okay, let's go over what I've done, what I regret not doing that I should do now. I went to Europe, but I've never seen the Neopolitan zoo. I've had multiple orgasms, but never told a guy I loved him. I e-mail my brother at least three times a week, but haven't spoken to my dad in over a year. F.J. Pizza came into sight. *I really regret fighting with Lashell yesterday about something as stupid as her opinion.*

Lashell had switched days with Jeff to study for an exam, which shaved off a little bit of Erin's stress. She got straight to work and realize neither Pat nor Tracy were there. *Man, who can I talk to? I'm about to explode.* Ed came out the office and she steeled herself for some statement calculated to piss her off, but not only was he not in his usual bad mood, he was doing something she thought she would never see: smiling. After he passed the counter, she asked Roger if he knew why Ed had been smiling.

"I neither know nor care."

Jeannie poked out of the office and waved Erin in.

"Fuck," Erin mumbled under her breath. *Death row prisoner to the gas chamber, please.* Jeannie closed the door, sending a fresh wave of panic into Erin's stomach.

"Am I fired?" *Part of me would be relieved—I'll be free and inspired to shoot for something bigger and better.*

Jeannie sat, paused, and then sighed. "No, you're not fired. You were late."

"Yeah, I had to go to the doctor."

"You didn't call in before you went."

"I know. I thought that I could make it to work in time. But it took longer than I expected."

"Still, if you had told someone yesterday you were going to the doctor's, we could have marked your being late as sick leave."

"Well, I really went to the doctor."

"I believe you Erin. And I also know that sometimes we don't know ahead of time when we need to go to the doctor. But it actually would have been better if you just called in sick and been out the whole day."

"Why's that?"

"Cause you didn't call in to warn us. It looks like you could have overslept and are using the doctor's visit as an excuse."

"No! No, that's not true. I can get a doctor's note if you want."

"I believe you, Erin. But You-know-who's going by the strict rules of conduct."

"So, what, he wants to fire me?"

"Remember when I said if you were late anymore then I'd have to write you up?"

"Shit."

"If it was just me, I'd ignore this because I believe you really went to the doctor's. But Ed doesn't believe you, so…" Jeannie slid a form to Erin. It was a probationary warning for constant tardiness and improper conduct.

"Improper conduct? What the hell is that?"

"Ed says you play music at work that has cuss words. I fought him on that one, too."

"This is bullshit. Everyone does that. He's just picking on me!"

"Hey, you're preaching to the choir."

"So, does that mean I can't be supervisor?"

"That's exactly what that means. I'm sorry."

"Jee-zus! Fuck'n Ed! Asshole!"

Jeannie shushed Erin. "You don't want Ed to hear that when you're on probation."

"I don't care. I should just quit. If I get three strikes I'm fired anyway, right?"

"Yeah, but after the probationary period, you go back to zero."

"And that's, like, three months from now? I can't be late to work for three months? This is bullshit! Even if I cleaned up my act and pulled a miracle out of my ass and came to work on time and worked hard, I still wouldn't be eligible to be a supervisor until God knows when." Jeannie didn't say anything, which confirmed it. Erin slumped back in her chair. "No wonder he was happy."

"Creepy, isn't it. Seeing him happy is like catching the devil in a good mood."

"Fuck!" Erin yelled thinking about how long she'd have to be at F.J. Pizza in order to be considered for advancement again. "Whelp, I guess I should start looking for something else."

"You and me both. I can't work in a place where my opinion always means nothing. No matter what I say, Sal always takes Ed's side because he's been here longer."

"We should both quit at the same time. That'll show 'em."

"So tempting. If only Velma and I weren't buying a house."

"A house? How? How can you afford it?"

"Velma got some money from her dad and I took out loans; found a great place in North Depot…"

As Jennie talked about the house, Erin realized there was no way Jeanie was going to leave anytime soon. *Although Jeannie complains about the same things we do, she's not one of us. Sal listens to Ed because she's only willing to push things so far. The Jeannie Renaissance is over.*

"…And with a back yard we can finally get a dog. Velma wants one that—"

Erin interrupted the dog story, "If I'm on probation, I should get back to work."

"Oh…All right."

I'd rather be working than hearing about how great your life is.

Barbara was cleaning the Plexiglas between the prep area counter and the dining room. *Now the way is clear for Ed's evil plan to make Barbara a supervisor.* Erin resisted the temptation to yell, 'Missed a spot!' and slam Barbara's head into the glass. Instead, she slacked off on a professional level: she hung out in the storage room pretending to get supplies when, in reality, she was relaxing on boxes and trying to fold napkins into origami shapes; she took a break instead of doing the midday register total, reminding Ed it was a supervisor's job, which forced him to do it himself; and she took her lunch break two minutes before the lunch rush. Usually, as a courtesy to the other employees, no one took their lunch then. When she came back the register line was out the door, and Ed and Barbara were struggling to take the place of Pat and Erin.

"Are you back yet?" Ed snapped.

Erin looked at the clock. "Sorry, 5 more minutes," she lied, heading to the back for a smoke. Ed's face formed into a scrawl.

Back at the register, her attitude was so bad, the tip jar ended the shift at a historic low. She never said thank you, never gave utensils unless asked, put change on the counter instead of handing it back, and rolled her eyes and sighed at any question. She pretended not to know the answers to Barbara's questions, and if a customer gave the slightest attitude, his or her pizza or drink would get a subtle splash of vinegar or salt—just enough for them to think the food tasted bad, but had not been tampered with. In a final act of defiance, she left early. She had figured out if she told Jeannie what had sent her to the doctor earlier was making her sick, Jeannie, who had kept saying how much she believed Erin, would have no choice but to let her go.

#

Back at home, she laid out a bunch of outfits she'd purchased for occasions involving dates. Her cute leather jacket had little green specks. *Crap! Don't let this be an omen: my dream date outfit has developed mold.* She tried to regain a little inspiration by holding up her other outfits. *And why should I be excited? Kevin's just asking me out because we like the same kinds of cartoons. At no point will he suddenly slap his forehead and say: 'What was I thinking —I'm not gay!'*

To keep from getting more depressed, she went online and checked her e-mail. Dave had again sent something gross but funny, the amount of spam continued to increase, and she had a letter from her mom.

> *Hey, Sweetie:*
>
> *Hope your exam went well. Dr. Balboa didn't freak you out with all her New Age talk, did she?*
> *I just got an e-mail from Josh asking for your e-mail and mailing address. I think he's going to send you an invitation to his wedding. They're going to have some kind of fancy-ass dinner thing next week where everyone's gonna get together. Like a his family meets hers kind of thing. I'm not really in the mood to see your father yet so I'm skipping that. Maybe by the wedding I'll have enough booze and balls to talk to him and What's-her-face.*
> *Anyway, let me know if you want me to send him your address. Maybe you can get some time off from work and go to that dinner thing (said your cowardly mother). ;) <3*
>
> *Later, Yo Mama*

Erin wrote back, granting permission to forward her information. Thinking about Josh annoyed her. She leaned back and thought about her mom's birthday numbers. *If Mom celebrated her fortieth in 1992, when she moved here like the nurse thought, and I'm twenty-one, Dave is twenty-three, and Josh is thirty, she must have been twenty-five when I was born, twenty-three when Dave was born, and...* Erin stopped adding. *It couldn't be true. The woman at the hospital must have made a mistake. But mom has been at the hospital*

*for six years, and why would she celebrate her forty-second birthday like it
was a milestone?*

"Oh, my God! That can't be right!" She re-added the
numbers and achieved the same result. "No way!" Erin felt like
she had walked in on the Loch Ness monster and the Ark of
the Covenant smooching. *Did she have Josh at sixteen? And why
would she have two more kids after that? Okay, sorry, dry spell, but I
need a beer!* She walked to the kitchen, but all they had was
water, soy milk, and one overpriced organic soda. She sat at the
kitchen table sipping the soda and sulking. *Why lie about her age?
No, that nurse was wrong. On the other side, that would explain why
Mom and Dad always argued since day one.*

Fabrianne breezed past and opened the refrigerator.
"Goddamn it! Where's my soda?"

"Sorry. It was an emergency."

Fabrianne closed her eyes and stood with her lips moving.
Finally she looked at Erin. "Oh yeah? What emergency?"

"Kevin asked me out on a date, my friend Lashell's mad at
me—and maybe you too, I took an AIDS test I won't hear
about for a week, I got written up at work which took me out
of the running for supervisor, AND I just figured out that my
mom had my older brother when she was only sixteen!"

Fabrianne stayed silent for a second, then sat down, slid her
soda away from Erin, and took a gulp. "No, wait! You got a
date with Kevin?"

"Yeah, I think it's more of a buddy-buddy thing."

"But that's good, right? At least you get a new friend."

"I'd rather have a fuck-buddy."

"Isn't that what Steiner was?"

"Okay, a fuck-buddy who won't cheat on me and I'll
eventually get to marry."

"Get him drunk in Vegas, you can live that dream."

Erin giggled. "What's highest on my freak list right now is
the mom thing; totally freaks me out."

"Did she tell you that today?"

"No, this nurse let mom's true age slip out. Get this: she
tells a nurse but not her own family?"

"Maybe she feels ashamed."

"My mom? She sunbathes topless at the lake. What would she be ashamed of?"

"Well, what would you do if you had gotten pregnant at sixteen?"

"Me? I'd get an abortion so fast the Supreme court would change the law."

"You say that now, but our parents lived in different times. Back then it's: get pregnant, get married—work it out! So, you gonna talk to her?"

"I guess, but what can I say? I mean, when Dave and me were born they were married. If anyone should be told it's Josh but man, this is gonna crush him. I mean, I'm always more than willing to drop a successful and happy, kinda yuppie asshole down a couple of pegs, but he's still my big brother, that kid who chased monsters out of my room with his toy sword and made fun of me skipping all the time. Hell, he's the one that started calling me Skipper."

"Maybe this should be between your mom and him."

"Perhaps. But I don't like being misled."

"Hey, moms make mistakes. Mine told me people shouldn't have sex until their wedding night. My first serious boyfriend turned out to be the worst lay in the world, so what if we'd married?"

Erin looked at the clock. "Speaking of lay, I gotta get going for my date." She started walking to her room.

"Oh, right. So where are you going?"

"Movies."

"That could get sexy."

Erin gave her a sarcastic look. "Fabe."

"Yeah. But at least a new friend."

"No more friends. I'm having a hard enough time keeping the ones I got."

#

The train ride to University Circle presented her with an opportunity to continue pondering what to do about her situations. For her AIDS test: *If it comes back positive, I won't fall into depression. Instead, I'll take my credit card and max it out in Europe, drinking and partying until the end. As for Mom, I need to talk to her to see if it's true. I also want to talk to Josh, just to hear his voice and to know, no matter what odds are against those born in bad situations, they can turn out all right. How did the unplanned kid turn out so well while the other two took drugs, skipped school, and tore up empty houses? Why am I always tearing shit up? Why can't I just have something normal? And why didn't I go to the bathroom before I left the fucking house?*

She tried to ignore her bladder as she ran down the stairs to the station's bathroom, which was locked to keep addicts from shooting up in it. *The center of 10th Street is only a few blocks; I can make it.* She started running again and tried to concentrate on anything except the mounting urine pressure: trees lit orange by streetlights, a group of gutter punks hanging out near a garbage bin, a guy playing a guitar, and a girl replying, "Oh, my god!" at something her friend said.

Kevin was standing in front of the theatre, looking the other direction. *What's a non-awkward way to scream "hi" as I dash past him to a bathroom?* She stopped when she noticed K. Y. Knots—Your Local Feminist Sex Shoppe was still open. *Tracy's friend J.J. works here. If she's there, I can duck in and use their bathroom.* J.J. was. Erin ran up as J.J. was putting a video copy of 'Be My Bitch, Boyfriend!' into a customer's bag.

"J.J.!" She yelled.

"Thank you for shop—Erin?"

"Bathroom!"

"Back!"

"Clean?"

"Enough," J.J. replied as she handed Erin a huge pink dildo with a key swinging from a ring piercing the glans.

"No chance of stealing that," the customer said approvingly.

Erin ran to the back through a blur of magazines, videos, toys, and dildos all geared toward female customers like her. She sat in the accurately described clean-enough bathroom. *I should come back when I have more time and less pee.* She discovered, when she wiped, she had just got her period. "Motherfucker!

Of course this happens on my dream date! And no fucking tampons! Maybe I should just run in the opposite direction and cancel the date altogether. *What else can happen today? Did I step on a witches foot last week?* She cleaned up as best she could and returned the key to J.J.

"Everything okay back there? I heard the M-F word."

"No, just a visit from my little friend."

"Little... Oh, oh that."

"Yep, and no pillows at the inn for her to sleep on."

"Well, maybe I have something." While J.J. rummaged through her purse, Erin spotted three dildos of different shape and sizes inside.

"Employee discounts?"

"Homework. Ah-ha!" She handed a tampon to Erin.

"Oh, my god. You are the coolest woman ever! This isn't some sex tampon is it?"

"...Sure, why not?"

After utilizing J.J.'s gift in the bathroom, Erin read some video box covers on the way back. "Lords of the Cock Rings?"she asked J.J.

"You here to use that gift certificate?"

"Not yet. I have it on my refrigerator with a note saying in case of emergency." She picked up a bottle of Sinnamon Hott. "What's this stuff?"

J.J. took a tester bottle from behind the counter, dabbed some of the red liquid onto Erin's wrist, and spread it around. "Taste it."

Erin licked it. "Mmm, it taste like cinnamon."

"Watch this." J.J. took Erin's wrist and gently blew on it. The wet area went from cool to warm.

"Whoa! That's awesome! I gotta get me one of those."

"You think that's got ass, you should try this mint stuff that makes your skin numb." She squatted down and returned with a tester bottle labeled, Mr. Mint's Butt-Numb. Erin looked outside.

"Holy Shit! I forgot my date!"

"What?"

"I totally spaced! I have a date waiting for me at the theatre!" She waved goodbye and ran out of the store. She stuck her head back inside the doorway. "Uh, I'm not leaving because I'm a prude and using the date thing as a lame excuse. I really do have one. I swear!"

J.J. brought her hand to her mouth and frowned as if deep in thought. "So you faked being on your period just to insert tampons while looking at porn covers and having a hot girl blow on your wrist? Man, what a pervert! Your kind makes me sick!"

"I take it that means you believe me?"

"Have fun. Baby doll"

Erin ran to meet with Kevin. *How the hell could I have forgotten the Dream Date? I've waited almost a year for this shit and I'm wasting time in a sex shop? Man, I gotta get some of that cinnamon stuff—there I go again, thinking about other things when I should be all excited. This is it, Erin! Forget about Your Mom, AIDS, Lashell, fucking work—I wonder how many midgets are in Lords of the Cock Rings? Stop it! Stay focused!* Kevin saw her and waved. *See! He's alone! It's a date! Then again, who's gonna come with him? Maybe I'm the only animation fan he knows. J.J. sure is cute. If I were gay—whoa! Where the hell did that come from? Focus, Erin Pierce, focus!*

"Hi, Erin."

Kevin's voice brought her attention to the task at hand—surviving the Dream Date. He gave her a shoulder hug, which she returned. *Huh. I thought if he initiated any kind of physical contact again, I'd faint on the spot. No fainting. Not even a tingly feeling like at the show.*

"Hey, Kevin. What's up?"

He laughed. "I saw you coming. Then you ducked into that sex shop and I was like, 'why in the world did she go in there?'"

"I know someone who works there."

"Must be a fun job."

"Beats where I'm working."

"Yeah. How's that working out for you?"

"Not so good. I'm thinking of quitting."

"Reminds me of when I was at Gothica. You use to work there, right?"

"No, it was the Acid Pit. Now that was drama," Erin said as she paid for her movie ticket and took a program.

Kevin had launched into his short history at Gothica. Erin listened, weighing his angst-ridden story against hers and finding it lacking. *I wanted to share my tales from the Acid Pit. How did he miss that?*

10th Street Theatre's interior had been restored to it's 1940's charm: Art Deco gold molding, velvet red-and-gold balconies, lights like hanging flying saucers beneath industrial-style paintings of angels, cherubim, and a woman who looked like a Valkyrie.

"This reminds me of the theatre in Prague," Erin said. "In Czechoslovakia—"

"I've always wanted to paint my bedroom ceiling like this. Imagine waking up to that," he said pointing up.

Erin didn't look up. *I never noticed that hairy mole on his neck. This is like looking at the Mona Lisa and discovering a Band-Aid on her forehead.* He continued yammering about all of the things he wanted to do to his apartment but couldn't for fear of losing his deposit.

"My landlord encourages us to decorate any way we want, and Fabrianne has done some really cool sh—"

"That's right, you're roommates with Fabrianne. We had painting class together. Do you like tempera or oils?"

"Oil paints give me a headache."

"I'm that way with zydeco music. If I listen to more than twenty minutes I—"

The lights dimmed and the trailers started. *Holy crap! They're going to play My Fist, Your Face 2 next Thursday. No, thank you.*

The festival began with Nocturnia Artificialia, one of the Brothers Quay's early films, and began ticking off their shorts chronologically. Erin enjoyed their surreal, black and white stop-motion animation, but she had always taken them in smaller doses. Back-to-back for an hour, the ephemeral stories began to blend, and her long day at work combined with her marathon stress binge caused her to doze off. When she awoke she glanced at Kevin to see if he'd noticed, but he was studying the film as if he would be tested on it later. *I'm glad he's not one of those people who talk through an entire movie, but he should at least look over and smile or frown or nod.*

Kevin finally tore his gaze from the screen. He lowered his eyes onto the bobbing head of the woman in front of him, who only stopped loudly munching her popcorn to giggle into her date's shoulder. Kevin's anger-twisted face looked like laser beams were about to shoot out his eyes and catch the woman's black curly hair on fire. *If Popcorn Lady annoys him that much, I can't imagine the whispering guys behind us not driving him nutso. Man, now I want popcorn. No—don't surround him with suck. Sit back, be good, enjoy the show.*

On the screen, a ball bounced down steps, vibrated and vanished.

"I'm going to the restroom," she whispered and went to the concession stand. When she returned with a small popcorn, she took a seat in the very last row so Kevin wouldn't lump her with the gauche Popcorn Lady. *What's wrong with me? So what if Kevin would scrawl at me for eating popcorn—we're at a fucking movie!* She watched the back of his head, waiting.

Okay, I've been gone maybe ten minutes and he doesn't even seem to notice! I could just head on home right now. You're lucky I like some of these films, Mr. Goldberg. She looked up at an animated doll head crawling across the screen. *Man this would be so awesome with pot, or at least a beer. Kevin would have a fucking baby if I came back with a beer. Why am I so afraid of him? I mean, if I was afraid that it would ruin my chance with him then I can understand that. But he's gay! And this is definitely just a buddy-buddy date. My friends accept all the stupid shit I do, maybe he should learn to deal with me, too. Even Steiner, although he was a cheating dog, put no pressure on me to act all perfect. I miss that part of him. I shouldn't have told him to beat it. I mean, maybe he came by work to apologize or redeem himself, and then that Suzan bitch fucked things up. I should have cut him some slack.*

After she had finished the popcorn she rejoined Kevin. He smiled at her briefly and turned back to the movie. *His smile didn't feel, "All right, you're back. I was worried," but closer to, "Who is that? Oh, it's you, whatever".* When the last film, The Cabinet of

Jan Svankmajer, ended, the lights came up, but Kevin sat watching the credits to the very end. *If there are no bloopers at the end or we're not planning to sneak into another movie, what's the point?*

Finally they left the theatre and started walking aimlessly. No one spoke until Erin realized they said next to nothing all evening. She rooted for a comment. "I like the rock videos they for MTV, the best."

"Me, too, though I have a soft spot for Gilgamesh."

"Oh, yeah." *I must have been asleep during that one. What can I pull out my ass to say about it?* "I like...the way they used doll heads."

"That was cool."

And the hail-Mary toss scores three-points! "Thanks for taking me, Kevin."

"You were the first person I thought of when I saw this in the paper. They also have a new print of Solaris coming up."

"I love that movie." *I hope he's talking about the American version, because the Russian one put me to sleep.*

"It's a date then."

Erin raised an eyebrow. *Hmm...Does he mean it's another date or this isn't date and that one will be? I've got to find out if I'm wasting my time. Shit, how come I have to analyze everything instead of just relaxing and enjoying myself?*

"Cat Head Saloon?" Kevin asked, nodding in the direction of the bar.

"Sure."

#

Kevin ordered a beer. When Erin asked for a ginger beer he acted surprised.

Did he expect me to order liquid crack or something? "The bar's not as full as it used to be. I guess the East River Valley is drawing away people searching for a new hip Mecca."

"Fine by me. More seats for us."

They sat near a window. Erin looked out at the people walking past. *This reminds me of being on a stage. The whole world is* now going to witness everything I've been working for all this time: my Dream Date conversation. "So…Pepe's working at F.J.Pizza again."

"Really? That must suck. Going from a record tour and a contract to a pizza parlor."

Wow. Not only did he not say, "it must suck having to work with such a horrible person", but he equated where I worked with the ultimate failure. It does suck, but to hear it come out of him is somehow more cruel. "…Well, there you go." The conversation stopped and Kevin did nothing to break the silence. *If I had some beer, words would fly out of me, but for once I want things to flow without drugging my superego. Okay, what to talk about? Nix on the AIDS test, my fight with a friend he doesn't know, and my out-of-wedlock brother—I should call Josh again. Or talk to Mom first? Maybe—oh, wait.* "Got any siblings?"

"Just a sister. She goes to law school in Texas." He drank his beer without asking her the same question.

What's going on with him? Is he nervous or something? Even Pepe shows more interest in my life. "I've felt like an only child since I moved out here. I rarely see my brother or my da…"

"That sounds like me and my dad."

How could my situation possibly be diverted into your life story? "I moved here to get away from mine. He's a cop, so you now how well I got along with him."

"My parents are divorced, but it wasn't a nasty one."

"Really?" *We've switched subjects?* "Why did they split up?"

"My dad came out of the closet."

Erin tried not to show shock or surprised. In her mind, a part of a huge puzzle had a final piece inserted. "After all of those years of marriage?"

"Yep. Twenty-five years and two kids. But they're still good friends. She visits him whenever she's in France."

"Oh, you're French?" Erin started to play with a couple of cardboard beer coasters, flipping them like playing cards.

"No, he just works at the embassy."

"Cool. I guess you've done a lot of traveling?"

"Yeah. Actually, I'm kind of sick of it. I need more stability in my life. You know what I mean?"

"Hmm, yeah," Erin said like a psychiatrist. She started stacking the cards one on top of each other, trying to form a tower. *What does he mean? Is he going through what his dad went through? Stop analyzing, Erin.* The tower of cards fell down. "Shit!" *Why hasn't he mentioned the 'I love Jews' statement from the art show?*

Kevin handed her a cigarette.

"Thanks." *I had no idea you even smoked. There's a lot I don't know about you.*

"So, what about you? You grow up here?"

Finally! "Naw. I grew up in Newark, New Jersey."

"Ahh, a Jersey girl eh?" He stood up. "You want another ginger beer?"

"Sure."

"Be right back."

Oookay. Barely touched base on my life. How selfish. She flicked cigarette ashes onto one of the coasters. *This is weird. Here I am on my dream date and I'm not excited.* She took a drag and exhaled a smoky sigh. *Maybe I should just clear the air between us.*

"Psst! Erin!" whispered a voice behind her.

She turned and saw Tojo from work. "Tojo! Hey!" She soft-punched him on the shoulder. Next to him stood two jock-type frat boys in college sweatshirts, the kind of guys F.J.P. employees made fun of when they came in.

"I see you're finally out on your dream date."

How does he know what Kevin looks like? Is the grapevine at work more talkative than I thought? "It's more date than dream," she replied as she looked at Kevin. He was talking to a girl at the bar, laughing and feeling her scarf. *Probably complimenting her clothes. You know, I'm not even a twinge of jealous. I've wasted a shitload of time chasing after him. I don't think I'd even like him as an acquaintance. Which means Lashell was right to advise me away from him, though she loses points for the super-rude way she did it.*

"Bummer. Well, if you guys are bored or something, me and my 'rads are going to a barbecue at Lake Charles." Tojo looked at his watch. "Matter of fact, it's already started. We'd better get going."

"Er, ah" Erin stuttered as Tojo and his friends started toward the door. She looked back at Kevin. *Would he be into going off to a hetero-bash full of probably sexist, homophobic, frat boys? Or, do I even want to continue spending time with him on this dead-end date?* "Wait!" she yelled to Tojo. "I'm coming with you!"

He stopped. "Huh? What about what's-his-name?"

Erin glanced at Kevin. Part of her said, *Tell him where you want to go and let him decide if he wants to come along,* while another part said, *You've wasted your time and embarrassed yourself chasing after him, and now you expect to develop—what kind of friendship exactly?* Erin moved toward the three guys at the door. "Let's just go before I change my mind!"

#

If one more frat boy asks if I go to State, I am quite prepared to scream; if one more guy asks if I want a beer, I am quite prepared to scream while kicking him in the balls. She regarded the sea of sweat-shirted men hooting and competing for the small supply of girls. She found many of the men attractive, and perhaps under other circumstances they would have had a chance with her, but each one she talked to eventually said something to embarrass themselves. *I'm not the type for any of these guys, but they keep hitting on me and trying to get me boozed up anyway. Barbara from work would fit in better, at least for getting taken to the back bedroom. But no cuddling or a phone call the next day from these predators.* One such bumped into her, nearly causing her to spill the red plastic cup of beer. She wasn't drinking, but had started using it as a decoy to prevent the beer question. He reacted to her full cup with the same face Kevin used during her soda order. *Is it so wrong not to want to get drunk and date-raped?*

Erin moved to the opposite side of the room and observed, fascinated, as the men showed off how many ways they could cram alcohol into their mouths: some made beer bongs, others did body shots, a lot used a funnel and a tube, and a few bit into the sides of the cans and sucked. Between drinks, the men and women danced hip-hop—the type, popular on mainstream radio stations—and waved their hands as if they were from the 'hood' itself, though the only minority Erin had had seen all night was Tojo. She watched as he took a hit on the beer funnel, raised his arms, and yelled. *How does he see himself among these guys? At work he exposes his arm tattoos and acts like an alternative hipster, but with his school and party buddies he's hiding that. I bet he's as unconnected to these yelling Republicans as he is to the yelling anarchists at work.*

She grew restless and left the living room to check out the rest of the place. The house couldn't have been more than twenty years old, probably built during the height of the great White flight, when people left the drugs and crime of the inner city to live out in the suburbs and raised kids who got into drugs and crime. Outside the upstairs bedrooms she smelled pot and heard a girl's loud sex noises. "Gross," Erin muttered, but she inhaled as much pot smell as she could in order to cop a buzz without technically breaking her fast.

Out the back, she found the house had its own dock. Guys were jumping off or being pushed into the water, sometimes barely missing the boat tied up alongside. After a scream and a splash, a big guy hauled a girl out and then started arguing with the shover. *Mustn't lose track of Tojo. There are no trains or buses for miles.* Avoiding the dock area, she took off her shoes and strolled along the sandy shore. The top layer of sand was a little moist from the rain, but dry under the surface. She spotted Tojo on the beach with a girl, about fifty yards away. *That was fast. I wasn't upstairs for long. Well, they're arguing, too, I have no desire to go back inside, so I guess hanging out here is good enough.* She stood, looking at the sky, where no one was likely to be arguing. The quarter moon made an appearance between the storm clouds, accompanied by a few stars. "This is beautiful," she murmured, "but not as enjoyable alone."

"Fuck you!" yelled Tojo's girl as she stormed back toward the condo. Tojo remained seated and raised his hand. Erin squinted in the semidarkness. *Did he just flip her a bird?* She walked towards him. *This whole thing is none of my business, but he's my ride and I'm curious.* "Hey."

He didn't acknowledge her presence.

She moved some sand around with her feet and tried again. "So…everything okay here?"

"Sucks."

"What sucks?"

"You do everything you can for someone, and then you ask for one fucking favor and they freak out on you!"

"What are you talking about?"

"Women! Man, you guys. You play your little games and you tease and the minute we call you on it you're out of here."

How the fuck did I get lumped into his drunken rant? Let's summarize: she's a sorority girl, he's a horn dog, she won't put out, the end. "She your girlfriend?"

"Girlfriend. She-yeah, right. I don't have a girlfriend." He threw a rock at the lake.

In the conversational lull, Erin started drawing a heart in the sand with her toe. *Louie Louie* replaced the hip-hop playing at the condo, signaling a shift to Whiteness. "Whelp, I left my true love at the Cat Head without saying goodbye."

Tojo looked at her. "Yeah, what was up with that?"

"I guess I panicked."

"Over what?"

"He wasn't what I thought he'd be. It was like seeing Santa Claus on the toilet."

Tojo began to laugh really hard. "That's rich. You're a trip."

"Thanks." She kneeled and added her initials plus a question mark to the heart.

"You know, it totally sucks what they did to you at work."

"I know."

"I mean, we all think you would have been a cool supervisor."

"Thanks. Who's we?"

"Everybody. Well, maybe not Cliff and Roger, but they're assholes."

"Doesn't matter anyway. I guess Barbara's in."

"Who's Barbara?"

"New hire. I don't think you met her."

"Yeah, different shifts. Like that guy Robert."

"Robert?"

"He works on your days off. You've probably never met him."

"Wait, Black guy with dreads? I think I saw him when I came in to get a check one time. He was busy, so I didn't say anything."

"He's cool. You'd like him."

"Oh, please. You ain't trying to hook me up are you?"

"Naw." He took a gulp of beer. Erin erased the heart with her hand and started over. She again put her initials in the heart. Tojo reached over and put his beneath.

"Whoa." She laughed. "I was going to put the lead singer of this group I like."

"Sorry. Maybe I'll join a rock band and then it would work."

"You got the tattoos for it."

"Yeah." He rolled up a sleeve and bared a tribal designs of thick black lines crisscrossed like black flames that ended in sharp points.

"Why cover them up around your friends?"

"I'm not hiding them. I just don't like people seeing them first and then making judgements on me."

"But isn't that the point? Aren't they like a billboard that says: Look at me, I'm a cool person?"

"Sorta. At school they say: Be afraid, I'll kick your ass."

"That's good too, right? The bad boy image?"

"But I'm not a bad boy. I go to college, get good grades, don't ride motorcycles or get into fights. It's like you. I don't look at your shamrock and go, she's saying she's all into the Irish thing but doesn't have red hair or wear all green on Saint Paddy's day."

I do have red hair. "You noticed my tattoo?"

"Well, of course. You wear tank tops and stuff. What I'm saying is—people shouldn't judge you on the way you look. Just because I'm half Japanese people think, 'oh he's Japanese, he must be smart and all into sushi and shit', I fuck'n' hate sushi!"

"You hate sushi?"

"Raw fish? Hell, yeah."

"Oh, my god, I looove sushi. If I were still eating meat I could eat that every day."

"You're a vegetarian?"

"Yep."

"Since when? I saw you sneak a pepperoni mini-pizza one time."

"Not too long."

"For health or animal rights?"

"Neither. I needed to clear myself out. Just like the booze."

"I noticed you weren't drinking."

"You seem to notice a lot of things about me. Are you stalking me?"

"N—no, course not. I just notice things."

"What else do you notice?"

"Lots of things."

"Like what? Tell me?"

"No way, you already think I'm like Freddie Krueger."

Erin laughed. "Go ahead, I won't say anything."

"Yeah, you will."

"I won't." She moved closer. "I promise I won't hold it against you."

"Well, let me think…that guy you like is gay."

"Duh. What else?"

"You live with Roger's ex-girlfriend. Before that with Mary Jo, and before that with your mom."

"Yeah, yeah, everybody knows that. What about something personal that I don't think anyone knows?"

"I don't know it, then."

"Come on, what do people say about me?"

"What you'd expect: chases a gay guy, kinda crazy."

"People think I'm crazy?"

"You know how people are. They think I'm crazy. If you're different, you're crazy."

"True, but what about sexy?"

"What?"

"Do people think I'm cute or sexy?"

"Oh, oh yeah, sure."

"Like who?"

Tojo grabbed his legs, and started to rock nervously. "Er-in, why are you asking me these questions?"

"I just want to know."

"Everybody thinks you're cute."

"Everyone? Even Brenda?"

"Well, not her. She hates everybody. Oh! Did you know Jeff has a crush on her?"

"Don't change the subject. Who else? Do you?"

"Do I what?"

"Don't act stupid."

Tojo buried his head into his knees. "Yes. Now shut the fuck up."

Erin laughed.

"Geez!" he moaned.

When she finished laughing, Erin patted him on the back. "That's okay. You're cute, too." Erin looked at scattered house lights across the lake.

"You think I'm cute, huh?" Tojo said raising his head. "Sure, why not?"

"Why not?"

Erin laughed again. "Gah, you're so sensitive."

"C'mon, I just got dumped. I need an ego boost here!"

"You got dumped?"

"You saw it. What did you think it was?"

She shrugged. "I'm pretty bad at reading people, as you may well know."

"Yes, we broke up."

She patted his shoulder again. "I'm sorry to hear that. Did you love her?"

"No—I guess not. You love that gay guy?"

"I'm sure I do."

"You have a strange way of showing it."

"I know. I just had to get away. I mean, you'd think I'd be stoked, but it was so unlike what I pictured: He had a mole on his neck, he was kind of boring, he had laser death eyes, shit like that. And he was all about himself. He didn't even ask me about my day."

"How was your day?"

"Don't ask."

Tojo laughed.

"It was stupid to expect him to be all perfect, but give me something to work with! Once I got past his looks, the rest was so…so normal, you know what I mean?"

"Sure, he burst your bubble—Santa on the toilet." They laughed.

"It feels good to laugh," she said covering her feet with sand. "I feel like I haven't laughed in years."

"You should laugh more. If you can't, what else you gonna do?"

"Well, there's sex." *Ooh! That was a point, not a suggestion, but now it's too late.*

"All right, if you say so," he said grabbing her arm.

She tried to giggle. "You know what I mean. There's so many other things out there besides feeling like shit. I just forgot about them. I use to laugh, have sex, be all happy and shit and there were no problems. Now I can't go out on a date without something going wrong."

"That's cause you ditched your date."

"That's not the reason, that's the result," Erin snapped.

"I didn't mean to harsh you or anything," he said rubbing her back. "You're right. It seems harder and harder to be happy now days. Fucking world messing with you. Girls—or in your case, guys—tripping out all the time. Yuppies moving in raising your damn rent. I'm sick of it."

Erin stood up, picked up a stick, and sat back down near Tojo. She began dragging the tip through the sand. "Me, too. Why can't people just be nice to each other? Why play so many games? Like, my ex-boyfriend apparently broke up with me because I was mean to him, but I didn't find that out until recently. In all our years together, he never told me to back off! He just took it like a pussy and then dumped me when I was at the airport about to go to Europe. If he would have said something I would have totally stepped back and been like, gee, you're right. I've been a total bitch."

"Uh…you sure? I mean, it's easy to say that now, but when you're in the thick of it…"

"I'm pretty sure. I'm not a bitch. At least I don't think I am."

"You're not, but maybe you hated this guy and wailed on his ass sometimes."

"I didn't."

"You sure?"

"Yes, goddamn it! Why don't people ever believe me?" She started to get up.

Tojo grabbed her arm. "Okay, chill. I believe you, you're not a bitch. I'm just saying…"

"Well, say, it to yourself," Erin grumbled. Tojo kept hold of her arm but didn't say anything. She looked over at the dock, but the partiers had gone inside. She sat again, and Tojo let go.

"At least you have cute feet," he said.

She wiggled her red painted toenails. "Do I?"

"Sure"

"You a foot fetishist?"

"I'm an everything fetish, totally open-out."

"Lips, eyes, tits, ass?"

"All of it."

"Ears, belly buttons?"

"Yes! I love women's belly buttons."

"See, I don't get that. Why do men want to see a girl's belly button? I don't like my belly, and I especially don't need a guy licking it or anything."

"Maybe they haven't done it right."

"Oh, and I guess next you're gonna say: I know how to do it right, let me show you."

"Sure." Tojo leaned over and tried to lift her shirt up to expose her belly."

"Whoa!" Erin leaned back and pulled her shirt down. She glanced at the house. The music and shouting had gotten louder.

"Now why you have to be like that?"

"Be like what?"

"All pull-back?"

"You made a pass at me. Of course I'm gonna pull back."

"Oh, but if it were Mr. Dream Guy, it'd be okay?"

"No, then I'd be confused."

"But I'm not confusing—you just don't like me."

"What I said was I don't like guys licking my belly button."

"So, if I kissed you I'd be okay."

"I didn't say that, either."

"What if I did?"

"You're gonna try and kiss me?" *How do I keep him calm?* "Maybe you've had a little too much to drink."

"It's 'cause I'm Asian."

"Wh-what? I dig all guys. I had a Black boyfriend in Eng —"

"But not me?"

"Nothing personnel, Tojo, but I ain't gonna make out with someone I have to work with."

"How about a kiss, then?"

"Geez, what's with you?"

He latched onto her arm again. "All I want is a kiss, Erin. One kiss. That's it"

"She-yeah, right."

"That's all."

"Just a little simple kiss?"

"Sure."

"And then you'll drop it and stop saying I hate Asians or some shit like that?"

"Sure."

Let's make this quick. "Fine. Just a peck."

"A peck? C'mon, how about a regular kiss? No tongue."

She considered. "No tongue, no groping, no licking, no whatever."

"I'll be a perfect gentleman."

Erin repositioned herself. She raised her right index finger. "No funny stuff, or I'll kick your ass!"

"Right." Tojo leaned forward, eyes closed. Erin kept hers open. When their lips met he kept his word and didn't try anything, but he did open his mouth just enough that her bottom lip fell between his. He used his bottom lip to massage and embrace hers. When she pulled back, her lips had a buzzing sensation and her feet felt like curling. Tojo looked smug. Erin looked back towards the house. The excitement of being caught only made her appreciate the kiss even more.

"There you go: I kiss Asian guys too," she stated, digging her feet into the sand again.

"What'd you think?"

"What, do you want a grade or something?"

"Sure."

Don't push it. "Okay, a six."

"A six! What? I deserve at least an eight."

"That's my grade."

"I get a do-over!"

"Tojo, you're already gonna tell everybody, 'Hey! I kissed Erin!'"

"No, I won't."

"If I were a guy, I would."

"I promise not to. Cross my heart." He leaned in. She turned her face and he kissed her neck instead. When she didn't pull back, he stayed on her neck, hitting one of her sensitive spots. She giggled and squirmed away. She turned to tell him to stop, and he seized the opportunity to kiss her lips again, this time clutching his left hand to the side of her head. He rubbed her scalp and played with her dreads.

I'll bet he's always wanted to do this.

This time he massaged her lips more intensively, still without any tongue. She restrained herself from using hers. *I'm going to hate myself in an hour, but right now he's triggering my sex button. The minute our tongues touch, it could be: hand on breast, hand on crotch, hand in pants, pants in hands, and so forth. But then what? Only the strong-willed can pull off dating a co-worker, and the awkwardness and reputation-hit from a one-night stand would be unbearable. Even what we're doing now will cause trouble.* Tojo lowered his hand to her right shoulder. *He's made it halfway from dreads to nipple. What do I do?*

Woo!" someone yelled. "Yeah!"

Tojo and Erin pulled apart. They spotted the yelling guy thumping down the pier, followed by some buddies. He jumped into the lake with all of his clothes on and his friends roared as if he had scored a touchdown.

Tojo jumped up as if he had been caught naked outside a playground. *Huh? We obviously aren't in trouble, or even in that compromising a position. Why'd he get up so fast?*

"Hey, yeah! All right!" he yelled.

He had added distance from her and positioned himself in front of her, as if refusing to admit her presence. He started walking away.

"Tojo, where are you going?"

"Just over there," he answered, still not looking back.

She stayed behind, feeling abandoned and rejected. *He kept his word, but to not try is a little...I mean, if I can reach the point of... if he just walked away with a hard-on, that was an insult.* Tojo joined his friends on the pier and they started throwing the smaller ones into the water. Erin put her head onto her knees and wished she could be buried in the sand.

#

During the car ride back, she had nothing to say to anyone. She wasn't concerned the driver had a BAC of 0.8 or the guy riding shotgun kept complaining about "that faggot" he saw on a corner two miles back. She was not in the mood to enlighten or argue. Tojo remained close-lipped as well and didn't look at her. *This screws up so much more. I'll bet he tells everyone at work I'm easy. Why did I let him take advantage of me? Am I easy? One thing's for sure—he's an enormous, pulsating asshole with sugar on top.* When she got out, the only thing she said was "bye" over her shoulder.

She bee-lined to the kitchen. Though she was dying to talk to someone, her roommates were asleep and she didn't want to wake them, especially since she'd just averted screwing up their friendship. She pulled Fabrianne's leftovers out of the fridge and peeled back the lid. From what she could tell, it was an Indian dish of some sort. Indifferent to whether there might be meat in it, she stuck it into the microwave. As it warmed, she checked the answering machine. There were three messages: Fabrianne's financial aid supervisor about a missed payment, Annette Dean announcing she had passes for an art show at the Neo MOMA, and one message for Erin:

"Hi, Erin, it's me, Kevin." His voice was hesitant, as if uncertain he had reached the right number. "I called to see if you made it home, or if you even went home. Call me back." The machine beeped just as the microwave dinged.

What did I do? First I ditch a nice guy and then whore it up with Tojo. She put the leftovers back into the refrigerator and went to bed.

#

Erin was already awake, looking at the ceiling and thinking about her short-sheeted bed covers, when someone knocked on the door. Like the alarm clock an hour earlier, she ignored it. Unlike the alarm, she realized, the person would open the door to check if she was dead or alive.

"Fine, come in."

"Erin?" Fabrianne said, "Tracy called. She wants to know if you're coming in."

"Tell her I'm sick."

"You can't lie to Tracy."

"It's not a lie, Fabrianne, I feel like shit." Erin felt under her stomach. This cycle's cramps were a little strong. *I should lay off coffee. No coffee, no drugs, no cigarettes, no meat. Why bother living?*

"Ahh, had too much spirits at a party, eh?"

"That's an understatement. I really fucked up, Fabe."

"What did you do?"

"I ditched Kevin at the Cat Head and went to a party."

"Oh, my god! You didn't! You were on your dream date and you O.J.'ed him?"

"Pretty stupid, huh?"

"Very. So, what are you gonna do now?"

"I'm doing it. I'm going to stay in bed until I die."

"Gee, it's going to be hard getting rent out of you."

"Ha…Ha," Erin said sarcastically.

Buster came into the room. He glanced around as if he had never been in her bedroom. Fabrianne petted his head. "Sit,

Buster." The dog sat and made a groaning noise. "Why don't you just come clean with Kevin and tell him you flaked? Like, you panicked or something and you were afraid of getting too close, or something like that?"

"That's just the simpler problem."

"Oh-oh. What else did you do?"

"I...kind of made out with someone from work."

Fabrianne ran over to the bed shook Erin's shoulders. "Oh, my god! Who? Who?"

"I'm not gonna tell you. You'll tell Roger and he'll tell everyone."

"At least I know it's not Roger."

"Yeah, that would happen," Erin said, rolling her eyes.

"Besides, he won't speak to me. C'mon, Erin, tell me. I won't say anything."

"Roger's not speaking to you?"

"Stop trying to change the subject. Who did you sleep with?"

"I didn't sleep with anyone, I kissed them."

"Kissed? What's the big deal? I kiss my friends all the time."

"Okay, number one: no, you don't, and number two: I don't mean no quick hello-goodbye kiss, I mean a long make-out kiss."

"Oh. With Cliff?

"No! Don't make me kill you."

"That hippie guy?"

"Yuck, no!"

"That big bald guy?"

"Pat? No, he's on vacation."

"C'mon, Erin, I don't know anyone else there."

"Good, let's keep it that way. It's irrelevant. All you need to know is I dumped Kevin and went to a party and made out with another guy."

"That's true, but, you know, it's not like anything was going to happen with Kevin, right?"

"No, but I blew him off and I feel like a total bitch."

The doorbell rang. *Thank goodness. This will give me a break from Fabrianne's interrogation.*

Fabrianne pointed at Erin. "This ain't over!" She left to open the door.

Erin rushed to the front window blinds. Kevin stood looking around as if wondering whether he had the right address. *How did learn where I live?*

"Yes? Oh, hi. Kevin, right?" Fabrianne asked.

"Yes. You're...Fabrianne? You were in Painting 101, right? You're Erin's roommate?"

"One of them."

"Is she here?"

Erin held her breath, afraid Fabrianne would rat her out in order to teach her a lesson.

"Ah, no. I think she's working today, so you may wanna try her there."

"Hmm, okay. Well, tell her I stopped by. Nice seeing you again, Fabrianne." He turned and headed back to the sidewalk.

"Bye, Kevin." Fabrianne closed the door.

When he reached the sidewalk, he looked back. Erin sunk below the window sill. *As if it matters. He may not have seen my face, but I bet he's seen my actions very clearly.*

"He's so sweet. I can't believe you made me lie to him."

"It's for his own good, Fabe. You know salt and sugar don't mix."

"So now he's heading toward your work and..."

"Work! Shit! Tracy's on hold!" Erin ran to the kitchen phone and picked it up before remembering she should be putting on a sick voice. "H-hello?"

"Ah ha!" yelled Tracy. "I heard all of you talking in the background. You ain't sick!"

"Ah, man, don't rat me out, Tracy. If I get another mark, I'm out of there."

"I would never do that."

"Thanks, man."

"But we're short staffed, so you better get your ass down here and do a half day."

"But I..."

"Butt—ass! I'm tired of covering the register. I have a great game of Solitaire going in the back."

"Fine. Whatever. I'll be there in thirty minutes."

"Thanks, Mademoiselle. Oh, and by the way, that gay guy came by here looking for you."

"What! When?"

"Fifteen, twenty minutes ago. I sent him to your house."

"Oh, my god! That means—shit! Well, so much for that."

"What?"

"Nothing, see you in thirty." Erin hung up. "He went to my work first! He knows you were lying and that I was hiding from him. So now I'm a flake, a cheat, and a liar to him and I have to go to work with a guy I made out with!"

"Oh what a tangled web we weave."

Erin buried her face in the couch cushion and screamed.

#

Work went a lot smoother than Erin had expected. The shorter workday went fast; Tojo was on the late shift, so she avoided him; and because she and Lashell were not speaking to each other there were no arguments or drama. *I wish I could tell Lashell to get over it, but she'd only react with insults.* Around 4:30 PM, three skinheads walked into the parlor. Before Erin could scream or alert the management, she realized they were more the antigovernment, anti-racist, Socialist type of skinheads. She also recognized one of them—Ned, the guy she gave a hand job to after Bebe's party.

"Mu-ther-fuck-er," she uttered slowly. She ducked down behind the counter.

"What are you doing?" Barbara asked Erin.

"Doing inventory. Tell me when those skinheads are gone."

"Are they dangerous?"

"Only to my reputation."

Lashell looked back, then down, at Erin crouching. Lashell shook her head in disbelief and smiled. Erin also smiled at her silly predicament.

"Hey, is Pat here?" Erin heard Ned ask.

Barbara looked down at Erin, who waved frantically and shook her head, and then at Lashell. "Is Pat here?"

"No, he's in England."

"England?" one of the other guys yelled.

"What's he doing in England?" asked the third guy.

"I think he told me he was going, but I didn't know it was this week," Ned answered. "Hey, is it true a gutter punk girl tried to vandalize your store?"

"Yeah," Barbara answered. "She broke our soda machine and ran out."

"See, I told you!" Ned said. "We're gonna have to do this without Pat."

Do what without him? Erin heard them walking, and then the door open and close. She stood up as though there was nothing at all unusual about cowering under a counter.

#

She had expected to see Tojo at the end of her shift, but he'd called and told Tracy he was running late. *Probably just avoiding me.* Instead of going home, she went next door to Café Olé to order a latté. A new girl was working counter. She was in her early twenties, had short black hair, and wore thick black glasses, almost like Lisa Ann's, and a black T-shirt with Big Black Cock-a-Doodle-Doo on it. *I wonder what her story is? Maybe, like me, she chased after the wrong guy or got hosed by her job or is waiting on her AIDS test. God, what am I gonna do if it's positive? Okay, chill out. Think about the problems you have now.*

She spotted Tojo heading to this car with a delivery. She jumped up and ran outside to meet him.

"Tojo!"

He acted like he didn't hear her at first. When she caught up to him at his Datsun and called again, he turned.

"H–hi, Erin"

"Can I talk to you for a sec?"

"Well, I kinda have four pizzas to deliver."

"It's okay, this won't take but a sec." Erin took a deep breath, looked at the ground and then looked at him. He was shuffling around as though he had to go to the bathroom. "Listen, about last night…"

"Hey, don't sweat it! We were both loaded. It won't happen again."

"Yeah, but…"

"It's no big deal, Erin. These things happen. I won't let it affect us working together." He got into his car and closed the door.

"But, we don't work together."

"Even better. Hey, I'll see you later, Erin—gotta go!" He backed out of the parking space and sped off toward the exit. The tires screeched as he turned onto the street. *Did a boy actually choose to run away instead of talking to me? Maybe I'm a bad kisser? No, that's not it. Besides, guys will fuck a bad kisser.*

On the drive home, she began to feel better. *Tojo just simplified my life. I never have to speak to him about the kiss, or anything else, for that matter. And he acted too embarrassed to spread rumors around about me. One problem in my life has solved itself.*

She recognized the Honda Accord parked in front of her house as Roger's because the back had a bumper sticker which read: 'If You're Going to Ride My Car's Ass, at Least Pay Me a Dollar.'

What the hell is he doing here? Revenge on his ex-girlfriend? Should I call the police? Inside she found him sitting on the couch watching a video with Fabrianne. *How did we get here? Well, whatever argument or drama between the two must have been resolved.* "Hi, guys."

Roger waved and Fabrianne smiled.

Seems like everything's all right. Erin departed for the kitchen. Tawnee was drinking a beer and reading a Clive Barker novel at the kitchen table, an empty plate next to her elbow. "Hey, Tawnee."

"Erin girl."

"Any food left?" Erin opened the refrigerator.

"Maybe some leftover pizza."

The F.J. Pizza box underneath a carton of soy milk was at least three days old. "No, thanks." She slammed the door. She walked to the answering machine, then hesitated. *Not one message has ever been good news. This blinking red light is like a beacon of doom.* She considered pressing the delete button and skipping the whole situation. *Then again, it could finally be good news. My week of doom could finally be turning around.* "We got a message," she announced to Tawnee, who checked for messages about as often as Erin cooked.

"Really?"

"Student loan people?" Erin hoped. Not that it would be good news for Fabrianne, but at least it would be a simpler problem to solve than relationships.

"Hello, Erin…" Said Steiner "…Remember me? I'm calling to say goodbye. I'm gonna kill myself tonight." There was a beep at the end of the message.

Tawnee and Erin looked at each other for a moment, then Tawnee went back to reading.

"Holy fucking shit!" Erin said, ignoring the other message from Lisa Ann telling them how much their answering machine pissed her off. "Oh, my god! What are we gonna do? I should call the cops or a fire truck, right?"

"Calm down," Tawnee said as she flipped the page.

"Calm down? Tawnee! Steiner's going to kill himself!"

"He's bluffing. Probably gonna do some stupid extreme night sport or something."

"How do you know that? When I met him, he was jumping off a bridge!"

"Bungee jumping. My point exactly."

"But, no. He called here. Right after I blew him off. Why would he call here if he was just gonna do some stunt thing?"

Tawnee didn't seem to have an answer.

"I got to do something!"

"Calm down. Just call his house and talk to him."

Erin picked up the phone and stared at the dial. "What's his number?" Tawnee got out of the chair, pulled the phone book off of the top of the refrigerator, and gave it to Erin, who started flipping pages then looked up.

"Oh, my god! Oh, my god! Oh, my god! I don't know his last name! I fucked a guy for a month and I don't know his last name! What kind of whore am I?"

"Hey! You're not a whore! It's Neubauten."

"New what?"

Tawnee grabbed the phone book, located the listing and dialed it for Erin. It rang and rang without pickup or an answering machine.

"Oh, my god! Oh, my god! Oh, my god! What if he kills himself because I blew him off!" Erin started pacing.

"Chill. He's not gonna kill himself. He's probably trying to get attention, like he always does. That's one thing I really hate about him."

"Tawnee! Don't say that. If he turns up dead, you're gonna feel really guilty. We gotta do something!"

Tawnee rolled her eyes. "Fine, whatever. How would he do it if he went through with it?"

Erin remembered how she met him.

"West Side bridge! He's gonna throw himself off!"

"Okay, you check that out, I'll try to call one of his friends and see if they've seen him."

"Right. Thanks, Tawnee."

Erin started to run. Tawnee picked up her book.

#

The Escort's engine backfired, sputtered, and stalled like a Model T as if it were on its last mission. Erin tried to ignore the death rattles and was stalwart in her rescue mission. *God is punishing me. I do something wrong to Kevin, and something bad happens to me.*

Traffic on the West Side Bridge was light, which made it easier to drive slowly without being honked at. She scanned the sides of the bridge for any human form or bungee cords. *Seeing nothing isn't necessarily a good thing. God, I hope I'm not too late.* She bought the car to a slower crawl. *Damn it, Steiner, why are you doing this to me?* She sighed. *Why did you call me? To teach me a lesson? So I can be the one to watch you die? Bastard!* "Hmm, unless you've already jumped, you're not here. I'll try the house."

She put the car into gear and sped up. "God, I hate you, Steiner!" *If he does kill himself, I'll be that ex-girlfriend, like Pepe. Sure, her boyfriend was an unstable heroin addict, but in spite of the hard shell Pepe puts on, it must still bother her to have a boyfriend who killed himself—like she wasn't good enough in bed or nurturing enough to keep him happy.* "So selfish!" She muttered, looking out the window.

She had a difficult time finding where he lived. She remembered he shared a house with a bunch of bike messengers on Pear Street in North Depot. Most of the houses in this part of town appeared to have been designed by the same architect. They were all blocky, '50s-style stuccos, what people in Neopolitan called garage houses. The garages, instead of being recessed, jutted prominently from under the houses, and the upstairs had doors to the top, allowing the owners to turn it into a deck for barbecue grills, potted plants, or whatever else people with actual yards did. Erin found Steiner's house, because of the screaming rowdies on the deck. The roof partiers had beer bottles in their hands and were hooting at the new arrivals.

What the—? Is there a party going on?

She slowed the car down. Even without the garage roof drawing her attention, she would have noticed the massive numbers of cars taking up all the parking in front, and there had to be a massive amount of college students living in this neighborhood, because she couldn't imagine anyone playing their stereo so loud without complaints.

A car in front left just as she drew close. Her brief celebration of good fortune ended when a beer bottle, thrown from the garage deck, landed on the street a short ways up. *I'm not going to be any safer at this party than at Lake Charles.*

"Excuse me," she said as she squeezed between two people blocking the front door. Her words were wasted because of the volume of the stereo and the loud voices.

"Fucking awesome party man!" someone told the guy she recognized as Big Dog.

Erin looked around the small, packed living room and the volume of drunken revelers. She recognized April, deep in conversation with some guy working hard to look sincere; and Tawnee and Fabrianne's drug-addicted ex-roommate, Hana.

She ignored Hana, who wouldn't know her anyway, and forced her way to April.

"Erin! How's it going, man?" she asked, giving Erin a shoulder hug. Her breath smelled of peppermint schnapps.

"I'm cool. Have you seen Steiner?"

"Who's Steiner?"

"He lives here."

"Oh, really? I don't know anyone—I was just driving by and heard the music."

"I'm here to kick a guy's ass."

"I like your reason better."

"Hey, Steiner," someone yelled, "cool party, man."

Erin excused herself and continued shoving through the crowd, getting angrier with each obstacle. "Scumbag, dick, whore, whorish dick-scum licker, asshole, asshole-bag," she mumbled. Steiner was sitting on the couch with the infamous Debbie Chan—the girl who always seems to be at every party —on his lap. They were laughing. *I don't know what they find so funny, but I'll bet it's the girl who broke it off with a boy because she really had no place for him in her life, and yet the minute he calls she comes running.* "Okay, stay calm. Do not make a scene," she repeated to herself. Steiner saw her. For some reason she expected him to make a run for it, but he smiled.

"Stein-ner!" Erin said through clenched teeth.

"Hey! You made it," he said as if he had invited her. Debbie Chan did better at reading Erin's face and looked worried.

"Y-es." Erin struggled against yelling. "Stein-ner! Why did you tell me you were going to kill yourself?"

"Well, I was," he answered cheerfully. "But, I decided to throw a party instead!" Some people nearby cheered when he said that. Debbie Chan got off of Steiner's lap and began creating distance.

"Stein-ner! I've been searching all over town to see if you were all right! You could have called me back."

"I'm sorry, Erin, I didn't know you'd think I was serious." He took a gulp of beer. "I was feeling down, but you know me —I get un-depressed pretty fast."

"That doesn't strike me as any kind of apology. It sounds more like bragging."

"Hey! Since you're here, just enjoy yourself." He tossed Erin a can of beer. She caught it.

She regarded the can of Olden Town Lite. She tightened her fingers around it as if it were an enemy's neck. *Dare I pour this on his head? Throw it through a window? Shove it up his ass?* She pondered, crinkling the can. *No! I have too much dignity.* Erin closed her eyes and started counting backwards. She felt better at six, She was in a place mentally where she could walk out without any more confrontation. She turned around and started to leave. "I'm going home, Steiner."

"Erin, wait!" he called out as she turned, grabbing her arm. "Hey, you're not mad or anything like that? Are you?"

It would have been better if he had called her a sucker. Like the Peter Fisher incident at the airport, when he'd known Erin really wanted to go to Europe, Steiner of course knew she was mad. Steiner was not in any way apologizing. If anything, he was, like Peter, telling her she was the stupid one, for taking him seriously. Erin didn't remember willing her hand to move; the air slipped between her fingers, a feeling of stubble crossed her fingertips, and then a sharp, fleshy sound.

The slap wasn't powerful, but he had not expected it. His drunken legs gave way and as he stepped backwards he tilted over the arm of the couch. To onlookers it looked like she had punched him. Someone said, "Whoa," another added, "Oh!, man!" and another laughed. Erin inhaled to yell out 'fucking asshole!', but a hand on her arm distracted her. Erin spun, and if it had been anyone but April, that person would have received a slap from the unrestrained hand.

"Let's go!" April yelled, It was less of a 'Let's go, crazy girl, you're so out of here!' tone than an 'I'm saving you, let's go before they call the cops' one. Like the Red Sea, people parted before the fleeing violent girl. Outside, April put her arm on Erin's shoulder. "What the fuck was that about?"

Erin almost sobbed but managed to regain control. "Nothing, he was being an asshole. I—he just got on my nerves."

"You can't go around slapping people for that, Erin. After the tenth, your hand gets numb."

"I know, I just can't take it anymore."

"Hey, if—"

Big Dog burst out the door at Erin. "There you are! What the hell did you do to my fucking cel phone?"

It took Erin a second to remember her drunken journey from a few weeks ago, where she threw the borrowed phone at a car.

"She gave your new one to Steve," April lied.

"Steve? You mean Steiner?"

"Yeah, that's the one. Go see him."

"Just like that fucker not to tell me!" he snarled, shoving back inside.

"Now, Erin, get out of here before he returns!"

Erin's ran to her car. She started the engine and checked the rearview mirror. Big Dog had emerged and was looking around, angrier than before. Her tires squealed as she pulled away from the curb, giving away her location. Big Dog started yelling many vulgar names, and then, when she was almost out of vocal range, something hard shattered her back left window, spraying her with tiny pieces of glass. "Fuck'n...!" Erin yelled. She stopped the car and looked back.

Big Dog seemed surprised. He looked around at the other party guests. Someone hooted approval and another pointed at Big Dog and yelled, "She's going to call the cops on you."

"Fucking asshole!" Erin screamed. A large part of her wanted to get out of the car, but her survival instinct had already stepped on the gas petal. *What am I doing?* she asked as the car sped off. *He broke my goddamned windshield!* She stopped the car. "He's gonna pay for a new one!"

She stayed in the car. *Okay, let's put this into perspective: I struck someone in front of millions of witness, my defense against stealing that guy's cel phone is that I destroyed it while damaging a random car, and the only way to get my window paid for is by involving the lame-ass NPD. If those lame-ass cops believe me instead of Big Dog's friends, who'll no doubt lie to cover for him, I'll go to court, and if I win I'll get $200 for the window, but he'll get $100 for the phone. Probably the lame-ass judge will fine me $150 from me to teach me a lesson about hitting people and* *stealing their cell phones, if he doesn't send my lame ass to jail. Bottom line: nothing good will happen.*

She shook out her hair and brushed glass off her lap. She felt a sting on her knee and saw a small, leaking nick. "Fuck!" She drove off. *How did I go from trying to save someone's life and end up with a broken window and a cut?* Wrapped in increasing anger, she drove on autopilot until it was realized she was heading back toward the West Side Bridge. *Did I forget a turnoff? Am I subconsciously wanting to visit my mother or Lashell?*

The textured steel of the bridge roared underneath her car tires. *It wasn't so long ago I met Steiner when he jumped in his mock suicide attempt. Back then, he was just a cute, wacky guy I wanted to use for sex.* The car backfired and stalled. She gripped the steering wheel and hunched over. *If one more thing goes wrong, I am prepared to crash through the guardrail and plummet into the murky depths of the Victoria.*

Then it happened: one year, three months, two days, seven hours, forty-five minutes and nineteen seconds after using her first pay check from her new job at F.J. Pizza to buy the car from a guy who had more than likely stolen the it, and after untold miles of driving, numerous dents and dings, and an unexplained moldy smell in the trunk—the car died. Erin turned the key repeatedly, she stepped on the gas, she beat on the steering wheel—nothing helped. The car crawled to an inevitable rest on the bridge. It didn't take long for people to start blowing their horns and driving around her with fingers upraised. Every honk increased her rage. "I can not fucking believe you!" she yelled at the car. "How can you possibly do this to me now? After all I've been through and you do this to me! You asshole!" She hit the dashboard. "This can't be fuck'n real!"

As passing vehicles continued to poke fingers into her sanity, she grabbed the sides of her head and closed her eye to shut them out. *What would make me feel okay? Leaving this son-of-a-bitch car right here would be a start.* She looked out her window at the traffic whizzing past, then crawled to the passenger side and got out. Standing on the sidewalk and looking at her dead car felt like viewing her own body lying on a coroner's table. *I* *need a tow truck. That won't be cheap. And what then? I don't want to spend money fixing a car that cost less than $300.* She considered removing the license plate and tossing it and the registration papers into the river. *Maybe I could walk away from everything, just like I did with Kevin. Leave the city and go somewhere else. Back to Europe, where people don't know who I am. Change my name, my personality, tell people I'm a writer or a music reviewer or something that people couldn't say 'Oh, really? Prove it' on the spot.* She looked at the car. *And if I'm in Europe, screw the license plate and papers!*

She made her way to the bridge's pedestrian exit and was about to take the steps to the ground level and her freedom from responsibility when flashing blue and red lights stopped next to her. A white spotlight found her.

"Shouldn't get out of your car when it breaks down," a voice called out. She shielded her eyes. *If I run, I could be shot or arrested on some trumped-up charge.* She looked at the rail. *It would be so simple to hop over it. A few seconds of rushing wind, a hard, quick end, and then silence. Maybe I'll be the one to cause them to finally build a suicide barrier; through my sacrifice, I would accomplish something positive.*

"Driver's license," the voice interrupted. She turned to the blonde police officer stepping out of the car. She handed it to her.

"Where you're coming from?"

"Party in North Depot." *Ugh. Now they'll think I'm a DUI.*

"How much have you had to drink?"

"Not a drop."

"Mind taking a breathalyzer?"

"Sure."

She fetched the device and instructed her to blow into it. She seemed almost disappointed when it came out clean. She still led Erin through a standard sobriety test, including walking a straight line and doing the alphabet backwards.

"Well, you sure weren't drinking. You mind stepping in the back seat, please?"

"Am I under arrest?"

"No, I just thought you might want to get out of the rain while I run your license."

Whoa! I'm so spaced out that I didn't notice. She stayed out, feeling each drop was washing her terrible week away, but when it started coming down heavier and became annoying, she climbed into the car. *Well, at least unlike the other time, in Newark, I'm not handcuffed and angry.*

The dark-haired policeman in front was speaking into his radio. "917A, West Side Bridge, lane one, 926."

Erin's dad had given her brother Josh a police scanner one Christmas. He lost interest and Dave inherited it. When he lost interest, Erin got into it even more than they did, following the coded adventures of life among the peace officers for hours on end, usually imaging herself as the bad guys, shooting and driving in car chases. She'd memorize some important codes, and while she didn't recognize 917, she knew it wasn't anything to do with a suspicious person or a crazy lady. Probably he had been calling for a tow truck.

After the dispatcher replied, he turned. "You shouldn't leave your car without emergency blinkers to warn people."

"Sorry, all the power went out."

"You check your battery?"

"I wouldn't know where to start."

"First you--" The radio interrupted his lesson in auto maintenance. The only things Erin understood were the codes 415G and 245, and '10th Street'. 415 was a disturbance and the G meant a gang. 245 meant assault with a deadly weapon.

"There's a gang fight on 10th Street?" she asked. *Why did I say that? Nothing's more suspicious than a citizen who knows police codes. Now he'll think I'm drug dealer who listen's to police band to get a heads up on a raid.*

"You know something about that?"

"My dad's a cop. I memorized some codes."

"Oh, okay."

He punched her driver's license number into the computer. Behind them the female officer had laid out flares. *Well, these two are obviously not being called to help at the fight.* Dispatch announced the gang fight had claimed one victim, a Ned Bard, age 26. *How many skinheads are named Ned? And how many come into my pizza parlor and say they have to do something without Pat? And he asked about Suzan's Coke machine vandalism, so I know who the other gang is.* She put her hand on her mouth and tried not to scream. But if she had screamed, the cops would not have heard her. They would have been too busy listening to the squealing tires behind them and watching the pickup truck trying it's best to avoid the back of Erin's car and failing miserably. Erin turned around in time to witness it plow into the back of her car. With the sound of breaking glass and metal against metal, it lifted her Escort and pushed it onto the sidewalk. What sounded like a million rocks hit the police car's back window. A bumper flew into the other lane. A white car was able to avoid it, but not the red one that mounted the bumper, drawing a trail of sparks down the lane. So much was happening, the cops, like Erin, weren't sure what to do. When the mayhem had settled, the policeman got out to investigate. Traffic had come to a halt. Erin wanted to get out, to see what horrible thing had happened to her car. She banged on her window and screamed: "Let me out! What happened?"

He shook his head. "No. It's too dangerous out here!" The blonde officer pointed to the police car's back bumper. "Oh shit!" the man yelled. He opened the door and pulled Erin out. "Get your ass over there!" he barked.

What made him change his mind? She circled to the back of the car. A flaming piece of something, perhaps from her car, had lodged itself under the police car. The officer grabbed a fire extinguisher from the trunk and extinguished the little fire.

The pickup truck driver stepped out onto the pavement, looking more confused then hurt. A can of Budweiser fell out behind him. *Well, that answers how someone could not notice flares and flashing police lights* Erin looked at the other drivers. The red car's driver appeared pissed but unhurt, as was the man from the white car, who was already on his cel phone. The policewoman busied herself, keeping the truck driver from wandering away from the accident.

This is getting too crazy. Oh, my God, why? Why is this all happening to me? What did I do, God?" This time she didn't walk away from the bad scene, she ran. She reached the pedestrian stairs and swiftly descended the concrete steps, past graffiti-covered walls and a sleeping homeless man three flights down.

On the street underneath the bridge, she continued to run. From above she heard a voice ordering her to stop. She had no real goal except away. She heard the distant, lower sirens of a fire truck or an ambulance approaching the bridge. On her right, she could see the river, reflecting the lights of ships and the city and shimmering on each crest and wake. She looked up, at the city. Lights, people, cars, office buildings. The clock tower and her adrenaline high reminded her of being drunk and drugged on Monster Day.

About a block away was a street she knew had a bus station. *If I make it there, I can use my credit card to buy a ticket and be out of Neopolitan within the hour. A new existence.* She looked over her shoulder for one last look at the events going on the bridge. More flashing lights had appeared, and one of the cops was watching her while speaking on his walkie-talkie. When she turned her head back around, she ran into the door of a police car parked on the sidewalk, knocking the wind out of her. She fell backwards onto her butt.

A Black female officer got out of her car, speaking into a walkie. "Suspect is in custody," she said reaching down and hauling Erin up. "Miss, I'm going to have to place you under arrest."

"Oh, my God. I don't know Ned Bard! Is he all right? It was only a hand job! I don't know those skinheads!" she cried

"I was going to say for leaving the scene of an accident, but we'll talk about that other stuff later.

#

Erin watched the woman, perhaps the slowest typist she has ever seen, peck the small bit of information Erin had given her about the accident on the bridge into the computer. *A regular person could have written a novel by now.*

"Which police department did your father work at?"

"Newark, New Jersey" she answered again, unsure whether the woman was forgetful or was trying to trip her up and reveal a deception. As the officer pecked away, Erin looked around. Like her dad's station, the Neopolitan police department was less hustle and bustle more DMV. There were no arguments or fights or dramatic speeches, like on the TV cop shows. Just a bunch of drunks looking for a safe place to spend the night and cops typing reports and playing computer games. The building appeared to be very old, perhaps from the early 1900s. Marble floor and columns made the station look like an old Italian bank and amplified the noises—you could hear walking, talking, coughing from across the room. She couldn't see what was going on behind her because the handcuffs restricted her movements. *What do sex fetish people see in these things?*

"Okay," the officer continued, "it looks like your dad is a policeman. So, how did you end up here?"

"Even cop kids are human."

"True. But surely a little bit of the right and wrong rubbed off. One of the officers said you seem to know a lot of the police codes. That at least means that you are aware of things like procedures, such as not running away from an accident scene."

"I know. It was just all the craziness going on. Trucks and explosions. I freaked out. I had to get away from all that."

The officer paused for a moment. "I can see that, I'll let you off on that one. Now, about Ned Bard. It was ...By the way, you know you have the right not to be questioned without a lawyer, right?"

"I know. They told me when they were putting me in the car. It's okay."

"Alright. Ned Bard. How do you know him?"

Erin described meeting him at Bebe's party, but not the hand job in her car, and seeing him again at the Pizza parlor with a group of skinheads, but not that they were looking for her friend Pat, and described Suzan as just some angry skinhead girl who had knocked over the soda fountain, but not that she knew her.

"Anybody else see him come in to the Pizza place or see you at that party?"

"For the party, you can talk to Bebe who works at the Acid Pit, and for the parlor you can call Lashell Bronson. She should be home right now."

"And that was the last you saw him?" The officer asked.

"Yep. So what happened? Someone knifed him during the fight?"

"He was shot."

"Oh, my God! Is he all right?"

"I'm sorry, Erin...he died."

She's mistaken, that's why she said that. She stared at nothing in particular, feeling like she was watching a familiar prerecorded video and seeing something new and horrible.

"Erin? Erin? Are you all right?"

"No, I..." She didn't cry even though she felt really bad. "I feel like..."

"Like what?"

Utter shock, cursed, or in a weird dream where nothing is real anymore. Is this how it felt to go crazy? Like all it would take is one wrong trigger to send me to a mental institution. Insane people make sense now: they're people who've had days—weeks—like this, and one person said or did that one thing and that made it seem reasonable to start a collection of heads in the freezer.

"You feel like what?"

"Numb."

"I'm sorry. I'm gonna check out your story. Could I have the numbers for the Acid Pit and your friend Lashell?" After writing them down, the woman took off.

Erin rubbed her handcuffed wrist with her free hand. *How the hell did I end up here? I swear, if I get out of this I'm going to change my life. No more doing stupid shit.* Another prisoner was escorted to a chair across from her. In addition to being handcuffed to the chair like Erin, her legs were also secured. Even with her head tilted to the floor, Erin recognized her.

It's Suzan! Erin examined her closer. Suzan was sobbing on and off. *She's different. She's not the tough, racist, vandalizing monster I'm used to. She's like a scared child. Is this who Suzan was before something turned her against the world and she joined a group of nonconformists in declaring war on anyone different? She looks like someone's daughter. She's me if she hadn't been sent away from New Jersey.* Suzan lifted her head. Her face looked like she had been punched. *Which of Pat's friends would hit a girl?*

"Suzan?"

Suzan turned her head, as if embarrassed.

"Suzan, what happened? Who shot..." Erin held back a tear. "Who killed Ned?"

Suzan cried a little more and then shrugged. "I don't know. One of the guys."

"But, not you, right?"

"No!" she yelled. "I never wanted them to get into guns. I just like breaking shit."

"And hurting people."

"Only people that hurt us."

"Like those Black guys that you ran out of town?"

"They started it! Niggers are always making fun of us, stealing from us, raping us!"

Erin closed her eyes and breathed. When she opened them she met Suzan's stare. "A White person shot and killed Ned..." Suzan looked away. "...A White friend of yours took a human life and you're going to go to jail as an accessory to murder."

"Hey, I didn't kill anybody!"

"No, but they know Ned came after you guys for terrorizing F. J. Pizza."

Suzan looked down at her handcuffed legs and began to cry again.

"Tell me: if you could, would you go back in time and take it all back?" Suzan nodded. "Me, too, but here we are—you up for murder, me for blowing up my car."

She looked up at Erin.

"Long story." *How far back would I need to go to avoid the trouble? To Kevin's house, when I saw the guy in his underwear? When I snuck into the NRT with Suzan? Meeting Steiner on the bridge? Snorting cocaine at Bebe's party? So many mistakes to correct.*

She regarded Suzan. *Her vandalization at F.J. Pizza starts the connection to the murder. And if the police also knew she helped start the fire at the boarding house, she's double fucked. One word from me, and Suzan will be put away. And then what? A confused little girl who thought she was tough meets the real thing—people like Ned's killer, people who will guide her from a vandal to killer, because the only Black people she'll know are prisoners trying to kill a skinhead racist in the shower.* "Suzan, tell me, if you get out of this, can you promise me one thing?"

"Leave your pizza parlor alone?"

"Naw, you can burn that fucker to the ground. No, I was wondering—this may sound corny, but I'm not asking you to promise to clean up your life, because I won't—but, I've dated a Black guy and White guys, kissed a Japanese guy, been in love with a Jewish guy, worked under Italian guys, and you know what?"

"They all suck?"

"Exactly! They all piss the fuck out of me! They all landed my ass here! Strapped to this fucking chair! All men are assholes! Period! No matter what race or creed, whatever, assholes every last one of them! Your White male friends got your ass here. You claim the Black ones want to steal your women or whatever? But, you know what? A White guy tried to rape me a while back! Men are men! And I fuck'n hate them right now!"

"So you're a dyke now?"

"Oh, no, don't get me wrong—a lesbian tried to feel me up in a bar, another woman turned into a total pussy and burned me at my job, A straight White woman knocked my soda machine off the counter, a Chinese woman hung all over my boyfriend, and a Black girl thinks I'm a dumb-ass. So you see my point: Women suck! Men Suck. People Suck! There's no color, religion, or anything that makes one better. Your White Nazi friends landed you in here. I bet you money they ain't gonna bail you out—everyone sucks super ass!"

"You need friends." Suzan looked down.

"Yes, but fuck race, sex, and religion! Right now, at this very moment, we need friends who will get our asses out of here. We need friends, Suzan, not race."

No one spoke for a long moment. *Was that for her or for me? I don't know how much Suzan absorbed—probably it went in one ear and out the other—but I sure feel better. Well, we're both cursed with a broken time machine that only goes forward.*

The officer came back and unlocked Erin's cuffs. "Your story checks out. As far as running away from the accident goes, it's going to be considered as misdemeanor and we're releasing you on your own recognizance."

"What about my car?"

"What's left of it was towed, The insurance stuff you're gonna have to deal with."

Erin rubbed her wrist and looked at Suzan, who winced as if at any moment Erin was to rat her out.

The officer sat down. "All-righty, then. If you see that skinhead girl from your pizza parlor again, give us a call."

"I will," Erin said walking away.

The rain had slowed to a few scattered drops blown by the cool breeze into Erin's face. Downtown North's lights reflected off the shiny streets and cars driving past produced a watery hiss under their tires. Erin took a deep breath. *To fix things, I have to go back to the beginning. Where did I first fuck up, and how do I set things right? Treating Kevin badly, I can start with that. I should apologize.* She headed toward the NRT station.

#

A light was on in the Peachtree Gardens apartment. *What will I say?* She kept walking. *Just be honest. Tell him everything. The worst he can do is say how silly I was and that all I had to do was be up front with him from the beginning.* She rang the doorbell and fought off the urge to immediately run. The door opened a little, then closed. She heard Kevin unlatch the chain and opened the door all the way.

"Erin?" He asked in a tone one reserved for strangers.

Erin stared at his Abercrombie and Fitch sweatshirt, unable to look up.

She took a deep breath. "Listen, I just came by to apologize for blowing you off at the bar and avoiding you. But the truth is…" She clenched her fists and pushed away the urge to flee again. *Clear the air and start your new friendship right now.* "…I was in love with you, even though you're gay and all. I just didn't want to get into a relationship with you and then you leave me for some guy or something."

She looked down at her feet, shuffling around. "So, anyway, that's what I came to say. If you want to hang out, I won't blow your calls off anymore. If you don't, I'll understand." *Now the ball's in his court. If he says something, it means he's willing to start over. If he doesn't, we should part company and move on with our lives.*

The silence dragged, and she'd almost decided to just leave and never look back when she heard him take a deep breath.

"Erin…"

"Hmm?" Her heart thumped. *I never realized that telling the truth could solve so many problems. This feels like a movie, where the music swells and the couple approach each other. We're not gonna kiss in this case, but we can start a new friendship that will be good for the both of us. I'm a new Erin, adult-friendship Erin. No more running away from things and swapping fantasy for facts…*

"FUCK YOU!" Kevin bellowed at the top of his lungs for everyone across the street and for perhaps a few blocks away to hear, and then he slammed his door shut.

First she felt stunned, and then the familiar numbness she'd experienced at the police department crept back. She hovered on the porch. Inside, music got turned on. Erin stared at the door. *My movie moment ended like that?* She replayed the scene again and again. *Did he say, "Fuck you!" or "Love you!"? No, it was a "Fuck you!…I want to fuck you? No, definitely 'Fuck you!'* She turned around and headed to the station.

#

"Oh, my God! There you are!" Tawnee yelled as soon as Erin opened the front door. "Your mom called looking for you. She said that you were arrested or something?"

"What? How the hell did she know?"

"No idea. But is it true? What happened?"

"Let's just say Steiner's alive and having a party instead of killing himself."

"I knew it! But seriously, you better call your mom. She was shitting bananas."

"Is that Erin?" Fabrianne asked dragging the phone as she came out of the kitchen. "It's okay, Lashell, she's here. Okay. 'Bye now." Fabrianne hung up the phone.

Lashell is concerned enough to call, but too prideful to talk to me?

"Jesus, Erin, Lashell said that the cops called her asking about some girl that vandalized F.J. Pizza."

"Whatever. Do you know a guy named Ned?"

"No," Fabrianne answered. Tawnee shook her head.

"Well..." *I'm not up to explaining the whole night's events.* "Never mind. Let's just say I struck out with all the men in my life tonight. I better call my mom." Erin went up to the bathroom to take a therapeutic shower and change her tampon. Afterwards, refreshed, she called her mother.

"Oh, my god, Erin! What happened to you?"

"What are you talking about?"

"I got a call from your father, telling me that you were in a car accident. And then I called Lashell and she said someone called her asking about some girl that vandalized your store and—oh, my God, what the hell happened?"

"Wait, how did Dad find out?"

"He said an officer called his office asking if you were his daughter, and after getting a summary he called me asking what was going on with you."

"It was nothing. My car stalled on the bridge, I got out, cops came by, drunk guy hit my car and it exploded. This guy I met at a party a while back was killed in a gang fight and I panicked and made a run for it. Got busted and released the end."

"Jesus, Erin! Why didn't you call me?"

"I don't know. I didn't have time. The cops came when my car broke down, and I got out of jail before I needed to make my one phone call."

"You actually get three, but Erin, I'm freaking out here. I'm sorry. Let me catch my breath." Erin also took the opportunity to breathe in and out. "Okay, I'm better. Are you all right?"

"I'm fine. If I'd been in my car after those cops came by, I'd be de...never mind."

"Dead? Oh, my Lord. Erin, please don't do this to me again. I was worried sick, and then your father calling me and acting like I've pushed you back into your old habits or something."

"Is that what this is all about? I embarrassed you in front of dad?"

"Don't be stupid. I was worried sick about you. And he was just concerned. He hadn't heard anything about you for a year, and this? Erin, you can't keep us in the dark, especially me. I worry about you sometimes."

"Mom, I'm old enough to take care of myself."

"I know. We talked about this on our trip to Mountain Springs. But we also agreed it's okay to ask for help when you need it."

"I know, but I had the situation under control."

"Erin..." Her mother paused. "Erin, I know how much you want to be independent, and I applaud that—I encourage it—but you don't have to be so independent that you alienate your loved ones and let things spiral."

"Mom, it's not like you don't keep things to yourself."

"Erin, I never, never hid Dan from you."

"I'm not talking about Dan."

"Then what?"

"Josh."

"What about Josh?"

"How old are you?"

"What? Forty-eight."

"Can I see your driver's license sometime?"

"What is this about?"

"You didn't answer me."

"Erin, what does my license have to do with Josh?"

"Not much, except you're not forty-eight."

"What are you talking about? I am too."

"Mom, I know you're forty-six and that you had Josh at sixteen."

"Who did you hear that from?"

"No one," she lied. "I figured it out. You've lied about your age all these years to hide the truth. That you were a teen mother."

"Erin, even if that were true, how is that the same as you almost getting arrested for murder?"

"Secrets, mom. We all keep secrets from each other."

"Erin, some things are secrets, others are things that take the right time and place to be revealed.

"So the thing about Josh is true?"

"If it is, I think it would be between me, your father, and Josh. There's no reason for you to be involved in any it."

"Then it is true?"

"Erin...I have to get ready for work. I'm glad you're all right. You should rest. We'll talk about this later."

"Mom, are you cutting me off?"

"A time and a place, sweetheart, a time and a place. Bye now."

"Wai—"

Erin kept the phone to her ear as if the dial tone was a mistake, then hung up. *Mom's never cut me off before. I guess I put her on the spot. Crap, I stressed her out and revealed her to be a liar about a part of her life. Way to go. And now my dad knows his wayward daughter, has once again had a brush with the law. So much for going home. I guess I've officially fucked everybody this week. Did I leave anyone off? Should I call Pat in England and tell him his friend is dead and I let an accessory to the crime walk?"* She went to her desk to see if anyone had sent her panicky emails. Coincidentally, the first was from Pat:

> *Hey! Mop Top:*
>
> *I'm in one of those cyber café's in London. Having a blast. Mr. Humphrey is a hoot. He misses you and wants you to visit. Mimi said she saw the Queen. I think it was just some old lady. After all, the Queen wouldn't be riding the underground. Gotta log off. This e-mail is costing me some pounds. Say hi to the Hee-Haw gang.*
>
> *Pip Pip, Cheerio, Pat*

The next was from Josh:

Hey, Skipper!

I would love to have you come to our dinner. It's a pity that Mom has to work those days. I know, with your job you can't afford a ticket, especially on such short notice, but no problem! At my company, we fly at the last minute all the time. I'm going to put your name in, so all you have to do is go to the counter, give them your ID and a confirmation number and tell them where you're going and you can be on the next plane with an unsold seat. The ticket will be paid for. (Just don't get crazy and tell them you want to go to Europe. Ha, ha.)

I'll send you the airline and confirmation number later. It would be great to see you.

Love, Josh

Erin felt as if she had won the lottery. "Fuck New Jersey! I'm going to Europe! For free!"

#

She entered F.J.P without much hope. Considering her reputation and current job status, she was gambling on a five-percent chance Jeannie and especially Ed would let her take her vacation hours, which couldn't be used until next month, for a short trip to Europe. Again, Lashell acknowledged her existence but didn't say hello. *There's still a grudge factor after showing concern for my safety?* Erin walked past the counter and went into the office. Ed was putting receipts together for the bank deposit.

"What do you want?" he asked.

"Oh, that's nice," she responded. *Whoa! Where did that sarcasm come from? Come on, girl, suck it up for Europe.*

"What?"

"I said morning, Ed."

"Erin."

"So, Ed….next month, I get my one week vacation."

"Unless you screw up and get fired before then."

"Er, yeah…*ass-hat*…anyway, I was wondering if it were possible to use some of the hours next week, like on Friday, Saturday, and Sunday. Pat will be back Saturday, so I'll only be gone one day, basically. Also, if you hire someone to take Mary Jo's place, they should be trained by—"

"No."

"What?"

"Are you deaf? No, you can't have any time off." He swiveled in his chair to face her. "You don't have any vacation time until next month, so until then you owe us sixty hours."

"Aw, come on, Ed. Can't you just push it up a month?"

"What for? You want to go to some punk rock concert or something?"

Punk rock? "No, I just need a vacation. I'm all stressed out and stuff."

"Welcome to my world." He took a sip of coffee. "If you want off that bad, you can always quit and reapply later."

"Oh, yeah, and what are the chances that you'll hire me back?"

"Let me show you." He opened a file cabinet drawer and took out a stack of manila folders and shook them in her face. "This is a drawer full of people who want to work here." He put them back in the drawer. "Now, get back to work and stop wasting my time."

She remained still for a moment. *I want to tell him what an incredible asshole he is. I want to take his folders and throw them in the air or stuff them into his mouth. I want to tell him that he's nothing but an insecure bully who compensates for the massive failures of his career and life and inability to control an underage-drinking, probably promiscuous daughter, and that he takes it all out on a bunch of minimum-wage slaves who wouldn't piss on him if he caught fire.* She managed to leave the office quietly.

"Lashell, the prep area is messy. Clean it up," Barbara was saying. Lashell returned a look that said, 'I know you didn't just give me an order'. Barbara either didn't understand or chose not to. "Doug, you need to make calls on your own time on your own phone"

"It's okay, I'm on break," he responded.

"If you're using our phone, you're on our time."

"I'm talking to Sam about our new baby. None of the other supes had a problem with me—"

"Well, that's them. If you're going to work with me, you're gonna have to follow my rules."

"Cut him some slack, yo," Lashell suggested.

"You guys are already too slack. I don't see why Ed hasn't fired you all. Erin, get behind the register already. Unless you'd like to change the toilet paper in the bathrooms, and while you're back there mop the floors?"

Lashell, Doug and Erin exchanged shocked expressions. Barbara had transformed from a new, annoying supervisor to a clone of Ed. Doug hung up and Lashell started chopping tomatoes, but Erin didn't acknowledge the yuppie at the counter. She just stared into the register buttons. *What am I doing here?*

Barbara walked over. "Erin, you have a customer." Getting no fast answer, Barbara snapped her fingers in Erin's face. "Hello?"

Lashell saw the confrontation building and lay down her knife. "Oh, no, you didn't just snap your fingers in her face."

Erin raised her palm to stop Lashell from getting into trouble.

Barbara raised her voice for the whole staff. "You guys think you're soooo cool and above everybody, with your alternative clothes, your tattoos, your slacking, and your loud, raunchy music, but this is a business, not a club house, and I expect you to do your job without copping an attitude. That's what we pay you for. You don't like it, talk to Ed. He's got a drawer filled with people ready to take your place."

"Amen to that," said the customer. Erin looked at him as if he had just farted. She then turned to Barbara.

"What?" Barbara asked. Erin remained silent. "Nothing? Then get cracking, chop-chop." Barbara spun to Lashell. "That's enough tomatoes. Start on the oni—"

"You know what?" Erin said quietly

Barbara looked over her shoulder. "What?"

"Last night, someone threw a brick through my car window. Later my car got hit by a truck and it blew up, just like in those action movies. Later I got mistakenly arrested in connection with a murder…"

"So, you had a bad—"

Erin held up her hand. "Don't interrupt. Earlier, I found out some personal secrets about my roommates and my mother, and I also had to go to the hospital, which cost me the job that you now have…"

"I still don't see…"

"You interrupted again. You had your little speech, now here's mine. On top of everything, I fucked things up with one of my coworkers. But the worst thing? All that trouble, and I have no one to cry about it to. You think we like coming here because of the music, or our hip fashion? This is a crap-ass job. The one good thing about it is my friends, and you're trying to make us miserable, to rob us of that little spark of goodness. I almost <u>died</u> last night. And another person I know <u>did</u> die. What can you do to me compared to that? Fire us? Fire us from this place? Don't you think we know that at any moment we can be fired from here? Let me spell it out for you: I-almost-died-last-night! Do you think I'm afraid of Ed? He's just a mean old dude that signs our checks."

Erin noticed the staff were now looking past her instead of at her. She turned, knowing what she'd see, and there he was, in his classic managerial pose, hands on hips and eyebrow furrowed.

"Your <u>last</u> check, Pierce. Hand over your apron and get out!" He said.

Everyone, including the customer, was silent. Even Cliff, the opinionated radical, didn't say a word. Erin expected someone to speak up, to support her or declare a strike— anything. But no one did. Ed put his hand out. She untied her apron and handed it to him. Then, she walked to the back to get her things out of her locker.

#

Erin wandered through the park, vaguely aiming for home. She felt neither sad nor depressed, just disappointed. *I thought for sure my friends would rally behind me and demand I not be fired, especially Lashell. Didn't the bit about losing a friend touch her? Then again, they all have bills to pay, as do I.* She turned onto a dock and sat looking at the pond through a veil of cold drizzle. *Where'd the ducks go?* She dangled her right clog on the surface of the water, moving it to spread ripples in all directions. The clog crept along her arch until it finally plopped into the water. Instead of sinking, like she'd expected, it bobbed back to the surface and floated away, pushed by the wind. The other shoe also slipped off and started following the first. "Bon voyage," she said.

#

"Flight 420 to Paris, Charles de Gaulle now boarding."

Erin ignored the announcement, as she had the countless others she'd heard the last two hours. There were several planes to Paris, but she hadn't built up the nerve to buy her ticket yet. With no job and nowhere else to be, she wasn't in a hurry, so she sat and watched people stream through the international terminal. The ones arriving were tired and complaining, but the ones departing were excited and had a spring in their step. *I want to hold onto that feeling of constantly departing, always having butterflies and being full of hope about starting a new adventure.*

She had one bag with a week's worth of clothes and a Walkman with enough music for a trip to Dallas or New York. She reached in and pulled out a pad of paper and read over the letter she had written.

> *Hi Josh:*
>
> *I guess you and everyone else is wondering why I didn't show up at your dinner. I'm very sorry, but I had to use your free ticket thing to take a different journey. I've had a really rough*

time lately and I feel that coming home will only add to it all.
There are some things that I want to talk to you about, but it's
not the time. Don't worry about the bill for the ticket, I plan on
paying you back as soon as I can…

She tried to think of what else to say. By her calculations, if
she mailed the letter from Europe, it should arrive the day of
or day after the dinner. By then, the other letters will also have
arrived. She flipped to Lashell's:

Hey, Shell:

Well, I guess I really fucked up. I thought my friends would
rise up and walk out with me if I got fired. Just like some movie
or something. The theme song to an Officer and a Gentleman or
Top Gun playing while all the customers cheered. What the fuck
was I thinking? Don't think I'm all sappy and everything, but
I love you, Shell, like a sister I've never had. That's why it hurt
so much when you didn't have my back. I guess I can't blame
you. You guys need the money and you are pissed at me. I
actually don't remember why we were even fighting. I've had such
a crap-ass life lately. How crap-ass? So crap-ass that I've left the
country and I'm not coming back! But how will you survive?
How will you eat, you say? Like you said, there are a million
shitty jobs out there, so I'm sure there's an F.J. Pizza in
Europe. I just hope there are no Eds. Too bad we couldn't talk
about this, perhaps it's for the best. This is a decision I need to
make on my own.
I'll write later and tell you where I end up.

The letter to her roommates asked them to take care of
Buster until she could find a way to ship him to her. She really
didn't look forward to having her dog in a long, customs-
required quarantine, but it was also unfair to burden her friends
with an abandoned dog. She added:

...I'll try to send some cash to pay for my missing rent, but If you need the money, it's okay to rent out my room and sell my stuff.

She wondered if they do any of that? *The last time they saw me was last night, and they won't hear from me for a day or two. No one will have any idea where I am. To them, I could be dead.*

She started to work on the letter to Ed:

Dear Ass-biting, boil-licking, King Turd of the Butt Pirates, You suck ass, you suck cock, you suck your mother's...

Insulting Ed made her angry about the whole firing episode. *I want to hold onto the giddy, adventure feeling But know this, Ed, your day will come, and you will be judged.*

To get back on track, she went over her letter to her mom.

Hi, Mom:

By the time you read this, I will be thousands of miles away. That sounds so cliché. (Did I spell that right?)

But yes, I am far away. I'm okay. I'm alive and hopefully in a place where boys like Kevin and Steiner don't exist, or at least the American versions of them. I just couldn't take anyone else lying to me or keeping secrets from me. I've been disappointed by everyone from close friends to my own mother, who I've always thought of as a close friend.

I wanted to fly to Newark for Josh's thing, but the thought of confronting Daddy right after I was arrested would not be a good scene.

Please check with my roommates and pick up Buster if they don't want to take care of him. I know he's my dog and I'll try to get him to me as soon as I get settled. I've given them permission to sell my stuff, but knowing them they'll try to put it into storage, expecting me to come back. I'm starting a new life. I just hope it's a life that Dad won't be ashamed of.

I love you, Erin
P.S. Say hello to Dan.

She started to tear up, but stopped by remembering this was all a good thing. She put her notepad away and imagined what everybody's reaction would be. Lashell would call her a dumbass, her roommates would be upset and perhaps crying, as would her mother. Josh would try to find out how much she'd charged to his company's account. Ed, she hoped, would kill himself.

"Hey, do I know you?"

She blinked out of her fantasy. "Huh? What?" Next to her sat a Black guy with dreadlocked hair. For a second she thought it was Kenneth Lukas. *What a perfect fairytale ending that would be: Kenneth come to take me home with him to England, where we'll live happily ever after in Manchester.*

"Yes, I do recognize you."

"Really?" She panicked, remembering the 'I love Jews' incident.

"You're Erin from F. J. Pizza."

"Yeah, and you are…?"

"Robert."

It took a second. "Oh, yeah, from the late shift. Nice to finally talk to you."

"Same here. I've heard a lot about you."

She buried her head in her hands. "Ah, yes, the F.J. Pizza great grapevine strikes again."

"No, it wasn't anything bad. At least, I didn't think so."

"What did you hear?"

"Just that you fell in love with two people and couldn't choose."

Hmm, a simple version, but accurate. He's kind of cute, but I don't like the fact that he follows gossip.

"How did it turn out?"

"Why do you think I'm at the airport?"

"You're leaving Neopolitan? Ahh, it can't be that bad?"

"Ha!" She scoffed. "Everyone either hates me or thinks I'm an idiot. You don't know the half of it."

"I know, you don't solve problems by running away."

"Who says?" Erin looked at the departure monitor across the room.

"I do. I've lived in five different places since I left Chicago, and, you know, what I discovered is that no matter where you live, there are still going to be good and bad people."

"Then why did you stay in Neopolitan? It's full of bad people?"

He laughed. "True. It took me a while to find the good people in Neo." He put his hand on her shoulder. "But I bet you anything, like me, the people you call your friends in Neopolitan are some of the coolest people you've known—Neo has too many assholes, we need to balance it out."

Yes, my mother kept a secret from me, but it's something between her and Josh. Steiner's a clown who's only good for sex and I took him seriously. Tojo is a coward. My relationship with Peter ended the first time we had sex. Yes, I got arrested, but being in their car saved my life and I may have even saved Suzan's life. Ned's death was tragic, but if Pat were working that day he could be dead instead. Lashell was right about me being stupid to think me and Kevin were going out on a date. Gay or not, he's boring, self-centered, and unforgiving. If my dad was going to rag on me about my life then he should do it to my face, and if he's too afraid to do that, then screw being afraid of him, and as for being fired from F.J. Pizza? Big fucking deal!

"So, you still gonna move away?" he asked

"Naw, I guess not."

They announced a flight number and he stood up. "Good."

"Yeah, so what are you doing here? Meeting someone?"

"Oh, I'm moving away. 'Bye."

As Erin watched him head toward the gate, she tried to figure out whether he was joking. *Well, even if all of his talk about how I should stay in Neopolitan was crap, I still feel a little better about my home for six years.*

She found a pay phone to hear if anyone had left her a message. Her roommates would still be at school so she wouldn't have to talk to them about leaving.

The first message was from Lashell:

"You dumb-ass! I can't believe you went through so much shit and refused to talk to me about it. What do you want? Me to apologize? You know I don't apologize. Everything I say I mean, just like I'm sure everything you say you mean. Get over it. I have. Now, getting past that shit, I had no idea Ed was going to fire you. I've always thought that he was all mouth and no balls; guess he showed me. Well, I'm gonna show him when I quit next month—two weeks notice, my ass! Don't you worry, though, I think this is your chance to brush your ass off and go to school. Fuck F.J. fuck'n pizza. I'm gonna start getting some brochures for you. Hang tight, bitch. Call me, a'ight?"

The second was from Tracy:

"Hey, Erin. I just found out that douche Ed fired you. Me and my girls are gonna get together to plan a proper retaliation. I don't know what we're gonna do, but I've always wanted to see him cry like a baby. So, chin up! J.J. said she'll put in a word for you at the sex shop and April will see if Jolly Rogers needs anybody. Ta, ta."

The last was from her mom:

"Hi, sweetie. I called you at work and they said that you were gone. Are you sick? Anyway, I'm sorry that I cut you off yesterday. That was rude, and I apologize. But, like I said, a time and a place. It has nothing to do with it being none of your business. It is your business. You're Josh's sister and I'm glad that you can come to terms with it. Just hold off until I can catch up to you, all right? I'm still growing up. Anyway, call me later, I love you."

There wasn't a fourth message. She'd hoped Dr. Balboa would call saying her blood test was fine and she wasn't going to die. *I know the doctor's probably right and I have nothing to fear, but I liked the idea where I was going to live my life in a fuck the consequences way. It's probably wrong to totally abandon all my responsibilities, but would it really cause any harm to just live my life with less fear?* Erin started crying after she hung up the phone. She became so emotional she had to sit down. She tore all the letters out of her notebook and threw them away, one by one, except the one to Ed, which she was still going to mail to him after it was finished.

After a spruce-up in the bathroom, she went to the airline counter. The ticket agent smiled at her.

"Hi," Erin said. "Do you have any cheap, round-trip tickets to Paris?"

"Let me check." The agent began searching the computer database.

Erin thought for a second. "Oh, another thing?"

"Yes?"

"I'd like a three day layover in Newark."

Preview

FLAMING JACKASS
Returns

Alexander G. J.

Part One
Jet Lag

"Pauvre con!"

Erin's French was bad, but even she knew that the cab driver who'd almost run her over had just called her an asshole. She racked her brain to remember how to reply in French. She settled for the American version and the accompanying sign language: "Fuck you! Pedestrians have the right of way, dickhead!" When she lowered her bird hand she noticed three old madams, also sharing the traffic island near the Place de Bastille structure. They stared at her as if she was the ugliest of ugly Americans "Désolé," Erin apologized.

The women turned to one another and muttered something in French as they scurried to the sidewalk. *Yes, I know. Even in Paris, I'm a horrible, horrible person. Don't worry, I'll be gone soon.* She rubbed her buzz-cut orange hair. It felt good and calmed her, like stroking a pet. Putting the incident with three strangers she'd never see again behind her, she dragged her luggage down the street and around the corner to the brasserie. Her heart started pounding and her hands shook—the same three old ladies were leaning on the bar, drinking Oranginas and smoking. One of them gestured to her. *Goddamn it, give me a break!* She took a deep breath and checked out the rest of the room. Only two people sat at the little round tables near the window. *I need to make it clear that I'm going to sit down.*

"Bonjour," the large, aproned man behind the counter said as he approached her.

Crap—I forgot to say 'bonjour' first, and after all those nasty looks thrown at me each time I forgot that part of the game. "B-bonjour..." she stuttered. "...J-je voudrais, uh...un café, and uh...ah pâtisserie? S'il vous plaît?"

"Pâtisserie? Vous voulez commander un croissant?"

The man spoke fast, and Erin almost broke out into a sweat. *'Croissant' rings a bell. He's asking me if I want a croissant!* "Yes—er-ah, oui! La croissant—merci. And café."

The man smiled and shook his head a little as he poured Erin a cup of coffee and put a croissant onto a plate. He rattled off an amount in Euros. Erin couldn't follow numbers, but her trick was to look at the register. The price reminded her that she was supposed to have mentioned eating at a table. She poked her finger in the direction of the tables near the window. "For er-ah—pour la table? S'il vous plaît? Merci?"

The man handed her the items. "Oui, vous pouvez les manger à la table." From his openhanded gesture she guessed that he had either already charged her a table price or was too nice or lazy to ring her up again. She put some Euros on the counter and he gave her change, which she didn't bother counting.

"Merci."

"Merci, Mademoiselle. Bonjour," he said, turning his attention to the old ladies who had started smoking their second cigarettes.

At her little table, her heart slowed back to normal and her hands became less sweaty. She looked out the window at the Parisians going to work on scooters, in tiny cars and little trucks that sped past in an anarchistic traffic pattern, and at the people, mostly in black, talking on cel phones, cleaning the streets, going to school and jaywalking. *So similar to rush hour in Neopolitan.* She sighed. *Tomorrow at this time, I'll be back in my own zone. There will be coffee, croissants and French people, but it won't look, sound or taste the same.* She lit up a cigarette, knowing a new law back home won't allow her to light up in restaurants and bars. *What crap. I can understand restaurants, but why do people go to bars if they don't want to be around smokers?* She took a sip of coffee. It was extra good. *Intellectually, I know it's not necessarily the special African beans they use or whatever, just my idolization of everything Parisian. I'm used to Europe, and my taste buds are telling me not to go. Yes, here bartenders make fun of my horrible Dutch, French, and Italian, but people in Neopolitan made fun of me without me having to speak.*

A familiar figure in a long black coat approached the window and waved. When Madam Marie Callier came in, Erin stood so they could kiss cheeks. The bangs of her shoulder length, dark black hair hid her sullen features.

"Bonjour, ma chère petite. How did you do?" She removed a long purple, silk scarf.

"Terrible. I said 'patesserie' instead of 'croissant.'"

"Ooh." Marie winced

"I just tense up whenever I have to talk to anybody."

"Il n'est pas grave…don't worry about it, at least you tried. You just need to be more confident." She patted Erin's shoulder and walked away. "Bonjour," she called as she went to the counter and, in a much more effortless fashion than Erin, ordered a coffee.

She returned and sat across from Erin and also lit a cigarette. *How does she smoke so much more elegantly than I do? She always looks bored, tired and older than her thirty-nine years, but I practice that look in the bathroom mirror and can't look that sexy.*

"Man, I'm gonna miss this."

"Paris or eating croissants?"

"Both. I'm not ready to go back."

"Ah, poor Eir-on. You can stay another week, non?"

"No, I can't. I have a crap-load of things I need to take care of."

"Oui, responsabilité—c'est bon."

"Plus, I'm sure you're sick of me in sleeping in your spare room."

"Don't worry about me. I like having your company. But you miss your home by now, no?"

"Some of it. I miss my friends and my mom. I miss my dog and I do like Neo. But I just don't like all of the loose ends."

"Loose ends?"

"It means things I left behind, that I didn't solve."

Marie rolled her eyes. "Oui, I know the saying 'loose ends'. I mean, what loose ends you have? You will stay away from those troublesome boys, you will talk to your mother about your brother, and you do not have that awful pizza job, non?"

"Yes, but I still have to get a new job to pay off the big fat bill coming from my brother, and my dad covered my rent, so he's blackmailing me into signing up for art school as payment. It's gonna suck."

"It is good that you are going to school. You are very talented. Look, see, I am wearing your necklace." She drew aside her coat collar to reveal a pendant of small, turquoise-colored turtles and tiny gold fish.

"I noticed. You know, buying the supplies in the arts and craft shop was even harder than ordering coffee."

"The first time you were here, you were getting over a boy. Now it is Steiner-Kevin. Am I only to see you again when your heart is breaking?"

"Oh, no-no-no! I hope not. I mean, I hope that's not the only time I come to Europe. That's funny, in England Mr. Humphrey said the same thing."

"Well, you know you are always welcomed. I like all of my friends from Nopolitón."

"I tried to call Salome, but she apparently moved, and Bob and Larry never gave me their numbers."

"That is too bad." Marie took a slow drag on her cigarette and gazed sideways at Erin.

Erin looked down. *That trying-to-look-at-my-soul expression always makes me feel weird.*

Marie put her hand on Erin's head. "Très orange." She finished her coffee and looked at her watch. "Tant pis. I have to go. Time to go see Danielle about some fabrics." She caressed Erin's hands. "I wish you could stay, ma chère petite."

"Me, too." Erin's heart sank and she almost felt like crying.

"You will e-mail me when you get home, oui?"

"Oui, definitely!" They stood and kissed each other's cheeks more than once. Marie departed for her job as a buyer/seller/shop owner. Erin actually never understood what Marie did for a living. She made tons of money, took long lunches, usually set her own hours, and had tons of friends who also had vague, high-paying jobs with long lunches and flexible hours.

As Erin looked out the window at the beautiful, cold February day, she tried to psyche herself up for her homecoming. *If you have to go home after a good vacation, I guess there's no place better to return to than Neopolitan.*

#

"God-damn fucking-son-of-a-bitch!" Erin muttered as the plane hit an air pocket and dipped so much, the flight attendant in the isle crouched to keep from falling...

ABOUT THE AUTHOR

Alexander G. J. grew up in Charlotte, North Carolina. He moved to Atlanta, Georgia and studied graphic arts at the Art Institute of Atlanta, then to San Francisco, Ca and served as a cartoonist and editor on *Splunge Comix,* a humor magazine which featured the comic series *Flaming Jackass Pizza,* the inspiration for this novel. He currently lives in Richmond, California.

Novels by Alexander G. J.

Flaming Jackass: Sex, Drugs, and Pizza
Flaming Jackass: In Love
Flaming Jackass: Returns

Mary and I: The Real Story of Miss Mary Mack

Blog:
www.flamingjackasspizza.blogspot.com

Facebook:
facebook.com/rabbitstudiosbigpush

Author's page:
amazon.com/author/alexanderg.j

Twitter:
twitter.com/rabbit_studios

Tumblr
rabbit-studios.tumblr.com